Published by:
Powder River Publishing LLC
1014 Black Mountain Road
Thermopolis, Wyoming 82443

Copyright © 2025
ISBN: 978-1-956881-62-2
Printed in the United States of America

www.powderriverpublishing.com

Sweet Compromise

a novel by
Neesa Lee

This book is dedicated
to my daughters, Taylor,
Kinley, and Giselle,
with all my love.

CHAPTER ONE

Nance L'Breck leaned against his kitchen counter with his coffee mug in hand, scowling at the old tin can sitting on his center island.

Stupid can.

It was mocking him, he knew. Nance glanced around at the tidy room that was open to the living room. Both rooms were done in white with green and blue accent pillows on the overstuffed couch and chairs. The pillows were a gift from his mother, and he had to admit he liked the colors well enough. They made it homier, he thought as he turned to look out the large sliding door that opened onto a patio that overlooked downtown Minneapolis.

He looked back at the can and scowled again. It used to be orange and Nance knew it was a coffee can, but was now mostly rusty. And annoying.

It had been sitting there for almost six months, silently mocking him, watching his every move, including his futile attempts to ignore it.

Why had he told his mother he would research its contents? Nance shrugged and decided he had a weak moment. He hadn't looked inside since he sat it there, months ago, but he knew the contents. Some old and faded letters, some brownish newspaper clippings, a couple of photos and a few old coins, supposedly hidden by his great-grandfather in a cabin his parents now owned.

"I wonder if anyone would notice if I tossed you in the trash?" Nance asked the can. Predictably, there was no answer, but if the can could talk, he was sure the answer would be yes, someone would notice.

Nance looked at his watch and sighed. He may as well

get this over, he thought, and plucked a business card off the island, picked up his cell phone and dialed the number on the card. It rang three times before a woman answered.

"Hello." The woman on the other end put a whole lot of impatience in that one word. Nance could feel it resonating from the phone. If she didn't want to talk to anyone, he wondered, why had she answered the phone?

He introduced himself. "I'm looking for Tia Carnes. She's a genealogist."

"Genetic genealogist, but I'm her," she replied shortly. "What can I help you with?"

"Kendall Rasmussen, one of our video techs at KMNN television station here in Minneapolis, recommended you and I'd like to hire you to help me with some family history research. I'm a meteorologist."

"I know who you are. I watch the weather." He could almost see her sneer, and her answer made it sound like she would rather get boils removed from her butt than talk to him. "I generally don't do family history research, but what is it you're wanting me to do for you?"

She had already made up her mind to turn him down, Nance decided, and Nance almost changed his mind, wondered again why she had even answered the phone. He looked down at the can still sitting on the island watching him.

"I was given an old can with some historical documents in it, and I'm supposed to find out who the people are and why the can was hidden under the floorboards of my family's cabin. All I know is that the cabin was built in the early 1900s by my great-grandfather."

There was silence as she apparently thought about it. Nance waited patiently for her answer.

She sounded slightly less impatient when she answered, but he could almost hear her run her fingers through her hair. "Okay, I suppose I can have a look at it. Just put the can in a box and ship it to me."

Nance nearly did a dance at the about face, but didn't question it, just wrote on the back of her card as she gave him her address. He needed to get this done.

Nance looked at the address in nearby Stillwater. "Why don't I just bring it to you? You're only about twenty minutes from me."

"I realize that, but no." She sounded adamant. "Ship it to me if you want me to look at it. And just to be clear, my services aren't cheap."

"Um, okay." Nance was starting to get a little impatient

himself, but didn't say so. "Fine, I'll ship it to you. You have my number?"

Tia assured him she did and hung up.

"I hope you're worth it," Nance told the can. "Maybe she'll be able to research it all without any help from me." That would be fine with him, he didn't need her attitude.

Nance checked his watch, rinsed his coffee mug and retrieved his sports jacket from the back of a chair. He checked his tie in the hall mirror, grabbed the can and left the apartment. He didn't want to be late for work and wanted to get the can shipped before he went to work. It would be Tia Carnes' problem then, he thought, smiling.

Tia hung up the phone and ran her hand through her bangs, shoved aside the hair that had fallen out of her low pony tail for the twentieth time this morning. She was in the middle of a crime case and the interruption of the phone had annoyed her. She was overworked and tired, and shouldn't have answered the phone. On top of that, the caller was Nance L'Breck.

She certainly did know him. She had seen him giving the weather reports and if she admitted it to herself, only watched to see him and listen to his voice, which was low, and made her heart flutter a little. He was one of the city's most eligible bachelors, and looked like he had just retired from a pro football team, which was close enough to the truth. He played football for the University of Minnesota before starting his career in the business of forecasting the weather, according to the internet.

Tia thought she should be ashamed for searching for his information on the internet when she first got to Minnesota several months ago, but she wasn't. She could easily picture him. He had blue eyes, nearly black hair and with a smile that should be illegal. The neatly trimmed beard and mustache made her want to drool.

Tall and broad, Nance L'Breck was big, but not fat, and Tia decided he worked out on a regular basis. She imagined almost every woman with a heartbeat in a three-state area likely had a crush on the man. She wouldn't admit to herself that she had that same crush, she didn't have time for that.

Tia also didn't have time for a private job, but admitted she was intrigued by the thought of a mystery in his family. And she liked Kendall. They had only met once, at a conference in California, but she was a sweet person.

Her concentration on the case broken, Tia decided it was time for a break. She looked around at the small bedroom that served as an office in her mother's home, now her home. It was packed nearly to the ceiling with boxes, papers and three-ring binders, hiding the bed and dresser that were there somewhere. She had managed to clear a little place on the cluttered desk for her computer, but after months of living here, there still was only a path from the door to the desk.

Tia pushed her hair back one more time as she rose and made her way through a path in the equally cluttered living room, into the sanity of the now-tidy kitchen, where she poured herself a second cup of coffee of the day.

It had taken Tia weeks to get the kitchen and bathroom cleaned and her mother's bedroom cleared enough to be habitable. That's where she was sleeping, clothes still in suitcases. Even the bathroom had been full of stacks of paper, as was the sunroom that ran across the entire back of the house off the kitchen.

She had come back to Stillwater when her mother was diagnosed with lung cancer, and had taken care of her the best she could until her death two months ago, sleeping on the couch in the living room that she had uncovered the first day. Her sisters, Dawn and Marvi, had come back for her funeral, but had gone back to their homes after it, Dawn to Gary, Indiana, and Marvi to Atlanta. Tia didn't blame them, they had families and jobs that required them to be at home, while technically she could work from anywhere.

Had it already been eight weeks? Tia felt the grief well up in her and swiped her eyes. She knew she should have come sooner, if she had, maybe her mom would have gotten well. It wasn't fair. Esther Carnes wasn't a smoker, but she had gotten lung cancer anyway. She hadn't told any of her children about the diagnosis until she couldn't stay alone anymore, and Tia admitted she had been angry about that. She could have convinced her mom to get more medical attention, and she might still be here.

Tia shook her head and took another swipe at her eyes. There was no use crying about it, and she was here now, trying to work and put Esther's affairs in order, but she would rather be back in her apartment in Sacramento, where she worked as a genealogist, helping law enforcement departments solve old cold cases through the DNA lab she worked for. She could work from here, and had already made that choice, but the house defied her every day.

She was just pouring her cup of coffee when a knock at the front door brought her back to the present. A moment later, her friend Erica emerged from the path in the living room in a swirl of a bright pink.

"Good morning, Sunshine, how goes the sorting?" Erica walked over to Tia, embraced her in a hug.

"Ugh, I'm never going to get done. I've got a case I'm working on, been at it since dawn."

After Erica let go, Tia held up her cup. "Want some coffee?"

"Oh no, I was just taking a break from the bookstore, and thought I would see how you're faring." She sat down at the table with a bright smile and Tia followed.

"I'm faring," Erica Helms was one of the few people Tia knew in Stillwater and the only person she would let in the house in its present state.

Tia loved the older woman, petite and in her fifties, with spiked, black hair shot with gray. Today she was dressed in a colorful red and orange patterned, flowing skirt with an equally flowing blouse.

"Are you sure about the coffee?"

Erica waved her hand and pushed up the neon pink-rimmed glasses she was wearing. "Nope, not even a little taste. I've had three cups already this morning. I got a new shipment of books in late yesterday, so I wanted to get an early start before the store opens."

"I'd love to come help, but I'd find sixteen books I would want to buy."

Erica laughed. "I would be okay with that."

The older woman reminded Tia of a gypsy, or maybe a nymph come to life. She had so much energy that Tia could hardly keep up with her.

"But really, you still have a mess in here, do you need some help?"

"It's going to take me years to clean this place up." Tia shook her head. "Mom kept every document she ever collected, every piece of paper, note or photo. But I think I have to do it myself."

Tia's mom was a genealogist as well, focusing on her own family and the history of her friends' families. She never made much money doing research, she worked as a cook at the local school until she was too ill to work anymore.

"You really should just get a dumpster and toss it all, make it easier on yourself." Erica peered into the living room. "I mean, I've seen it worse, but it does take a lot of time if you're sorting as you go."

Tia thought about a dumpster every day but couldn't bring herself to do it. The research had been Esther's life after her husband died of a heart attack, and Tia thought she owed it to her mother to sort through it all, organize it. Tia also confessed to a small case of obsession that made her have to do it for herself.

"You know why," Tia said. "We've had this conversation. On top of the obvious, I can't settle Mom's estate until I find her personal papers in this mess."

"And you're trying to work while you're at it," Erica continued. "Are you sure you don't want me to help?"

Tia shook her head. "I'll get it, but I think I need to get some plastic totes to put stuff in, maybe some file folders." She stood and walked to the refrigerator, opened the door and looked in. Erica peered around her.

"Dang, I'm hungry."

"You really need to get some serious groceries," Erica observed. "I would whip you up something right now, but I don't see much to work with. French toast maybe, but that's not going to hold you for long."

"Yeah." Tia looked at the bottles of salad dressings that were likely expired. There was half a loaf of bread, half a bottle of wine, and a carton with three eggs in it. She didn't have to look in the freezer to know it was empty except for a couple of ice cube trays. Tia had cleaned out the refrigerator after Esther's death, and most evenings she walked down the street to a riverfront restaurant that had awesome food. She wasn't sure why she left the salad dressings. She shut the door and turned back to Erica.

"So, on top of everything else, you'll never guess who called me this morning, before I had my second cup of coffee."

Erica raised her perfectly sculpted brows as she sat back down at the table, cradled her chin with her hand. "I have no idea, but now I'm curious. Tell me."

"Nance L'Breck."

If Erica's eyebrows could have gone up any higher, they would have. "Really? He just called you out of the blue? What could he possibly want? This should be good."

"I don't know, something about an old coffee can and some old letters he wants me to look at." Tia sat back down at the table with her friend. "I don't have time to do family history. I'm so far behind in my cases, I feel like I'm never going to get caught up."

"Did you turn him down?" Erica breathed. "I wouldn't

have. I would love to get to know that man. And when I say man, I mean, living, breathing sex in a suit."

Tia put her head in her hands and shook it. "I was crabby when he called because he interrupted my work, but I heard that sexy voice and I caved, fell right at his feet, so to speak. And now he's sending me a rusty coffee can."

Erica laughed. "Maybe you'll be able to answer all his questions in a couple of hours, email him your findings, and move on."

Tia looked up. "You think?" Her voice was full of hope. "I mean, I admit I'm intrigued now, but I can't meet him. I'm sure he would notice if I drooled on his shoes."

Erica laughed. "You hear his voice all the time, see him on the news, and now after one phone call, you've fallen in love with him?"

"Maybe not love, but lust for sure. It was his voice on the phone that did me in."

Erica shrugged and Tia saw the interest in her eyes, but she said nothing for a minute.

"You'll just have to do it all on the phone, and what a shame, wasting a chance to have a close-up look at that body." Erica looked at Tia, sitting with a cup of coffee, hair falling around her face, wearing sweatpants and a t-shirt. "Have you had anything to eat this morning?"

Tia thought about it. "Yes, a bagel."

Erica stood up. "Go get a shower and some clothes on, and I'll pick you up in an hour. We're going to get you some groceries."

"'Do I have to?"

Erica cocked her head. "Yes, you have to get out sometime."

"I get out. I come see you, I ride my bike."

"You can manage a few people in a grocery store."

Tia sighed. "I suppose, but I'm going to have to get some totes," Tia added. "I need totes. I've got to get this place under control."

Erica pushed Tia towards the bathroom before she left. "I'll be back," she called out just before she closed the front door.

What would she do without Erica? Tia wondered as she stood under the hot water of the shower. She was the only sane thing in this whole craziness Tia called her life. Not that she couldn't afford to lose a few pounds, but Erica was right, she had to eat. Her mother had always called Tia her 'big girl.' She was a good five-feet nine inches tall and had the hips and bustline to go with the height. She turned off the water and dried off. Tia didn't consider herself fat, she preferred muscular, but she would never be thin and didn't necessarily want to be.

Tia examined her face in the bathroom mirror as she applied moisturizer. Blue eyes that turned gray on cloudy days, a nose that tipped up just a little at the end but was slightly off center from a break when she was thirteen. High cheekbones, full lips and a chin with just a little cleft in it. It was a good face, Tia thought as she put the lid back on the moisturizer, and it was hers.

Fifteen minutes later, she had dressed in jeans and a gray sweatshirt. She added a pair of scruffy tennis shoes and was ready to go. Her hair was dry and back in a long braid, but her bangs and the usual wisps around her face had already escaped. She went back to her computer and worked until a car's honk reminded her she was going shopping. She grabbed a bright blue coat and met Erica at the front door, then squinted when she stepped outside, letting her know she spent too much time indoors. She pulled a pair of tortoise-shell sunglasses out of her bag and put them on.

The house sat in a tiny neighborhood at the edge of the river. Trees blocked the view of the river from the front of the house, but Tia knew it was there. The river was the best part of living here, Tia often told Erica, even though she didn't take advantage of it like she should. Her mother's house sat on the Minnesota side of the St. Croix River just outside of downtown Stillwater. The sunroom looked out over the river and there was a nice stoned patio outside as well as steps down to a small beach and a dock.

If she could only finish cleaning the house, Tia thought as she got in Erica's SUV. Today was Friday, she promised herself that Saturday would be spent cleaning out the rest of her mom's bedroom, the one she was using now, and was still so filled with clutter that it was all she could do to find the bed. She would like to start cleaning the living room and actually get some of the clutter stored away.

The house had an attached garage that was remarkably clean, holding only Tia's small SUV, her bicycle, and a few lawn tools. She thought she could store some of the stuff in the garage, if she had some totes. Luckily, she hadn't had to do much with the lawn except scoop snow.

What started as a simple trip to the grocery store turned into several hours of shopping.

"My feet hurt," Tia told Erica as they carried the last bags of groceries into the house, and it looks like I'm inviting an army platoon to dinner."

Erica laughed. "It kind of does look like that, especially since we packed some of the bags in the plastic totes you bought. At least I'm assured you have something to eat in the house. I believe you've lost weight since you got here."

Tia held out her arms. "Do you think so?" She pulled on the waistband of her pants.

"See, you've got a pretty good gap there." Erica walked around Tia and nodded. "It looks good on you."

Tia tried to twist around to see her butt. "If you say so, but if I've lost weight, it's probably stress related."

"Oh, I don't know about that. Okay, maybe some," Erica amended when Tia rolled her eyes. "But the bicycle riding is good for you, and even though you've been eating out, you're obviously making better choices."

One of the things Tia liked about this town was that it was small enough she could ride her bike, snow notwithstanding. There were times when she had to drive, like going to get groceries, but if she didn't need to drive, she didn't. She preferred the bike.

Tia wouldn't dispute that she still ate bagels for lunch, but it was easy to walk a block or so down the street to a local restaurant and order a salad for dinner. They also had a tasty grilled walleye that Tia had come to enjoy. It was her go-to meal unless the See-Food Inn had a special. Tia loved a good steak, but it wasn't something she could afford on a regular basis. The walleye was a good value and the portion was large enough she usually had leftovers for the next night.

"I do like the food at the See-Food, and the bike riding helps too, I suppose," Tia conceded. "Maybe I should start lifting weights too." She flexed her arm.

Erica laughed that sweet laugh she had. "You mean like heavy boxes? You have a few of those."

Tia joined her laughter. "Maybe Pilates. I'll look into it, but it's boxes for now. I'm going to tackle the boxes first thing in the morning."

"Are you sure you don't want to go out for drinks later with Allie and I?" Erica asked a few minutes later as she gathered up her things. Allie was Erica's daughter, and they tried to get together once a week, usually on Friday evenings, allowing Allie a chance to get away from her three young children.

"Of course I do," Tia answered, "but I think once I get

all this food put away, I'll just fix myself something to eat here. I have food now, and I still have several hours' worth of work I want to get done tonight. That way I can devote the whole weekend to cleaning and organizing."

Half an hour later, the groceries were put away, the freezer was full and Erica had gone back to the bookstore. Tia sat down at her computer and was immediately engrossed in a murder investigation in North Carolina, thoughts of Nance L'Breck and cleaning the house forgotten.

Nance flagged Kendall down in the lobby as they were both leaving the station for the day.

"Hi Nance, ready for the weekend?" Kendall was a video technician at the station and a whiz at her job, younger than Nance, always cheerful and friendly. She stood out in a crowd with her long, bright pink hair that showed her natural deep brown color closer to her head. She wore a plaid fedora hat most of the time, along with big, black rectangular glasses that still showed her bright brown eyes. Bright pink lipstick always highlighted her lips.

Nance nodded. "I am, but I had a question or two about..." He pulled the business card out of his pocket. "Tia Carnes. How well do you know her?"

"Weren't you able to contact her?" Kendall asked instead of answering the question.

"I did, and she said she would help me, but she acted like it was a pretty big inconvenience."

"Ahh." Kendall adjusted her glasses. "Well, I know she's busy, so if she agreed to help you, you're pretty lucky. She's also pretty private."

Nance nodded. "I briefly checked her out and apparently she's not on social media."

"Well," Kendall replied, "I know she works with a lot of law enforcement agencies, private detectives and the like, so she probably prefers to stay out of the public eye. She's kind of shy, sat in the back row of chairs at every meeting we were at together."

"So, you've met her?"

"I have, yes. I met her at a conference on search technology." Kendall shrugged. "I wanted to send her name to features for a possible story idea, but since she lives in California, Tia didn't fit our market."

"What's she like?" Nance hated that he had to ask.

Kendall shrugged again. "I don't know, she's tall, and blonde, and... well, maybe your age, and she's really smart."

"Wait." Nance just realized what Kendall said a few seconds ago. "She lives in California?"

"Yeah, that's what she said. Sacramento, I think." Kendall blinked her eyes and looked confused.

"Thanks Kendall, I have to go. Have a good weekend." Nance left the young woman standing there looking even more confused. He strode out of the building and stopped on the sidewalk, pulled out his phone and looked up the phone number on the card.

"What the hell?" The area code came up as a California number, but the rest of the number didn't come up at all. "If she lives in California, why did I ship the can to Stillwater, Minnesota, only about twenty miles away?"

Nance walked the few blocks to his apartment and let himself in, fuming, but no one would know that from his actions. He laid his overcoat on the back of the couch, took off his suit coat as he strode into the spacious bedroom and pulled off his tie, unbuttoned the top button of his shirt. Today was one of those rare days in a Minnesota winter when the temperature was warm enough to go without a heavy coat. It wouldn't last, he thought, next week they had a huge winter storm coming in.

Ten minutes later, Nance was in sweats and the white t-shirt he wore under his dress shirt at work, seated at his computer in the corner of his living room.

If he lost that can, his mother would kill him. Why hadn't he made copies of everything and sent those? How stupid could he be? Nance shook his head. "Just that stupid," he told the computer as he typed in the woman's name in the search box.

Two hours later, Nance rubbed his eyes and got up, stretched and went to the kitchen. He wasn't hungry but he needed something to drink. He grabbed a beer out of the refrigerator and found a bag of pretzels in the cupboard, poured them into a bowl, and took it all back to the couch. He had missed dinner, had been too engrossed in the research that he had forgotten the steak he had thawed out in the refrigerator.

Except for the fact that he had talked to her, and Kendall claimed to have met her, Tia Carnes didn't exist. What was he going to do now? He needed to get that can back, Nance thought as he flicked on the television to a basketball game. He would think of something in the morning.

CHAPTER TWO

Nance sat straight up in bed. The address. He had this Tia person's address. He ignored the bedside clock that said it was three in the morning and padded to his computer. He sat in the blue light the screen created and looked up the address.

It was there, in Stillwater, next to the river. From the pictures he found, Nance could see it was a modest cottage and fairly old. The siding was clapboard and there was a dock that ran from the back of the house out into the water, and a little beach area as well, but that's all he could see.

Nance clicked on the county tax website and looked up the property. M.N. Franklin. Not Tia Carnes. He looked up that name on the internet, but there were dozens of them across the country. Nance rubbed his eyes and shut down the computer. That was a dead end. He supposed this Tia could be renting the house, likely was, but what was she doing in Minnesota?

The answer came to Nance as he poured himself a cup of coffee the next morning. He banged his fist on the counter and nearly spilled his coffee.

"She's investigating some cold case from around here that needs her expertise. That's it." Nance suddenly felt better about the whole thing. Still, maybe he would drive out there, see if she had gotten the package.

It had been a good idea three hours ago in his caffeine-deprived state, Nance decided, but maybe not now as he pulled his SUV up in front of a white, clapboard house. It was older than all the rest in the secluded neighborhood and a little rundown. The rest of the houses were newer and much larger, fancier, and the neighbors probably wished someone would tear it down so something fancier could be built. It sat with its back to the river as did a couple of the neighboring houses, and Nance could imagine the view from the back was incredible.

The house looked pretty much as it had on the internet, Nance decided as he sat and tapped his fingers on the steering wheel. Would it be weird to go to the front door and knock?

"Not only weird, but creepy," he said out loud, and sighed. He was tempted, but there appeared to be no signs of life. He turned around in the driveway and headed back to the city. He would wait and call her in a few days to make sure she had received the can and its contents.

Tia had started early in the morning sorting boxes, then decided she needed human interaction and a shot of ambition, so she rode her bicycle downtown and spent half an hour with Erica at the bookstore. She sat on a stool at the counter while she drank a cup of coffee and munched on a homemade blueberry scone, one of Erica's specialties.

She loved Erica's bookstore, Pages, and the folksy vibes it gave off. Erica had several deep and cushy reading chairs near the rear window where customers could read their new purchases and enjoy a scone and a cup of coffee or tea. The area opened to a covered area with tables that faced the river. If it wasn't so cold, Tia would have sat out there.

Everything was decorated in pale orange and white with green and brighter orange accents, and rows of shelves held everything from romances to history and self-help books.

"Are you procrastinating?" Erica finally asked her between customers.

Tia denied the accusation. "I've worked hard already this morning and I decided I deserved a break. And it was too nice of a morning not to get out of the house for a minute."

"It is that," Erica said as she looked out the window. "I don't suppose it'll last long, but I guess we should take advantage of it."

Tia stayed a few more minutes, then gathered her coat and backpack and headed out the door, pedaling back to the river. She was just about home when she saw a big, black SUV driving down her street. FBI? she wondered briefly. What would they be doing here? Although she occasionally worked with the FBI, in-person encounters were rare. Just as she was about to turn, the SUV made a left turn and sped off down the highway.

Tia gripped hard on the brakes of her bicycle and managed not to fly over the handlebars as she skidded to a stop to avoid being run over.

"Jerk," she called out. That maniac could have killed her. Tia shook her head as she pedaled the last few yards to her home.

"Stupid drivers," she said to the sky as she stowed her bike in the garage and went into the kitchen. She swung her backpack off and onto the kitchen counter and hung her coat on a peg by the back door.

Tia had made some progress in the bedroom before she left for her bike ride and managed to fill several trash bags with papers that held no value. Most of them were full newspapers Tia's mother had saved, and as far as Tia could tell, contained nothing pertaining to any family's history.

She carefully separated other papers into file folders, then marked them and boxed them alphabetically. Tia used the boxes as a filing system and sorted others into the plastic totes she bought yesterday.

Now that she was back home, Tia was ready to dig in again. By noon, she had a substantial number of trash bags ready to haul to the dumpster. It was one of the smaller ones, so only a few would fit at a time. Tia stashed the others in a corner of the garage to go into the dumpster over the next few weeks. She had also unearthed about ten boxes of Christmas decorations in one corner of the room and spent a little time just going through them and remembering all of the Christmases they had as a family. This year there had been no tree, no decorations. Tia hadn't had the time or the energy to decorate, even if she had known where to find the decorations.

She lovingly repacked them into several totes and hauled them to the garage. There simply wasn't anywhere else, she decided, since the cottage didn't have a basement or an attic.

Wait. Was there an attic? she suddenly wondered. She went back into the bedroom and looked up. There was one of those little cut-out things in the ceiling. It was probably just a crawl space, she decided, but couldn't help herself. She went back to the garage and got a ladder, set it up and crawled up it. The piece of wood on the ceiling stuck a little, but came loose with an extra push. She squinted to see, but it was pitch black. She crawled back down and retrieved a flashlight from the kitchen, then went back up the ladder for another look.

Tia groaned. The flashlight illuminated a small area,

and maybe she could have seen more, but the space was filled with cardboard boxes. Many cardboard boxes. She pushed her hair back and rubbed her forehead with her fingers.

"What is all this?" she whispered, then boosted herself up and into the space. It wasn't exactly an attic, she decided since she couldn't stand up, but she was able to get to the closest box. She opened the top and shined the light in.

"Crap, crap, crap, crap, crap." Tia reached down into the box. Papers. More papers. She shined the light around the rest of the dark space. Boxes and more boxes. They were going to have to come down and be sorted.

She backed out of the attic space and crawled down the ladder. There was no way she was going to be able to get them out of there by herself, she was going to have to get help.

But first, she was calling Marvi.

Her sister answered on the first ring.

"Tia, hello, how are you and how's Minnesota?" Her voice was light and happy.

"I'm good, thanks, Minnesota is cold. I just had something I wanted to talk to you about."

"Okay? Is everything all right?"

Tia assured her it was. "Except..."

"Except what? Did the pipes burst?"

"Nothing like that," Tia replied. "I'm going through Mom's stuff as you know, and doing a poor job at it, if the truth be known. There's just so much of it to sort."

Marvi was sympathetic. "I know, and I'd come help you if I could, but I just can't get away right now."

"I understand completely, and some days I feel like I'm making progress, but then...well, did you know this place has an attic of sorts?"

There was silence for a moment before Marvi spoke. "I guess I've never thought about it, but I'm thinking you've found one?"

"Yeah, there's a little opening in the ceiling in Mom's bedroom. I just realized it, and thought I should have a look." She backtracked. "I was taking Christmas decorations to the garage for storage and muttering about there not being a basement or an attic." She took a breath, "So I looked."

"Oh, no, don't tell me..."

"It's full of cardboard boxes." Tia pushed her hair back from her face. "I looked in one and guess what, it appears to be more papers.”

Marvi groaned. “How did she even get them up there?”

“I can only think that they’ve been up there for years and Dad helped her put them there.”

“That makes sense,” Marvi agreed. “I have no idea why she would have kept them at the cottage instead of at our house.”

“Shoot,” Tia said, “I thought you might know exactly that.”

Tia could imagine Marvi shaking her head. “Nope. But keep me posted if you find anything interesting.”

Tia assured her that she would. “Thanks for listening. I guess I just needed to talk to someone about it. I’m going to have to find someone to help me get them down, but I think they have to come down. I won’t be able to sleep knowing they’re up there.”

After she hung up, Tia surveyed the living room and moved boxes around to make a space to put the attic boxes. She would call Erica, see if her son Toby would be willing to help.

For now, though, she was going to finish the bedroom. She would have to clean it out in order for Toby to get the boxes down. Tia folded up the ladder and set it against the wall in the living room for later.

She tackled her mother’s closet next, stopping only once to open a heart-shaped candy box, the kind people receive for Valentines Day. In it was a stack of hundred-dollar bills, fourteen total. Tia sat down on the bed and stared at the money. She had no idea her mother had this kind of cash in the house. Esther had never mentioned it. She put the money back in the box and set it on the dresser.

She went through the dresser with her mother’s toiletries on the top next, using a small plastic tote to collect Esther’s personal items... her watch and wedding rings, a small jewelry box with several pieces of costume jewelry in it, and several pressed corsages from special events, tucked inside a stack of lace-edged handkerchiefs.

Tia pulled out the old, yellowed newspaper that lined the drawer. She would replace it with new shelf paper. As it came out, Tia took a quick inward breath. She picked up the scattered bills, eight in all, totaling six hundred dollars.

“Mom, really?” Tia asked out loud. “You hid money in your drawers?” She put the money in the candy box with the rest, and started on the next drawer. She pulled out stockings and slips, then pulled up the paper at the bottom of the drawer. There was another stack of bills, more than a thousand dollars worth. "How did I not know this? You never said a word."

The bottom drawer was next and didn't disappoint. Under the colorful array of shorts and t-shirts and the corresponding paper was another nine hundred dollars.

With the clothes from the closet and the dressers in trash bags, Tia would be able to finally unpack and put her own clothes away. Up until now, her clothes had been in suitcases with her most-worn pieces of clothing on top of the dresser she had just cleaned out.

Tia systematically sorted through the taller dresser, the only other piece of furniture in the bedroom besides the bed. She came away with several thousand dollars more and shook her head in disbelief.

"I wonder if my sisters knew about this?" She looked at the money in the candy box. "Nope, I bet not, or they would have said something. They're going to be surprised as I am when I tell them."

Tia looked around and groaned at the realization that her mother could have stashed money anywhere. She had found a stash in the kitchen in a cookie jar, but she thought that was the only place Esther kept her money. Sure, there was several hundred dollars, but most of it was loose change, to use if she needed extra cash. That made sense. This didn't.

"There could be money anywhere." She sighed and put the money in the box with the rest. "But that means..." She turned and looked into the living room. All those boxes just sitting there, full of who knew what. This was going to take more time than she thought, and it was already taking forever.

Tia hauled the full trash bags out to the garage, put them next to the others. She had thought to donate some of the clothing to charity, but most were too worn to be useful to anyone. When she moved into the cottage, Esther had apparently gotten rid of all the old clothes she didn't wear anymore.

"That's something I suppose," Tia muttered.

Tia wandered into the kitchen and made herself a grilled cheese sandwich for supper, ate it standing in the jumble of boxes in the darkened sunroom as she watched the river in the moonlight. She knew it wasn't frozen, it didn't really freeze, and she could see it moving slowly downstream.

This was her home now, for better or worse. It was hard to believe. A year ago, she had no intention of ever living in

Minnesota again, happy in Sacramento, and not missing the months of cold weather that came every winter. Her parents had purchased the cottage when Tia and her sisters were little. They had enjoyed weekends here during the summer, and Tia had fond memories of playing at the river's edge, fishing with her dad, grilling on the deck.

Their home in Elgin, Minnesota, was a big, sprawling house that had two stories, a full attic and a full basement. After their dad died, Esther had moved here permanently since the girls had moved away from home and the big house was just too much work. She had loved it here, and it had been her idea to put the cottage in her oldest daughter's name so they wouldn't lose the property if she died. It was older than the rest of the homes in this area, at one time it had been the only home on the street. Now, modern, classy houses lined the street that curved around and back to the main highway that ran through town.

Marvi and Dawn had decided when Esther got sick, Tia would come home to take care of her and would receive ownership of the cottage in exchange. The paperwork was in motion. Tia didn't mind, she was the only one without a family of her own, and she always got along well with her mother. They spent hours on the phone, and later, in person, talking about family trees and the history of their own family.

Esther's hobby had actually been the catalyst for Tia's career. Tia had majored in genetics in college and knew the field well, but she also loved the personal side of genealogy, just like her mother.

So, here she was, and it was a good life, or it would be once she got the house in order. She missed her mom every day, and Tia knew Esther had a lot of files, but the extent hadn't been clear until they all had to fit into a small, two-bedroom cottage.

Fortified by a chocolate bar for dessert, Tia headed for the second bedroom, also known as her office, and started cleaning there. She was sure there was a bed and a dresser in there along with the desk, but she hadn't found them yet. When Tia fell into bed near midnight, the desktop was clean, and she was another two thousand dollars richer. Some of boxes she hadn't made it through sat in the living room, along with an ever-growing pile of garbage bags that hadn't made it to the dumpster yet. Maybe Erica was right, Tia thought right before she fell asleep, she should get a bigger dumpster, at least temporarily.

CHAPTER THREE

"How's the search going?" Paula L'Breck asked her son when he wandered into her kitchen for a couple of beers Sunday afternoon.

"What search?" Nance replied, confused.

"You know, the search for answers with the contents of the tin can Jill found?"

Nance usually spent Sundays with his parents. After church, his mother would treat him to lunch, then he would stay and hang out, or watch football or basketball on television with his dad, and today was no exception. His dad, Allen, claimed he needed another beer to get through the rest of the game, so Nance offered to go get him one.

"Hello, the coffee can?" Paula repeated when he didn't answer.

Nance groaned inwardly, wished he hadn't offered to get his dad a beer, because the can was the last thing he wanted to discuss. On the other hand, Nance knew his mother well enough to know she would want a progress report. She had been asking for one for several months now.

"I hired a genealogist to look into it." Nance sighed and held up his hands as Paula started to speak. "I know, I know, I said I would do it, and I looked at everything and decided I didn't even know where to start. I just don't have the resources or time to hunt it all down."

"I was just going to say that was a good idea," Paula replied. "I didn't know where to start either. Has he found anything yet?"

"She... and no, I just contacted her. She said she would look at it."

"Oh. Is she local?"

Mentally, Nance groaned again. He nodded and hoped he wasn't lying to his mom. "Kendall Rasmussen from work recommended her. I believe she lives in Stillwater. I'm hoping to talk to her more about it next week. She does a lot of police work and said she was pretty busy, but she would do it." He didn't mention that she acted like it would be an imposition.

Paula patted Nance's arm as he opened the refrigerator. "I'm sure she'll do fine. Now go enjoy the rest of the game, I think your dad's waiting for his beer."

Nance knew he was lucky to have his parents nearby. Paula and Allen still lived in the house he, Jill, and Jan had grown up in. It was a split level in an older, but modest, neighborhood in Minneapolis. They always said they didn't need fancy, just a place to live. They spent a lot of time at the hospital where Allen was a surgeon, and Paula a dietitian. It was where they met. Both loved their jobs, but weekends were for themselves and their family. Nance's sisters both lived in Mankato, a couple of hours away and had families, so they didn't spend as much here as Nance. He enjoyed his Sundays, they gave him a chance to relax and get ready for the next week.

Nance kissed his mom on the cheek as he pulled two beers from the refrigerator, then headed back to the family room, the can forgotten as the game got wild.

"Hello? Anyone home?"

"In here, Erica," Tia called.

Erica stepped into the living room and stopped. "Wow."

"I know, right?" Tia sat on the couch with her stockinged feet propped up on the now visible coffee table. She held up the glass of wine in her hand in greeting.

Erica looked around the room. The wood floor, polished, was visible, most of it anyway. Boxes still covered part of it where Tia had neatly stacked boxes along the walls, and the newspapers were gone. There was an empty space by the ladder.

"What's with the ladder?" Erica asked.

"Oh, that, well, apparently there's an attic of sorts in this house."

Erica raised her eyebrows in question.

"Yes, it's filled with boxes. They all have to come down." Tia pointed to the corner by the ladder. "I'm saving that space for them, but I'll have to have help. I was wondering if Toby could come help. I'm happy to pay him something."

"Sure, I'm sure he will be happy to, and I'll see if Jamael will help him."

Toby, Erica's son, was a high school student and was always happy to help. Tia had already hired him to do yard work once spring came. Jamael Buckley was a college student who worked part-time for Erica. He was studying criminal justice, but loved books, so the job suited him.

"That would be wonderful," Tia replied. "It's a bit of a

tight fit through the trap door, but someone has to be on the ladder. I feel like it might take three people.”

“Well, they’re your guys then. Both of them are slender enough, I would think.”

“I still have to go through the boxes, but I feel like I’ve accomplished something.”

“You should,” Erica said. “This is amazing.”

“Would you believe my mom had money stashed everywhere?” Tia asked. “I think I could be rich by the time I’m done here.”

Erica raised her eyebrows and whistled. “Rich, huh?”

“Well, maybe not rich, but I can pay for help.”

Erica looked around the room. “So, you could have money stashed anywhere?”

Tia nodded as she followed Erica’s gaze.

“Well, that takes care of the dumpster idea. And it’s going to slow you down for sure, but you’ve made a huge dent in it.”

“I’m celebrating. Do you want a glass of wine?” She held up her glass again.

Erica shook her head. “I’m not staying. I just stopped by to check on you since you didn’t answer your phone.”

“My phone.” Tia lifted her feet off the coffee table and put them on the floor. “Where’s my phone?” She checked the cushions on the couch for it and came up empty. She stood up. “I hope it’s not out in the garage in one of the millions of garbage bags I put out there.”

Erica pulled her phone out of her purse and hit Tia’s number. It connected, but neither heard Tia’s phone ring.

“Oh, no, this isn’t good,” Tia said. She went into the office and then into the bedroom. “Here it is,” she called from the bedroom. “It was under the bed.” She walked back into the living room while scanning missed calls.

“Uh, oh.”

“Uh, oh, what?” Erica asked.

“Nance L’Breck called three times.”

“Did he leave messages?” Erica peered over Tia’s shoulder.

“No,” Tia replied. “I wonder what he wanted.”

“Maybe you should call him back,” Erica suggested.

Tia checked the time. “It’s really too late tonight, I’ll call him back in the morning. I can’t help him with anything yet since I don’t have his information.”

“Well, good luck with that,” Erica said, “and it is late, so I’m going, now that I know you’re still with the living.”

Tia called Nance the next morning. "I haven't received your materials yet," she explained when he answered.

"I figured that," Nance replied, "but I talked to my mother yesterday and she pointed out that I didn't give you enough information to get you started."

Tia pushed her hair back from her face and randomly wondered why she didn't find a new hairstyle. "What do you mean?"

"None of the items in the can connect to anything except my great-grandfather, John Beckwith. He was born in 1900 and grew up here in Minnesota. We have a family tree drawn out."

Tia pictured Nance sitting at his desk in one of the suits he wore on television, broad shoulders pushing at the fabric. It was too bad he never worked without his jacket. Tia figured she would be able to see the muscles ripple when he moved. She shook her head and pulled her attention back to the conversation.

"You'd be surprised what I can find with just a name and a date," she said, "but yes, more information would be helpful. Maybe you could email me his information?" Tia made a couple of notes on a pad of paper.

"I can, and I will," Nance replied, "but the fact is the information in the can doesn't mention anyone in our family. There are a couple of letters addressed to him, but we don't know anything about the person who sent them."

"What does that mean, exactly?"

"It's kind of difficult to explain on the phone, but maybe we could go over it together when you get the can," Nance suggested. "You are in Stillwater, correct?"

Tia's hand stilled the pen. How did he know where she was? And meet Nance L'Breck? In person? Tia didn't think that was a good idea. She would likely stutter and possibly drool. She imagined he was even more imposing in person than he cwas on television.

"Hello? Are you there?" His deep voice interrupted Tia's thoughts.

"Umm, yes, I'm here, and yes, I live in Stillwater. How did you know that?" She was trying not to panic. She liked her privacy.

"You gave me your address to send the can to," Nance reminded her.

Oh, yeah, she did do that. Her only excuse was that

she was in a hurry. "I remember, but I generally don't meet people face to face. In this day and age, it's really not necessary."

"I understand that, but since you're this close, well, maybe I could help you with some of the research. You know, two heads are better than one and all that stuff."

Tia groaned inwardly. That was the last thing she wanted. She preferred to work alone.

"Why don't you let me have a look at what we have for information and then we can go from there?" Tia remembered something. "Once I have a look, I'll send you a contract. And there's one more thing."

"What's that?" Nance was starting to sound impatient.

"You'll need to accept the findings even if they show... irregularities. DNA doesn't lie."

"Oh, sure, and I guess I can wait for the contract. I'll just send you the family tree stuff."

Tia thought he sounded disappointed, but didn't know what to do about it. She preferred to work alone, and that was that. She gave him her email address and they hung up.

"Great," Tia said to the computer screen in front of her. "This is just great. I'm pretty sure he's going to insist on working together, and I'm going to agree and then regret it."

She laid her phone on the desk and went back to work but she couldn't shake the feeling of... what? Doom? Anticipation? She sighed and put him out of her mind.

Nance ended the call, sat and looked at his phone. He didn't know why he was disappointed, but he was. He had been honest with his mother, he had neither the time nor the resources to search for information on the people mentioned in the can, but he admitted he was curious. More curious now that he had actually put the wheels in motion to get the research started.

Nance rolled his eyes. Who was he kidding? He was more curious about the genealogist, the voice on the phone. Her voice intrigued him and he wondered what she looked like. He laughed out loud. She was probably sixty years old with gray hair and lived with six cats. No, wait, Kendall said she was about his age. He smiled and thought, okay, then groaned. She probably still had the six cats. He shuddered.

"Are you okay?" An intern... Mike, he remembered, stopped in front of his door. Nance looked up.

"Yeah, I'm okay, but thanks for asking. I just had a thought that struck me as funny." The intern nodded and wandered away. Nance sat there for another minute, turned back to his computer. Within a minute or two, all thoughts of a tin can and the mysterious Tia Carnes vanished. The storm he had forecasted on Friday appeared to be taking on a stronger personality. By the end of the week, Minnesota was going to be buried in snow, with strong winds adding to the situation.

Tia was engrossed in her work when the doorbell rang. Muttering under her breath, she answered the door and signed for the box the delivery driver handed her. In less than thirty seconds, Tia was back at her desk and the box was sitting on the floor next to the front door.

A little after five, Tia's alarm sounded. She shut it off and rose, stretched and walked into the kitchen. She hated it that she set an alarm so she wouldn't miss the weather report. Tia clicked on the small television on the counter and listened to Nance L'Breck talk about high and low temperatures as she drank a glass of water.

She should have taken a break earlier, but she was on a roll with her research into the cold case from North Carolina. She believed she had found the identity of a college student who had been murdered years ago. She would double-check her information in the morning and send the information on to the lab she worked for.

Tia watched the man on television but wasn't really listening until he pointed at the low-pressure system out west.

"Snow?" Was he talking about snow? Lots of snow? Tia turned up the volume in time to hear him tell viewers to batten down the hatches and get ready for a January snowstorm.

"It's March, so what are you talking about?" she asked the television.

"Yes, I know it's March, but this is one of those storms that will make you think it's January," Nance explained like he was talking directly to Tia. He went on to say that the temperature would drop and the wind would pick up. "Much of the state could be covered with a foot of snow," he finished.

The storm was several days out, Tia realized, so no worries tonight. When the station cut to a commercial after announcing sports would be next, she put her shoes and coat on and strode towards the door. She was ready for dinner.

It took only a few minutes to walk to the See-Food Inn. The gravel in the parking lot crunched under her feet and the sun had already set. There were a few cars in the parking lot, but the restaurant wasn't nearly as busy as it usually was.

Tia stepped into the restaurant and paused. She loved this place. It wasn't fancy, instead it was a place for families or a casual date. The square clapboard building was nearly a hundred years old and had survived numerous floods over the years. Like her house, it sat on the river and was built up off the bank to allow for the water that would rise during rainy years. Thanks to dams and reservoirs upriver, the flooding threat had mostly diminished.

The old-style bar formed a rectangle in the middle of the room, and there were booths and tables placed around the outside walls. Windows let patrons enjoy the view and big glass doors led out to a patio on the river's edge.

It was empty now, but whenever it was warm enough to dine outside, people flocked there to enjoy the view. Tia preferred it empty, admitted to a slight fear of being around a lot of people.

The whole place was decorated with an eclectic collection of vintage fishing equipment, from nets and lures to her favorites, a canoe and an old rowboat that both hung from the ceiling.

"There's my favorite customer."

"Just a customer?" Tia asked as a handsome older man engulfed her in a hug and kissed her cheek, then stepped back and held her hands.

"Never just a customer, and you know you're my favorite person in the world." He cocked his head to one side as he considered her. "How many times have I asked you to marry me?"

Tia laughed and kissed him back. He was a charmer and if she was inclined to get married, she might seriously consider Danny Holcomb. She stood eye to eye with him and in his mid-sixties, Danny was all muscle. He wore his white hair neatly cut short and his equally white beard and mustache were neatly trimmed close to his face.

"I've lost count, but you know I appreciate your efforts." She smiled. "And you should be thanking me for turning you down. One of these days the right woman is going to walk through this door and steal your heart."

Danny sighed and kissed her again. "I hope you're right, but it better be soon. I'm not getting any younger." He hooked his arm with hers and led her to a table. "For now, I'll bask in your beauty and grace whenever you stop in."

Tia laughed as he held the chair for her while she sat down.

"Do you know what you want this evening, or would you like to be surprised?" Danny asked as he reached for a pitcher on the next table and filled Tia's water glass.

Tia considered. "Do I get wine with this surprise?"

Danny laughed. "Of course, we wouldn't have it any other way." He glanced toward the kitchen. "Micah's been working on a new recipe, and he was hoping you would come in so you could taste test it for him."

"Then surprise it is." Tia nodded as she looked up at him. "Now I'm intrigued."

"And hungry?"

"Always hungry, you know that." She considered the rest of the customers, chatting and eating. "Do you have time to join me?"

He smiled, a genuine smile that could make women melt into his arms. Yep, if she were looking...

"I would love to, just let me tell Micah it's a go."

He stepped away and a moment later she heard a whoop from the kitchen. Along with all the other customers, Tia looked towards the kitchen, then smiled. Micah must be pretty excited about this new dish.

Danny brought a bottle of wine and sat down across from her. In a few minutes, Micah, Danny's son and head chef, brought out two plates and placed them in front of Danny and Tia.

"Goodness." Tia didn't know what else to say. She looked down at her plate, beautifully dressed with maple-glazed salmon with pecans and a helping of sautéed asparagus. "It looks wonderful." She caught the scent in the steam rising from the plate. "It smells wonderful." She took a bite and closed her eyes, relishing in the texture and flavors.

"I think she likes it."

Tia opened her eyes when Micah spoke. They were both smiling broadly. "You look like Meg Ryan in that movie."

Tia blushed. "'Sleepless in Seattle'," she said. "I remember that scene. She was pretty loud about it and that was fake anyway. This..." She speared another piece of salmon. "This could be for real."

Both men laughed again, and Micah bowed before he turned away

"He is one great chef." She watched the young man walk back to the kitchen.

"I agree, but you know that I taught him everything he knows." Danny helped himself to his own salmon.

"Didn't he go to Paris to a culinary school?"

"Well, yes, but you know."

Tia raised her eyebrows.

"I taught him first," Danny replied, and joined in with Tia's laughter.

This is what she liked about living here, Tia realized. Friends like Erica, who came to check on her, and Danny, who made sure she was fed on a regular basis. She didn't have many friends, so she cherished those she had, like Erica and Danny. Erica and Danny, Tia thought.

"Why didn't I think of that earlier?" she breathed.

Danny paused with his fork halfway to his mouth. "What was that?"

Tia smiled, eyes sparkling. "I just had a thought."

"I could tell that from the expression on your face." He leaned across the table. "It looked like a 'eureka' moment."

"Maybe." She smiled and changed the subject. She wanted to think about the Danny and Erica situation. "You'll never guess who called me today."

"The 'Rock' Johnson."

Tia laughed. "I probably would have led with that. Nance L'Breck."

Danny's brow furrowed. "Isn't he the good-looking weatherman on Channel Four? Why would he call you? I mean, not that he wouldn't, but... what don't I know?"

Tia laughed again. "He wants to help me solve a family mystery from a hundred years ago."

"Interesting. He's definitely good looking," Danny pointed out again.

Tia looked down at her plate before replying. "Yeah, I guess he's good looking." She shouldn't have said anything, she decided.

"So, that is interesting," Danny replied as he gauged her reaction,

"Maybe, but you stop that," Tia scolded. "We've only talked on the phone, and really, he probably has a million girlfriends."

"So, there's a chance?" Danny wiggled his eyebrows.

"I said stop that," Tia repeated. "I can't see that a guy like him would ever be interested in someone like me."

"I think you underestimate everything you have to offer." His tone was serious.

"Well, we only talked on the phone." Tia wished she hadn't brought it up. "And I'm not going to be anyone's million and one."

"Nor should you be," Danny replied. He looked up as Micah approached with two plates.

Tia followed his gaze. "Is that dessert?"

"It is," Micah replied. "Especially for you, for bringing sunshine into our otherwise gloomy existence."

"Oh, you," Tia replied, but basked in the compliment. Micah was a younger version of his father, slim but strongly built, but with sandy hair instead of Danny's distinguished gray. She knew it fell in curls to his shoulders, but tonight it was in a ponytail and tucked under a chef's hat. Micah had a girlfriend, Ashley, Tia remembered. She had only met her once, here at the restaurant, so she didn't know much about her.

Micah placed dessert plates in front of them, and it was all Tia could do not to pick it up with her hands and shove it all in her mouth.

Five-layer lemon cake with lemon frosting, from the looks of it, Tia thought.

"Oooh, I feel like it's my birthday," Tia said, picking up her fork. "I might be regretting eating all of my salmon, especially since I was hoping for leftovers for tomorrow." She cut a bite and put it in her mouth, sighed.

"Good?" Micah asked.

"Will you marry me and cook for me forever?" She looked up at the man who was picking up their empty dinner plates.

"Hey, now." Danny picked up his fork and waved it at Tia. "If you're going to marry anyone, it's going to be me. I asked first, remember?"

Tia laughed and Micah joined in. "He has a point, you know. But as to the leftovers, I'll put something together for you."

By the time Tia finished the cake, licking the last of the frosting off of her fork, she was full. Maybe too full. She sighed.

"What's wrong?" Danny asked.

Tia's smile was sad, but the sparkle was still in her eyes.

"I'm going to have to waddle home, I'm so full."

After Tia walked the short distance home, she put the box of food Micah had packed in the refrigerator and wandered out to the sunroom. This room had to be next, and once she went through the stacks of papers, she would move the boxes into the living room and stack them with the rest. She had planned on working tomorrow afternoon, but if it was going to snow, she could use part of that time to clean out here.

She wasn't really worried about a snowstorm, she had grown up in Minnesota, after all, but it made her miss Sacramento and its lack of winter weather. She didn't mind scooping snow, but she hated that the wind blew with every snowfall. Tia made a quick check of her emergency supplies just to make sure she would be okay if she got stranded, or if the electricity went out. There was plenty of wood in the garage for the fireplace since she hadn't used it much.

"Only because I didn't want to burn the house down," she muttered out loud. Getting rid of papers and stacking boxes away from the fireplace made it safer if she needed to use the fireplace.

On her way to the bedroom to get ready for bed, Tia realized the box Nance had sent was still sitting by the door. She retrieved it and took it into the office. He had also sent her an email that she still had to look at but decided to at least see what was in the box.

As Nance had said, it was a very old, orange coffee can made of tin, but in surprisingly good shape. She didn't see any rust on it as she twisted the old metal and pulled the lid off. She looked inside. Tia couldn't resist and reached in for the contents. She left the coins in the bottom of the can, she doubted they would be of any help, but there were several letters tied together with a string. She could see the top one was addressed to John Beckwith. There were also a couple of pictures, including one of a young girl that had one word written on the back, "Helen."

Tia shrugged and set it aside. She was afraid that wouldn't be much help either. There were several newspaper clippings as well, all brown and very fragile. Tia sat and looked at the small stack of items, each begging her to look closer. She was now intrigued and was already thinking about the research needed.

"No, I'm not starting this tonight, and I have things to do tomorrow." She found a folder and put everything in, labeled it and set it up on a shelf above the desk with the can.

CHAPTER FOUR

T ia was up early the next morning, showered with hair dried and back in a ponytail. She put on black leggings and one of her favorite shirts, a magenta long-sleeved knit shirt. She had promised herself a bike ride on the trail beside the river after lunch if the weather was still as nice as it was yesterday. First though, she had to send of the results of her research and would have an on-line meeting with the North Carolina officials who had hired her through the lab.

The ride along the river had done wonders, Tia decided as she put her bike away. It was truly a beautiful area, even though right now, the grass was dull, and the trees were empty. She loved the river and couldn't wait for summer to be able to enjoy it more. When she first came back, it was already early winter, and every minute had been spent with her mom. Even that wasn't long enough.

Tia took a big breath to stop the tears that threatened and looked at the stack of garbage bags. She sighed, picked up two and hauled them to the dumpster. She threw them in and went back for two more. That would do for now, Tia thought, and went into the house. If she was truthful with herself, it would take weeks to get rid of all of them, and she wasn't close to being done sorting things.

She settled down to clean up files from the case she had just finished, organizing them and putting them into one big file, so that if she was asked to confirm her information or called to testify at trial, she had it handy. It took about an hour to do and when she was done, she sat back in her chair. It always felt good to finish a case, but she was already looking forward to the next.

Tia stretched and wandered to the kitchen. She found a bagel, took it and a soda to the office. The can beckoned, despite the fact that the letters and newspaper clippings weren't in it. Tia sighed. She couldn't help herself and reached to retrieve the file folder from the shelf.

She scanned the letters and their corresponding envelopes into her computer and printed the letters off, did the same for the newspaper clippings and the photos. She labeled everything and put all the originals back in the can. She was actually surprised Nance hadn't done the same and sent her copies. She decided he originally wasn't that interested in the project, but that appeared to be changing.

"I wonder if he read any of it," Tia said to the can. The can didn't answer. She sighed and printed out the family tree Nance had provided. She entered the names and dates into a database, and from what little she had read while making copies, Nance was right. The people in the letters and clippings didn't match any of the Beckwith names.

It would make the search a little more interesting, Tia decided, and looked at her phone to check the time. She had time before dinner to find John Beckwith's obituary, Tia decided. It took exactly three minutes to find the obituary from 1972, another five minutes to save it to her computer and print a copy. She read through it and decided it wasn't much help.

Born in 1900 in Henderson, Minnesota, he served in World War I, married Lillian Hills, had four children. He was a blacksmith like his father, according to the obituary, and in the 1930s, moved to auto mechanics. He lived in Henderson all his life and was buried in the Henderson cemetery with his wife and parents, James and Ethel Beckwith. His children all lived in the area at the time of his death.

It wasn't much more than what she knew from the family tree, Tia decided, and put the paper copy in the file, patted the can. "Later my friend, later."

A few minutes later Tia turned on the television and listened to the news, most of which was about the upcoming snowstorm. She heated up her dinner, leftovers from last night, and sat down at the table as the weather came on and the image of Nance L'Breck filled the screen. She looked away, then back at the screen. Something was different. Tia sat up straight and stared. The beard and mustache were gone, and the man behind them was truly gorgeous. Why had he shaved? she wondered.

He was also talking about snow. Maybe she should wait until next week to talk to him about his family. He was probably going to be pretty busy the next few days. She also was starting a new case in the morning, so maybe it was better that they waited. Tia would choose a box after she cleaned up the kitchen, put a movie on and do some sorting. One box a day and in... possibly two years... she would be done. She reconsidered. Maybe she should do two boxes a day.

Nance went through the computer models for the third time in as many hours, rubbed the back of his neck as his shoulders protested.

"Anything new?" Nance's fellow meteorologist Adam Scott stopped at the door of Nance's office.

Nance looked up and smiled. Adam was tall, as tall as Nance, but thin. He was about ten years older and wore wire-rimmed glasses. He had a receding hairline and was the nicest guy Nance had ever met. He had a wife and three children, and worked the evening newscasts after Nance's noon and afternoon reports.

"It's hard to tell," Nance replied. "The models are all over the place and I can't get a good read on wind speed, except to say it's going to be windy." He rubbed his chin.

"Missing the beard?" He gazed at the younger man. "I never thought you'd shave that off. What happened?"

Nance shrugged. "I'm not sure. I just got tired of it."

"Well, you can always grow it back if want," Adam replied. "Anyway, it's too bad we can't just say it's going to be a doozy of a storm."

Nance was still chuckling a couple of hours later as he shut down his computer. Adam had it right, it would be a doozy of a storm once it got going. Not necessarily for Minnesota, but certainly for March. It wasn't exactly a proper meteorological term, but in this case, it worked.

"Damn." He rose and stretched, looked at the clock on the wall. He had stayed longer than he intended and now he was going to have to walk home in the dark, and yes, the snow that had started not so long ago. He needed sleep as well, had to be back here in less than six hours for meetings before going on the air at noon.

He grabbed his coat and headed out into the night,

breathed in the cold air. There were no cars moving on the street, and he was the only person out. It wasn't frigid, and wasn't going to get horribly cold, but there was just enough wind to swirl the fluffy flakes of snow around in the soft glow of the city's lights.

The scene reminded him of a gently shaken snow globe, Nance decided as he entered his apartment building. It wouldn't last, he knew, by this time tomorrow night they would be in a full-fledged blizzard. The warnings had already gone out.

Nance let himself into his apartment, shook the snow out of his hair. He took off his dress shoes and frowned. He should have left them at work but admitted he had been too tired to think about it.

He padded into the bathroom carrying the shoes, and dried them off with a towel. He would have to carry them to work tomorrow, but for now, he was ready for bed.

Minutes later, Nance was in bed and asleep, certain he had done what he could to warn residents about the storm.

"You made it in." Kendall greeted Nance as he stomped off his boots just inside the door of the station's lobby.

"I did, and so did you." Nance felt like a cross between Minnesota's famous logger legend Paul Bunyan and a Yeti. He was covered in snow, including his eyebrows. He wore a pair of farmers' coveralls under a heavy coat. His stocking cap was pulled low.

"It's why I live close by," Kendall replied. "I kind of like that Paul Bunyan vibe you have going on, by the way, but you're missing your beard."

Nance laughed. "That's exactly what I was thinking. I totally feel like the big man, but yes, I'm missing my beard. I should have waited until spring to shave."

"To be honest, it is spring," Kendall answered. "Or it's supposed to be spring."

"Exactly." They walked together to his office, then Kendall continued on her way. Nance set down the backpack with his shoes and a few extra necessities in case he got stranded at the station.

He pulled off his gloves and scarf, took off the stocking cap. Even a few blocks made a difference in this weather. If he had much farther to go, he wouldn't have made it walking. The city was already out trying to get a jump on snow plowing, but the wind was blowing, and the snow was now falling at a pretty steady rate. He expected it to continue the rest of the day and through tomorrow, finally letting up by Sunday morning.

Nance took off his coveralls and boots once he got to his office, hung the coveralls up on a hook to dry. He would work in jeans and his flannel shirt until just before airtime, then change into the suit that was hanging in a closet just for occasions like this. Most of the on-air meteorologists and newscasters had offices like his, with closets and a bathroom to change in.

Nance sank into his chair and pulled up the latest weather models. He would consult with Adam, but he was pretty confident with his timeline.

Tia shook off the snow covering her and got out of the layers of clothing she needed just to try and keep the sidewalk and driveway cleared. She helped herself to a cup of coffee and flexed her shoulders. She went to her bedroom to put a flannel shirt on over her t-shirt, added her pink furry slippers.

She hadn't missed this weather when she lived in Sacramento. The only good news was that the snow should melt quickly since it was nearly spring. In January, the snow would last until, well, March.

Tia was pulled out of her weather musings when her phone rang. She planned to call Erica and see how she was doing, but to Tia's surprise, the caller was Nance L'Breck. She didn't think about it, she just answered.

"Hello?"

"Hi, Tia, it's Nance L'Breck, how are you?"

To her own surprise, Tia laughed. "I'm a little snowed in at the moment. Did you have anything to do with that?"

He laughed as well, a laugh so low and sexy that Tia plunked down onto a kitchen chair.

"Everyone asks that, but you know I can only tell you it's on the way, right?"

"I do know, but we all feel like we have to blame someone, and you're the guy."

Nance laughed again. "It's a good thing I have broad shoulders then."

From what she could see on television, Tia was sure he did. She decided Nance must have to get his suits custom made because she was sure his shoulders were too broad for an off-the-rack suit. She almost asked him, then shook off the thought of his shoulders. She was glad she was still sitting down.

"So, what can I do for you today?" she asked instead, fanning her face with her free hand.

There was a pause. "I was just wondering if you've had a chance to look at anything from the can."

"I did," Tia replied immediately. "I actually made copies of everything so you can have the original documents back, and the can too."

"Oh, that's great. I probably should have done that myself instead of sending you all the originals."

He sounded a little embarrassed and Tia took pity on him. "It's not a problem and I can send the can back if you like. Well, maybe not today, because, you know, snow."

He chuckled, and goose bumps formed on Tia's arms.

"I could probably swing by and pick it up, maybe after the snow stops." He paused. "Maybe tomorrow afternoon?"

Tia glanced into the living room. It still looked like a hoarder's paradise. No, he was not coming here.

"Umm, I don't think so."

"Oh, well. We could meet, have dinner."

"Sure, and I could bring my husband and six kids," Tia replied.

"You have a husband and six kids?"

Tia heard the panic in his voice and laughed. "No, but I could have. You don't know much about me. Maybe I'm a mass murderer."

He actually laughed, and Tia felt it all the way to her toes.

"I doubt that, I feel like I would have heard about it on the news."

"I suppose you're right about that, unless I was very good at it. Anyway, why don't we meet at a restaurant right by my house? The See-Food Inn? We could meet there about six."

"I've heard of it," Nance replied, sounding a little disappointed. "We could do that, and then we could discuss the case."

"The case?"

"Yeah, my great-grandfather and those mysterious letters."

"Sure, the case." Tia could have kicked herself for losing track of the conversation. "That would probably be a good idea."

"Have you found anything to get us started?"

Tia considered the question. "I really just made copies and glanced through the clippings, but I agree with you.

Several of the letters and clippings, even the photos, don't seem to have any connection to John Beckwith."

"Weren't there a couple of letters addressed to him?"

Tia nodded, then realized he couldn't see her. "There are, but they don't make much sense right now. Anyway, I won't be able to dig into it until next week, so I haven't wanted to get too far into it. I have plans for the weekend."

"I understand, I'm a little busy right now myself," Nance replied, laughing again. "The good news is that I'm predicting warmer weather next week. Wait. You have plans for the weekend? Aren't you snowed in?"

It was Tia's turn to laugh. "Yes, I am. I'm doing some reorganizing here and once I get started, I want to get it done."

"Understood. Do you need some help? I'd be happy to lend a hand. I'm pretty handy at moving furniture."

Tia looked around. She remembered all the boxes in the sunroom and was tempted. "I appreciate the offer, but it's more organizing than moving, and besides, if I'm snowed in, you are too."

He laughed again. "I guess that's true, so I'll let you get to it."

After Tia hung up, she refilled her coffee cup. She was surprised that talking to Nance L'Breck on the phone was that intimidating. But his voice. She could lose herself in just his voice. She imagined what he would be like in person and shivered.

"Stop it now," she scolded herself. "You know he likely has a girlfriend. He would never be interested in you." She put the thoughts out of her mind and walked into her office. As long as she didn't lose electricity, today was a perfect day for working, and it went by quickly.

Tia stopped for lunch, a grilled cheese sandwich and some tomato soup, then bundled up again and ventured outdoors into the snow. She scooped the driveway and sidewalk up to the house, just so she didn't have to do it all at once. She didn't mind scooping snow, but she didn't like the wind blowing it all over the place as she did so.

She worked most of the afternoon and as darkness closed in, shut down her computer and took a glass of wine into the living room to watch the news.

Nance wasn't on for the weather. She looked at her phone for the time and realized her alarm hadn't gone off, so she had missed the early news.

She shrugged and watched anyway. The snow would continue overnight and was predicted to end by morning.

Good news, she thought. She should have shoveled the walk one more time before it got dark, but she had been too engrossed in her new case to think about it. It was an occupational hazard and why she set her alarm as a quitting time.

Tia spent the evening snuggled up watching a couple of movies and fell asleep on the couch, the television casting moving lights across the room.

Tia opened a shade in the sunroom, then quickly pulled it part way down. The sun was shining off the snow that was as sparkling as the rhinestones on a wedding dress. It was absolutely beautiful, Tia thought, but she would be glad to see it go. As far as Minnesota standards went, it wasn't really cold, only twenty degrees or so, but of course the wind was still blowing. As soon as her eyes adjusted to the brightness, Tia opened all the rest of the shades in the sunroom and groaned. She had a lot of work to do in here. She sighed and got started.

It took several hours, but by lunchtime, Tia was pretty happy with the results of her work. Two white wicker chairs sat on either side of a small table, also white wicker. A larger wicker table and chairs also graced the space. All of the furniture had been buried under mounds of papers and hidden by stacks of boxes.

Tia had moved all the boxes to the living room and most of the rest of the papers had gone to the garage and into the pile of garbage bags. Despite the fact that the living room was back to having a path through it, Tia was happy with herself. It had taken months, but she finally felt like she had a handle on the clutter.

She settled on a bagel for lunch since she still needed to scoop the rest of the snow. When that was done, she looked at the room again, and decided she should mop the floor so the sunroom would be done.

By the time she was done with that, Tia's shoulders and back were screaming with fatigue. A shower took care of most of it, and after she was dressed, she went back out to the sunroom. She couldn't wait to show Erica her progress.

They had talked on the phone a couple of times a day during the snowstorm and Erica, who was holed up in her apartment above the bookstore, assured Tia all was well. After all, she had lots of books and was able to catch up on some reading. Toby, who still lived at home, was keeping her company.

Tia sat down in one of the wicker chairs and surveyed the area. This was a great place to relax. She remembered sitting out here when she was young, reading and dreaming little girl dreams, watching the river go by. The five of them had sat at the table and ate lunch, laughed and talked about everyday things. She could almost hear the voices of her parents, and Marvi and Dawn as they argued about hair styles, a favorite topic of the young girls. She sniffled at the memory.

When it got warmer, she could open the windows and enjoy the breeze off the river. That was not an activity for today though, Tia decided, and stood up. She would have loved to sit longer, but she was supposed to meet Nance later at the restaurant. There wasn't much choice for clothing, so jeans, boots, a long-sleeve t-shirt, and a heavy coat would have to do.

She was just trying to decide if there was anything she could do with her hair when the phone rang. It was Nance.

"I'm so sorry, but I have to reschedule," he said as soon as Tia said hello.

"Is everything okay?" She tried to keep her tone light, but she was a little disappointed. As much as she hadn't wanted to work with him in the beginning, Tia admitted she was now looking forward to it.

"Our evening weatherman had a family emergency, so I'm covering for him. We've got someone else coming in for the ten o'clock newscast, but it means I'm not going to get home until late."

"It's not a problem," Tia assured him. "It's still pretty rough going on the roads by the looks of it, and there's not much traffic moving." Although there was seldom much traffic on Tia's street, she could see vehicles going in and out of the marina next to the restaurant.

"I checked the road reports and I could make it, but now this..." Nance's voice trailed off.

Tia thought he sounded disappointed but didn't know why unless he was still worried about the coffee can and its contents.

"We can try another day," Tia said. "Do you want me to wait on the research until we can talk about it in person?"

Nance considered it. "Are you okay with that? I actually thought you might have solved the whole mystery by now."

Tia laughed. "I'm good, but maybe not that good. I don't think it's going to be as easy as poking a few keys on the computer. The information we have doesn't give us much to go on in my opinion, so I think there's some work to be done."

"But you do this for a living, right?"

"Sort of, but actually I do a lot of DNA research in my work." She paused. "I'm usually trying to identify a particular person, using their DNA to compare to others from the same family. This is more of a challenge to identify the people in the letters and photos and see how they connect with your family. Building family trees was more my mother's expertise."

"I see," Nance replied. "Would you rather I talked to her?"

Tia started to shake her head, then realized Nance couldn't see her. "My mother passed two months ago. She did genealogy for fun mostly, but that's how I got interested in it."

"Oh, I'm sorry. I didn't know." There was genuine sympathy in his tone.

"You couldn't," Tia replied. "I'm still dealing with her affairs, but I have to work. There are lots of people out there looking for answers about their own family members."

"So, how long have you been doing this professionally?" Nance asked. He hated that he was curious.

"About eight years, since I got out of college. I work with a DNA lab out of Sacramento, but it's mostly behind-the-scenes stuff."

"Interesting," Nance said. "I was wondering if you were a type of private detective."

"It's more forensics," Tia explained. "I'm usually working to identify murder victims from old cold cases."

"It sounds complicated," Nance replied. "I can see why you weren't very excited to take my case."

Tia remembered how impatient she had been when they first talked and felt her face get hot. "Sorry about that. I was very busy when we first talked. I've got some time now for this too."

"Good." He paused. "Look, I've got to go get ready for the next newscast, but I'll give you a call tomorrow evening to reschedule."

Tia assured him that would be fine, then hung up. Well, shoot, she thought, I'm all dressed and ready to go. She made a decision and put her hair into a thick braid, grabbed her coat and donned her stocking cap. She would go out for a bite anyway, since that's what she had planned. Otherwise, dinner would be another grilled cheese sandwich.

CHAPTER FIVE

Tia jumped and put her hand over heart. Someone was knocking on her front door. Loudly.

"What the heck?" she asked out loud as she pushed her hair back and willed her heartbeat back to normal. She had been engrossed in her research that she was unaware of what was going on outside. Of course, most people would ring the doorbell. Most of the snow had already melted already so everyone was out and about. Maybe it was a delivery person, Tia thought as she stood, but she didn't remember ordering anything.

The knocking came again, and Tia went to the living room, unlocked the door and opened it.

She stepped back in surprise at the same time Nance L'Breck put his hand up to knock again.

"Oh, it's you." Tia stuttered just a little. "What are you doing here? Did we have an appointment?"

Nance dropped his hand and shook his head.

Tia blinked. He was wearing jeans with heavy, lace-up black boots and a light blue long-sleeved polo shirt, covered by a black leather jacket. Tia licked her lips.

"No appointment," he said. "I just thought since I was out and about, I would pick up the coffee can and get it out of your way."

Tia blinked. Just as she had predicted, Nance L'Breck in person was a completely different animal than the one seen on television. She instinctively took a step back.

"I did call," he continued. "Twice."

Tia blinked again.

"And I texted." Nance smiled and Tia felt her knees

wobble. He was intense up close and his eyes were so blue they matched the blue of the sky. The television didn't show that.

Another blink. "I never heard my phone, but come in," she finally got out. "I've probably lost it again somewhere."

Nance raised his eyebrows as he squeezed in between two stacks of boxes. One of the stacks wobbled just a little and he steadied it. "It seems a little crowded in here."

Of course it was. Tia was instantly angry and mortified at the same time. This was exactly why she didn't want him coming here. Erica understood the situation, but to anyone else, Tia likely looked like a hard-core hoarder, and she didn't need anyone, least of all Nance L'Breck, judging her. She backed into the office and glanced around for her phone. Unless it was buried under the stack of papers she was using to take notes, it wasn't there.

She tapped her hips with her hands before she realized she had no pockets. The pair of dark gray leggings had no pockets and neither did the pink and gray, oversized pullover sweater that she had chosen for comfort. She was wearing a pair of gray suede ankle boots and was now glad she had put shoes on instead of her pink furry slippers. She had a meeting early that morning and preferred to dress for them instead of wearing sweats and a t-shirt. She also thought that dressing contributed to a better workday.

"I could call you again." Nance pulled his phone out and hit the call button. They both turned their heads as a faint ring came from the back of the house somewhere.

"Stay here, I'll be right back." She felt him watching her as she weaved through a path in the boxes. She returned a few moments later with her phone in her hand.

"I guess I left it in the kitchen," she said. "Look at that, nine missed calls."

"I only called twice," Nance pointed out.

She looked up at him. Even with the heels of her boots adding an inch or so to her height, he was still taller. And very close. She licked her lips again and turned into the office.

Tia lifted the can off the shelf and turned around, only to realize Nance had followed her into the room. She crashed into him, the can smashing into her ribs.

"Oomph."

"Sorry about that." He steadied her and looked around. "There's not much room in here, is there?"

Tia looked around too and immediately regretted mov-

ing some of her mom's boxes back from the living room into here. She had decided she should separate personal papers from general information about random family history. It turned out there were more personal papers than she realized. She knew it would be faster and more efficient in the long run as she sorted, but right now? Right now, she wished all the boxes would disappear.

She handed Nance the can and for a brief moment hoped he would just go. "Don't you have to work today?" she asked.

Nance shook his head. "I have the day off since I worked over the weekend. I have some time to go over things if you have a few minutes."

She thought about that for a moment. "Sure."

Now that he was here she may as well get started on his case. After all, he was paying for her time. "Let me just clean this up and save my work, then we can look at the information I've found so far.'

Nance stood quietly while Tia finished up. It took her longer than it should have, but the man made her nervous. She hoped her deodorant held up, and for just a moment she thought about running to bathroom for an extra shot of protection.

"Why don't you sit here?" Tia pushed her chair at him.

"Don't you need to sit too?" He moved the chair out of her way and sat down.

"Umm, yeah." Tia pushed her bangs out of her eyes. "I'll be right back." She rushed out of the room and came back a couple of minutes later with a kitchen chair. She saw him smile as she sat down, chose to ignore it.

"I don't get many visitors, so I don't usually need an extra chair in here."

"Maybe you should rethink that, it could come in handy." He smiled, showing straight white teeth, and Tia realized they were way too close. She scooted her chair over a few inches, like that would help, and turned to her computer.

"There's nothing out of the ordinary about your great-grandfather. We talked about that, but there's something off about this Elizabeth Perkins. Or Brownell. I believe that was her maiden name."

"Some of the letters are from her, right?"

Tia nodded. "But they weren't sent to him, they were sent to a woman named Mildred Olson in Lexington, Minnesota."

"That's somewhat close to Henderson where my great-grandfather lived, but who was she?"

"I don't know yet. I don't know if she was a friend or a relative or if that was her maiden name or her married name. I haven't really started on that yet. I don't think she's related to John Beckwith."

"Why would he have these letters then?"

Tia shrugged. "I have no idea." She shuffled through the letters. "I would say someone gave them to him, but I don't know who or why."

"Mildred Olson?"

"Possibly, but since I don't know who she is, or if she even knew John, I don't know how that would have happened." She examined the postmarks on the envelopes but didn't see anything that would help answer his questions.

"And there were a couple of letters to John too, right?"

"Yes, but they're from a woman who lived in Chicago. I don't know how she connects yet either." Tia looked at the can Nance had set on the desk. "None of these people lived in Henderson where John lived, and none of them lived in the same town as any of the others. I'm not sure where Elizabeth lived before she went to Ohio, but this Mildred lived in Lexington." She cocked her head to one side as she worked through that in her mind.

"Do you think this could have all been put under the floorboard of your family's cabin by someone else?"

"That's a good theory at this point, but it doesn't explain the letters to John, does it?"

"You're right, of course." She looked at him, then back at the computer. "We can read a couple of letters if you want. Ready?"

"Read on."

Tia took a paper out of the folder. It was addressed to Mildred Olson, from Lizzie Brownell, living in Mt. Vernon, Ohio.

To Mildred Olson
Lexington, Minn.

From E. Brownell
Mt. Vernon, Ohio
December 20, 1918

My dearest Mildred,

I hope you and the family are well and are planning for a nice Christmas. I have heard nothing from my own family and I'm afraid that were you to visit me in this Christmas season, you would find me in utter despair.

There is no news from my love and my heart breaks with each passing day. I have been exiled to this place and while my aunt and uncle are kind, it is not home. The babe grows inside me and what am I to do? I am losing all hope. Aunt and Uncle keep me well, but to what end, dearest Mildred? They say there are fine young men here and marriage is still an option, but at what cost? The cost of my heart? Oh, how will I survive without my love?

I must wipe my tears away and finish now so that I can mail this letter to you before anyone can intercept it.

My love,

Lizzie
P.S. Give the little ones kisses from me.

"So, Olson is likely Mildred's married name." Tia wrote a note on a paper tablet.

"How do you get that?"

"She has children, little ones, so I say married."

Tia bent her head to study the letter.

Nance looked around the crowded room and shuddered, then spied a photo on the shelf above Tia's computer, picked it up.

"Your family?" he asked, looking at it.

Tia looked up when he spoke. "Yeah." She sighed. "Happier times. That's my mom and dad, my sisters Dawn and Marvi."

Nance's eyebrows came together. "Marvi? That's an odd name for a girl."

Tia laughed. "It's worse than that. Her name is actually Marvelous Night."

Nance opened his mouth, then closed it, but couldn't stop himself.

"Was your mother on drugs? Why would she do that to a baby? Wait, is it a family name?" He couldn't imagine any family name that had Marvelous in it.

Tia smiled. "Mom was in her Quaker era, she loved the old names."

"At least you were spared."

Tia heard the relief in his voice and was puzzled by it. Odd reaction, she thought, but she answered his question.

"I wasn't." She paused. "Tia is a nickname. My real name is Thankful Day. Thankful Day Carnes."

There was silence. Tia waited for the snide remark that was sure to come.

"Well?"

"I actually like it."

"Really."

"I do. Thankful. It's nice." He caught Tia's skeptical look. "I'm serious. So, what about your other sister? Dawn, you said."

"Glorious Dawn."

"Wow." Nance carefully sat the photo back on the shelf.

Tia shrugged. "It could be worse."

"Really?" Nance looked at Tia and back at the photo. "How so?"

"I've seen a lot of names during my research. Freelove, for instance. Or Obedience, Discipline."

"Okay, I get the picture." Nance turned to Tia. "It could be worse. But I do like Thankful."

Tia wasn't sure he wasn't mocking her but decided not to press it. She turned back to the letters. "Shall I continue?"

"Absolutely." Nance started to say more but his phone rang. He stood up. "I'll just step outside."

Tia shook her head. "Stay here, I'll go get us each a soda, if you want one."

He nodded as he spoke to the person on the phone.

Nance was already putting the phone back in his pocket when Tia came back with the sodas. "I don't have much choice for flavors, just Coke."

"It doesn't matter. I'm going to have to go. My dad apparently fell, and my mom needs some help."

Tia sat the sodas on the desk. She was strangely disappointed. "Oh, okay. I hope he's okay."

"I'm sure he is, but I suppose I better go check on them. What about this?" He gestured towards the computer. "We were just getting started."

"Well, I can look at Mildred and see if she's related to Lizzie or John and I can look at Lizzie too. That seems to be the place to start. I have her obituary, so I'll build her profile and see who all she's related to."

"Yeah, that was in the can, wasn't it? That sounds good." Nance nodded and stepped out of the office and into the living room. He gingerly made his way to the front door. "Give me a call if you find anything."

Tia assured him she would and started to shut the door behind him, then hesitated and watched him walk to his vehicle, a big, black SUV. Her eyes widened. That was the same big, black SUV that had almost run her over a couple of weeks ago. Her lips clamped shut and her eyes narrowed to slits.

"Nance L'Breck. It was him. Nance L'Breck nearly killed me. The big jerk." She paused. "Okay, not nearly killed me, wait, yes, he could have killed me. And what was he doing here in the first place? I didn't even have the can yet."

The can. He left without taking the can. She stepped back into the office. Yes, it was still there. Tia moved the coffee can back to the shelf and sighed. She would have to see him again. The idea thrilled her, but then again, she had been a little intimidated by him when he was here.

"Admit it, you have a huge crush on the man." Tia sat down at her computer. "You need to stop thinking about it and get back to him... work, get back to work."

"I can't believe it, my genealogist is a hoarder." Nance shuddered as he drove to his parents' house. He wasn't a snob, but he preferred everything in its place. "How can she live that way?"

The boxes. So many boxes. He shook his head as he pulled his SUV into the elder L'Brecks' driveway.

Still, the meeting had been enlightening, for more reasons than finding out about the hoarding. Tia Carnes wasn't old, in fact, she didn't appear any older than him, just as Kendall had said. She was good looking and even if she seemed the nervous type, she was mostly friendly and he could tell she enjoyed her work. And best of all, as near as he could tell, she didn't own six cats. He couldn't help the lift of his lip into what others might call a sneer.

"Maybe she does and just can't find them." He laughed. He doubted that was the case, and if he was truthful with himself, Nance admitted that he actually liked cats, so if she had one or two, he would be fine with that. "But six? Nope. And no wonder I couldn't find her, Tia's a nickname."

He decided that M.N. Franklin must be Marvi. Marvi was the one who owned the house, and then he had another thought. If Tia didn't own the house, if her sister did, it might mean she was just living there temporarily and would have to find a new place to live once her mother's estate was settled. Maybe she would move back to California. It was something he hadn't considered. And really, why did it suddenly matter?

Nance put the matter out of his mind as he walked up to his parents' house. He needed to make sure his dad was okay and find out what they had been doing to cause his dad to fall.

It turned out they were trying to change a light bulb in the laundry room and Allen stumbled coming down from the step stool.

"It's just a little ankle twist." Allen adjusted his leg on the footrest of his recliner.

"I thought he should go have it checked out, but he refused. He could have hurt something else too." Paula pursed her lips and crossed her arms on her chest.

"Good grief, Paula, I'm a doctor. I didn't hurt anything else, it's just a little sprain." He pointed to his foot. "I've got it elevated, and I've got a cold pack on it. There's nothing else to do for it, except rest it. By tomorrow, I'll be up and back to normal."

He looked up at Nance. "I told her not to call you at work. It wasn't necessary for you to rush over here."

Nance looked from one to the other and tried not to smile. "I actually have today off, so I didn't rush over from work. I rushed over here from my meeting with the genealogist. I don't want to make either of you feel guilty, but I had to work hard for that meeting."

"So you just showed up at her doorstep, did you?" Allen smiled to take the sting out of the question.

"Guilty as charged." Nance smiled back. "She didn't really want to meet at all. I get the feeling she's a bit of a hermit." And a hoarder, he thought to himself. Definitely a hoarder. He was also sure Tia didn't care much for him, so maybe the clutter was a moot point.

"But?" Paula lowered herself into a matching recliner next to her husband. "You just barged into the house?"

"Well, I did knock, and she did answer the door." He smiled. "After the shock wore off, we settled down and got to work."

"Well, I'm sorry we interrupted, but we're glad you came."

"Thanks, Mom." He wasn't going to mention Tia still had the coffee can and he still had to get it back. "Are you guys good to go now? I should be getting out of here."

"Why don't you stay for dinner since you're already here? I'm making fajitas." Paula's fajitas were a family favorite.

Nance considered the offer. He might as well since the day was almost over. There definitely wasn't time to go back to Tia's. "Fajitas it is, if you'll let me help."

Nance loved cooking with his mom. It was something they had shared since he was young.

"Absolutely. Let's go."

"What about me?" Allen asked as his wife and son turned towards the kitchen.

Paula returned and gave him the remote, and Nance came back a moment later with a beer.

"Thanks, you two, I'm good now. Go cook." Allen waved them away.

Nance enjoyed spending time with his dad, they played golf and watched sports together, either in person or on television, but that didn't compare to the time in the kitchen with his mom. His sisters could both cook, but they did it out of necessity, not for the love of it like Paula and Nance.

"So, did you find out anything about the photos and letters?"

Nance shook his head and started chopping peppers. "We were just getting started when you called."

"Oh, I'm so sorry." Paula's expression showed her distress. "I guess I shouldn't have called you."

"It's not a big deal." Nance shrugged and dumped the peppers into a bowl, picked up an onion. "We'll get back to it."

"So, what's she like?" Paula asked. She had noticed Nance's expression softened when he talked about Tia.

He paused with the knife in his hand. "I don't know. She knows what she's doing, but I don't think she likes me very well." He started cutting the onion.

Paula looked at Nance. "Why do you think that?"

"It's just a feeling, nothing concrete." He shrugged again. "She's professional, but not very friendly. She acts like working with me is a burden."

"I'm sure she's used to working alone."

"That's what she said, and she doesn't usually do family cases, her work centers on crimes, identifying people who were found dead, or trying to find who killed someone. And…"

"And what?" Paula asked when he paused.

"Her house is very crowded."

"Crowded? As in ten people live there, kids, dogs, cats and all?" Paula looked concerned.

"No." He hesitated. "She lives alone, I think. She said something about moving back to take care of her mother, who recently died. There's just a lot of stuff."

"Stuff." The light bulb in Paula's head went on. "Oh. Well. That would make it hard for you then."

From his chair in the living room, Allen laughed. He obviously was listening to their conversation. "That's funny," he called

"It's not funny," Nance insisted. "You know how I feel about clutter. I mean, I'm okay with a little, like pillows on the couch and plants and a few knickknacks, but not random stuff, and certainly not to the point where there are only paths. It's the one thing I can't do."

Paula patted her son on the arm. "Can you walk through the house?"

Nance shook his head. "The two rooms I was in were full of stacked boxes. I could barely get in the front door."

Allen's chuckle came from the living room.

"Still not funny, Dad."

"And are there cats?"

Nance's expression was pained, and his voice was low. "I don't know. I'm not sure I want to find out."

"One of my favorite stories from your childhood is that one about the cats and your great-aunt Annie," Allen chortled from his chair.

"You stop that Allen, and don't forget, she was your aunt, not mine," Paula shouted back.

Nance cringed. That story was brought up at least once a year, they never let him forget it, and even now, he remembered it like it was yesterday.

Annie Dixon had lived across town when Nance was little, and he had offered to mow her lawn in exchange for some spending money. It was a unique opportunity for an eleven-year-old boy and Nance had been looking forward to it. He hadn't expected his dad to drop him and the mower off and leave him there alone.

Still, he was proud that his dad trusted him with the

mower and the responsibility. Aunt Annie was old, in her eighties, and lived alone. She sat on the front porch and watched his progress, and when he was done, invited him inside for some lemonade.

Nance knew she had a couple of cats, but he didn't mind cats, so he accepted. Annie told him to sit in the living room, and she would be right in with the lemonade. The cats circled his feet as he entered the house, four or five of them all swirling around his legs.

More joined as he stepped into the living room. He remembered stopping and being in awe of all of the things in the house. There was a path to an old recliner and another to the couch. He could see a television set over a pile of newspapers but shrugged it off.

He supposed it wasn't any messier than his room, so he went to the couch that was strewn with stacks of couch pillows. He picked one up to move it so he could sit down, but there was a cat sleeping under it. He pushed a little and it didn't move, so he poked it and jumped back. He peered closer and realized with a whoosh of breath that the cat was dead. He looked around the room, past all of the cats to the kitchen where he could hear Aunt Annie talking, and made a decision.

He replaced the pillow as fast as he could, then gingerly picked up another pillow and peered under it. No cat there. He moved the pillow and sat down, ignoring the cats still trying to get his attention.

Nance accepted the glass of lemonade when Annie brought it to him and drank the whole glass down before the old woman had time to sit down in her chair. He remembered saying something about waiting on the porch and nearly ran out of the house, cats chasing after him. At the last minute he remembered the glass still in his hand and set it down on a small table next to the door.

When his dad came to pick him up, Nance said nothing, just sat there while Allen went back in to tell Annie good-bye. He came back with the money Nance was owed for mowing, and Nance took it, stuffed it in his pocket.

"It took me a good three days to get the story out of you." Paula laughed. "You spent that time holed up in your room cleaning."

"Still not funny, Mom."

Paula patted his cheek. "I know it was traumatic for you, but I never had to tell you again to clean your room."

Nance rolled his eyes and kept chopping.

"We always knew it was traumatic for you, but do you know, you've never asked what happened to the cat."

"The dead cat?" Nance heard the amusement in his mother's voice. He lifted one hand to rub his jaw. "I have never once given that cat a thought." He shrugged. "I guess I thought it always stayed there and Aunt Annie went to her grave with the cat still on her couch."

Allen laughed from the other room. "I knew it, you never knew what happened to the cat."

Nance carefully placed his knife on the counter and walked to the living room to confront his father. Paula followed.

"So, what did happen to the damn cat?" He put his hand on his hips.

"Well, now, that's a funny story," Allen answered as he straightened in his chair. "After we finally got the story out of you, your mom made me go to Aunt Annie's to check it out."

"That was what? Four days later?" Paula piped in.

"You didn't believe me?"

"Oh, yes, we believed you," Paula answered. "But you have to admit, it sounded like you may have exaggerated."

"And?" Nance asked.

"The dead cat was right there, just like you said, under the cushion. It had started to smell by then, but you know Annie didn't have much of a sense of smell by then." Allen shrugged. "She was as surprised as you were."

"Your dad put it in a garbage bag and brought it home, buried it in the backyard."

"You did what?" Nance nearly shouted the words. He looked at his parents, one at a time in disbelief. "It's been buried in our backyard this whole time? And you never said a word? I don't believe it."

Paula nodded. "It's true. We waited until you were in bed and buried it under a bush."

Allen chuckled. "We thought it was better not to bring it up again."

Nance turned and went back to the kitchen, shaking his head the whole time. "And yet they bring it up every chance they get," he muttered to himself.

"Did you see any cats at Tia's?" Paula asked after a few moments of silence.

"Well, no, but then, I really couldn't see anything with all those boxes sitting there."

Paula was quiet for a moment. "Oh, well, it's not like

you're going to spend a lot of time there, and maybe that's part of her hesitation with you. She senses judgment. You know you can handle everything by phone if you want."

Nance didn't know how to reply, so he kept chopping. He loved Tia's voice, he got lost in it when she was reading the letter from Lizzie to Mildred. The rest of her was equally enticing and she had the sweetest smile when she took the time to do that. He liked that when they stood toe to toe, she was only a few inches shorter than him.

Her shirt had been baggy, but her legs. Her legs went on forever. He was almost positive she would feel good in his arms. He immediately regretted the path his thoughts were taking and pulled his attention back to his mom and the food prep. He wasn't going to think about Tia or cats.

CHAPTER SIX

T ia didn't know why she got irritated every time her phone rang, but she did. Especially if she was working. Sure, it was Saturday morning, but still. She looked up from her computer. It was Nance L'Breck. Since she hadn't heard from him all week, she accepted the call.

"How's your dad?" Tia put her phone on speaker and turned back to her computer, moving her mouse over information she had typed in a few minutes earlier.

"He's fine. It was just a sprain, and they didn't really need me. My mom apparently had a moment of panic."

"It's nice that you're close so you can check on them."

Tia heard his rumble of laughter and shivered, rubbed the goose bumps off her arms.

"It's more of them checking on me, I think. My sisters, Jill and Jan, have their own lives and live far enough away that Mom can't be there all the time. They talk all the time, but it's not the same, according to Mom. I'm lucky I'm not still living in their basement. If Mom had her way, I would be."

"I was away from my mom for a few years, living in California, but I know all the changes she had to make after my dad died. We talked often, but not every day."

"I'm sure you miss her."

"I do. We had a lot in common, and it was hard when she got sick, but it's even harder now that she's gone." Tia sighed.

"I'm sure," Nance replied. "I called to see if you've made any progress on Lizzie."

Tia adjusted the phone and brought up another screen

on her computer.

"Elizabeth Brownell, born in 1902, grew up in LeSeur, Minnesota. In 1919, she moved to Mt. Vernon, Ohio, to live with her mother's sister and her family, according to the letter. I thought at first she was working as a nanny, but our letter indicates she was likely sent away when her parents found out she was pregnant. It was common practice back then, so no one would know and there wouldn't be any scandal."

"Do you think it was John's baby?"

Tia shook her head, realized once again that Nance couldn't see her. "There's no way to know. It sounds like she was seeing someone, likely from her hometown, and I don't see how John would have met her. There's no mention of John, just this love of hers, and no evidence that John knew either Lizzie or Mildred."

"How did he end up with the letters then?"

"I have no idea."

"Hmm." Nance paused to think about it. "Have you read the rest of the letters?"

Tia wanted to lie and say yes, but she hadn't. "I thought we were going to read them together since you want to be part of the investigation."

"Thanks for that. I didn't think I would be interested in learning more about this, and I know it's an inconvenience for you, but..."

"Not at all."

"Really?" She heard the surprise in his voice.

"Well, maybe a little, but only because I generally dive head-on into the research. It works though, as long as you don't mind that the research takes a little longer."

"I'm okay with that."

Tia looked up at her shelf. "Did you know you left the coffee can here? Again?"

Nance laughed. "I realized it before I got to my parents' house, but I didn't want to take the time to come back for it. I would have had to explain to my mom why I took so long and quite frankly, I never told her I forgot it in the first place."

"Ahh. I take it she wouldn't be happy?"

Nance laughed again and Tia felt it all the way to her toes. "I'm not going to find out."

"So, do you want me to read the next letter now? I can."

"I thought maybe we could meet again, but..."

"But what?"

"I don't have any time right now, so yeah, why don't you

go ahead and read it now?"

"Okay. Just a minute." He heard papers rustle in the background. Tia removed the second letter from the file and smoothed it out.

To Mildred Olson
Lexington, Minn.

From E. Brownell
Mt. Vernon, Ohio
May 30, 1919

My dearest Mildred,

I hope this letter finds you well and your little ones too. The influenza has hit hard here and so many people have died. I have given birth to a beautiful little girl, but I was only allowed to hold her for a short time before she was taken away from me and now my heart is broken.

Aunt and Uncle have found a nice family to adopt my dear little daughter and I have had very little say in the matter. My heart breaks to know I'll not see her again, not be able to watch her grow up.

Have you heard anything from those brave men fighting for our country? I hear only of those from here and have fallen. I weep to think they will never return to their families.

I must go now if I am to get this in the post without anyone knowing. I have wanted to write to my love, but I know not where to send a letter. Please kiss the little ones for me.

My love,
Lizzie

Nance had closed his eyes and lost himself in her voice. He could listen to it all day. She spoke smoothly and with confidence, with just a hint of huskiness. He felt himself fall just a little bit.

"Hello, are you there?"

Nance jumped. "Yeah, yeah, I'm here." Her impatient voice was back, and Nance wondered how long he had been sitting there lost in the thought of her. He reminded himself that she didn't like him very much and wouldn't want to know what he was thinking. "Interesting. So, now she's had a baby and her parents are making her give it up."

"Again, that wasn't uncommon. I need to dig a little deeper into our Lizzie, see if I can find out what happened to the little girl. I can work on that this evening."

"Is that possible? Wouldn't she be dealing with adoption then?"

"It's possible, but I don't know how successful we'll be finding anything on it. There weren't many adoption records back then. Adoptions often didn't go through the courts, an agreement was made and that was it."

Nance heard that familiar impatience in her voice coming back. "Why don't we read the next one while we're doing it?"

"Sure, read on."

To Mildred Olson
Henderson, Minn.

From E. Brownell
Mt. Vernon, Ohio
June 25, 1919

My dearest Mildred,

I am to be married the week next. He is a good man, I know, and I expect I will have a good life with him, but my heart yearns for my own love, gone these many months. If he has returned, I have no knowledge of it, and no way to learn of his fate.

Does he remember me? Does he think of me? I fear not, but if he does, what can I do about it? I am consigned to my fate, my life a dark, dreary path stretching ahead of me.

I blame the war for separating him from me, taking my love away, and no little one to even remember him by. There is no one to shout at, and no use in carrying on, I suppose. I must accept my fate and go on with life, for the alternative is without license.

Wish me happy, my dearest friend, for I shall need it. Remember me in your prayers as I will surely need those as well. My love to your babies.

My love,
Lizzie

"Oh boy," Nance said as Tia's voice trailed off. "That's

sad."

Tia sniffed. "It is. She sounds really depressed."

"So, what now?"

"There's one more, to John from Silas Perkins, from 1929."

"Isn't that the guy Lizzie married?"

"It is." Tia reached for the letter. "It's a fairly short letter."

"Go ahead and read it then," Nance said.

Tia smoothed out the old letter.

John Beckwith
Henderson, Minn.

Sir,

This is a difficult letter write, but I feel it is my duty, indeed my fate, to inform you of the passing of Elizabeth Brownell Perkins.

She only spoke to me once about you, but made me promise that if anything should happen to her, I would inform you. I made that promise, and now I have fulfilled it.

Elizabeth was a wonderful person, giving and kind. She made a vow to her husband and family that she would be true and tend to her duties, and she never broke that vow, but the depths of her heart belonged to another.

She also asked that the items enclosed be sent to you and I have done so. I now feel my duty is fulfilled. It saddens me to write this, so I will finish with the hope that you may find some solace in Elizabeth's death.

Respectfully,
Silas Perkins

"That's odd," Nance said when Tia was done reading. "Her husband wrote the ex-boyfriend a letter."

"I've never heard of such a thing. Making your husband promise to inform an old flame of your death." Tia folded the letter back up.

"It gives support to the fact that they may have had a baby together, although he doesn't say that."

"Now what?" Nance asked.

"I can check for adoption files, and see if any are available for that time. It would be helpful if we had this Helen's last name. I'm assuming she was the baby."

"If you have time, that would be great, but let's continue looking at Lizzie and the others first." He hesitated. "Could we get together this evening? We could go out to dinner." Nance didn't really want to go back to Tia's house.

"I have a better idea. If you come by this afternoon, we could work on the research, and I could fix us dinner."

Nance shook his head. It was if she read his thoughts. "I suppose we could do that."

"But?"

Nance ran his fingers through his hair. Maybe he could do it, Nance thought, maybe the house wasn't as bad as he remembered. But if it was...

"But nothing. I was just thinking we could meet at that restaurant you mentioned. What was it?"

After they hung up, Nance sat and looked at his phone. The restaurant was a definitely a better option. He wasn't positive he could spend an afternoon at her house. He generally didn't judge, and sure, there was that incident when he first met his soon-to-be brother-in-law, but he had just been looking out for his sister Jill, checking out her new boyfriend to make sure he was suitable for her.

It had been a spur-of-the-moment decision and all had ended well. He hadn't been judging exactly, he justified, was just concerned. Jill had a difficult time with her first husband and Nance didn't want her to make the same mistake twice and get hurt even more.

No, he wasn't judging, Nance decided as he stood and walked into the kitchen for something to drink. It was as he was opening the refrigerator that he realized it was later than he thought. He was late.

"Hey there, Benny, how're you doing?"

"Good, Uncle Nance." The little boy pointed to the basketball court. "My dad's right there. It's Trey's last game of the season."

Nance sat on the bleacher next to him. "You sound pretty happy about that."

The seven-year-old nodded. "I'm tired of just sitting here."

"Maybe we can shoot some baskets when they're done." Nance ruffled the sandy-colored hair that was the same color as his dad's.

He turned his attention to the man coaching his son's youth basketball team. Reid Denning was his best friend, had been since they played high school football together.

They took that friendship to the University of Minnesota where they played football there together too, both playing tight end. Reid went to the pros after college, stayed with the Vikings for seven years until his dad was badly injured in a car accident. His wife, a top model from New York, had apparently gotten tired of the football life, her husband and her kids, and left, so now Reid taught high school science and coached the school's football team while raising his two sons alone.

"Looks like the game is almost over," Nance told the little boy.

Benny nodded. "You were late."

"I was, but I'm here now." They turned their attention to the game, and both clapped when Trey made a basket. There was more running back and forth than actual play, but they were learning, Nance knew, and they would get better.

He spotted Trey dribbling the ball and doing a pretty good job of it. Benny squirmed impatiently next to him and Nance reached into his jacket pocket, pulled out a pack of Starburst candies, and offered them to Benny.

Benny accepted the candy and settled down to eat it, handing each wrapper back to Nance to dispose of it in his pocket.

They stood up as the game came to an end and Trey came running over to them.

"Uncle Nance," he exclaimed. "Did you see me make a basket?"

"I did. You were great." Nance gave him a high five and Trey skipped off to rejoin his teammates.

"Thanks for coming." Reid strode up to his friend, shook his hand.

"No problem. You know I love these boys."

Reid nodded. "How did I get so lucky? They amaze me every day."

Reid had a strong, square jawline above that strong neck football players were known for, and his brown eyes sparkled as he grinned.

"Dad says we can get pizza, do you want to come along?" Trey was back.

"You bet, but Benny and I are going to shoot a few baskets while you guys get your gear together."

They eventually made it to the pizza joint, and after wolfing down two slices of pizza each, the boys ran off to the arcade machines.

"You spoil them," Reid told Nance as they watched the boys go.

"Every chance I get," Nance replied. "I hope someday I have kids that are as good as they are."

Reid grunted. "You apparently have low standards. They're good, better in public, but don't be fooled. They can get out of control very quickly if you don't watch them."

"I still say they're amazing," Nance insisted. "So, what's new with you?"

"We made it through the great March snowstorm, thanks so much for your hand in that."

Nance laughed. "The storm or your survival of it?"

Reid laughed with him. "Both. I was snowed in for days with those two. Mom and Dad were snowed it too, so it was just us."

"I love your mom, and she's helped you so much with the boys since Brianna went back to New York."

"I can never repay her for that." Reid was suddenly serious. "She's been my rock. I couldn't have gotten through Brianna's leaving, the divorce, the custody hearings, all of it."

"I thought once Brianna left and went back to New York, that would be the end of it." He shrugged. "She always said she didn't want kids, didn't want the responsibility, and didn't want me once I was no longer playing football."

"I wish she had told me that before we got married and when we were talking about having a family." Reid pinched the bridge of his nose. "She only wanted them once she thought she wasn't going to get them, and be able to collect the child support money."

"The joke was on her, because she actually makes more money than you and has to pay both alimony and child support, which is hard to believe, since you made the best rookie deal ever and when you re-signed your contract, made even more."

"I'm pretty much set financially, that's for sure, but I still would like to be playing. He flexed his knees. A bad hit did his knee in, and between that and a car accident that left his dad in a wheelchair, he decided it was time to retire. He took his dad's coaching job at the same high school he and Nance attended and was loving every minute of it.

He looked to where the boys were happily spending Nance's money. "Hopefully, it's all in the past, but there's always a little black cloud that seems to be hanging on the horizon with her name on it." He looked back at Nance.

"So, what's new with you? Have you found the people in

the can?"

Nance laughed. It was a standing joke between the two that the coffee can that lived on his kitchen island was going to be the death of him if he didn't do something with it soon. Reid was certain Paula was going to kill Nance if he didn't do his job and find out about the stuff in the can.

"I've actually made some progress on that," Nance replied as he picked up another slice of pizza.

Reid raised his eyebrows in disbelief.

"It's true," Nance assured him.

"So, you're actually looking into it."

"Well, I've hired someone to look into it."

Reid's eyebrows went up again. "You hired someone."

Nance laughed. "What else was I going to do? And just so you know, Mom was fine with it."

"Really."

"Seriously, she's fine with it. I've even been helping with the research."

"Okay, tell me she's a seventy-year-old grandma doing this as a hobby."

Nance shrugged. "She's not. She's a genetic genealogist with a bunch of experience in finding people. She's smart and shy."

"And pretty?"

"Well, yeah, but if it makes you feel better, she doesn't like me."

Reid slammed his hand down on the table, rattling their beer glasses, and making the other customers look their way with alarm.

"Oh, that's funny," he said when he got done laughing. "Is she alive and breathing? I mean, a woman who doesn't like the great Nance L'Breck?"

Nance just laughed. He wasn't offended. "I couldn't believe it either, still can't."

"And now she's a challenge?" Reid slapped his friend on the shoulder.

Nance considered the question, then shook his head. "No, I don't think so. I really like her."

"Whoa, whoa, whoa." Reid's tone was stern. "Don't go down that road."

"What road?"

Reid leaned in close. "Have you forgotten Missy?"

Nance sighed. He hadn't forgotten Missy, he doubted he ever could, and what kind of name was that for a woman anyway? he asked himself now.

She was slim and petite with shiny mahogany hair that

was always perfect, big brown eyes that were easy to lose yourself in. She wore designer clothes and always looked good.

Missy was bubbly and hung on every word he said, reveled in his every touch. The flame burned fast and bright and Nance couldn't get enough of the woman. She seemed so independent, worked as a retail store manager in Minneapolis and lived in an apartment downtown, just like him. She had roommates, she said, but she hated being there, preferred to spend time with Nance and he was okay with that.

She loved fancy things and Nance was happy to buy them for her. They went out for dinner nearly every night and then back to his apartment. He admitted even now that the sex was fantastic and his ego loved that she wanted him.

Then, little changes started. Missy began texting or calling him a dozen times a day, started leaving her things at his apartment.

His mom warned him Missy wasn't what she seemed to be, and he was moving too fast. Nance wouldn't listen, he was in love with her beauty. Then she quit her job and one day she was just there, at his apartment every day and every night. He ignored the changes she made there, from leaving her things in the living room to taking over his gym room for a closet.

Nance finally saw the light when she started tracking his every move with a tracking app on her phone, but by then she was firmly embedded in his apartment and wouldn't leave. He tried to break it off with her by telling her he was moving and that was it, they were done.

She finally had to move out of the apartment since he was leaving, moved in with a friend, she said. Thinking he had gotten rid of her, Nance stayed in the apartment. A few weeks later, he came home after a trip to Seattle, and there she was, back in his apartment. It was a nightmare, and he finally had to get the police involved, had to get a restraining order to get her to go away. Last he heard, she had moved to Chicago, but that didn't stop him from looking over his shoulder in case she showed up again.

"I just don't want to see you go through that again," Reid said.

"Neither do I," Nance agreed, "but I don't think Tia's like Missy. She's pretty down to earth and seems to live modestly. Most of the time I don't think she likes me much." He decided to leave the hoarding part of her life out of his story.

"Anyway, I'm taking her to dinner tonight," he continued.

"She agreed to go even though she doesn't like you?" Reid asked incredulously. "Oh man, you're headed down a slippery slope."

Nance tried to look at the situation from Reid's point of view and admitted he could see the other man's point. "I'm treading lightly, but I wanted you to know that this might be something I want."

He changed the subject with a question.

"So, what's going on with your love life?"

Reid hooted. "My love life? You're assuming I have one."

Nance grinned and Reid groaned.

"Benny."

Nance couldn't contain his laughter. "My man, you have no secrets, so tell me all."

Reid shrugged. "There's not much to tell. I met Kayla at a science educator's conference. She teaches across town, she's divorced and has two kids as well, but it's nothing serious. You know having kids complicates things."

"Really, nothing serious," Nance retorted. "Benny seemed to know a lot about her for it not being serious."

"Yeah, well, he's pretty nosy, when it comes to things like that, but the boys haven't even met her yet. Again, it's nothing serious."

"I guess we'll see."

The boys came running back then to jump up and down in front of their father. "Can you come help us, Dad?" Trey asked,

"Yeah, we need help to win a stuffie," Benny pitched in.

Reid and Nance shared an amused look... they both knew the boys had so many stuffed toys already that they didn't need anymore... then let the boys drag them into the arcade.

CHAPTER SEVEN

Nance was already seated when Tia walked into the restaurant that evening.

Danny greeted her with his usual hug and kiss.

"Your friend is already here, and I feel like I know him from somewhere." He glanced towards the man in question. "I know, he's the weatherman on KMNN. He doesn't look very happy, are you late?" Danny cocked his head. "Actually, he was friendly and in a good mood until just now. Ordered a beer, we chatted a bit about the weather. You are late, aren't you?"

"I'm only a little late, so I'm not sure what the deal is, but you're right, he doesn't look happy." Tia's eyes locked with Nance's and she couldn't look away from the scowling man.

"He's a fine specimen of a man," Danny continued. "Is there anything I should know?"

Tia pulled her gaze back to Danny.

"Just business," she said, then patted his cheek and walked towards Nance. "Just business, remember that," she muttered to herself. Every time she saw him, she wanted to melt into him.

She could hear Danny chuckling behind her, ignored him as Nance rose to greet her. She set the can on the table.

Nance scowled as they sat down. "You're late."

"Sorry about that, I was involved in some research for a client." She sent him a pointed look.

"Oh." He picked up the menu the waitress had left when she took his drink order. "What's good here?"

"Everything, in my opinion, but my new favorite is the

maple-glazed salmon. It's awesome."

Nance flipped the menu over. "That's not on here."

"It's not?" Tia looked at the menu. "Huh. Micah must have decided against it." She sat the menu down. "In that case, I'm having the walleye."

"Is that the man who was hanging all over you?"

"Who?" Tia was confused.

"Micah."

"Micah is the chef. The man who was hanging all over me is his father, Danny Holcomb. And you are jealous." Was that why he was acting like a jerk? He was jealous? Naw, that couldn't be. Maybe he just had a bad day.

"I'm not jealous," Nance retorted. He would have said more, but the waitress came back to take their orders and Tia was happy for the interruption.

"Hello Kahlia, what's good tonight?"

The petite young woman with kinky black curls pulled back into a ponytail laughed and her nearly black eyes sparkled.

"Everything's good, as you very well know." Kahlia was working her way through nursing school and liked the flexibility of working at the restaurant. Danny paid all of his staff a good wage so they didn't have to depend on tips.

"I do know," Tia replied, and placed her order for the walleye dinner. Nance opted for a sirloin steak.

When Kahlia had gone, Tia changed the subject.

"So, how was your day?"

She watched Nance flex his shoulders and release a deep breath as he visibly tried to relax.

"Actually, it was good. I spent some time with friends and played a little basketball. "How was yours?"

"It was okay. I did chores after we talked, then worked on your family history."

"Find anything interesting?"

"It's all interesting to me, but with the exception of a possible illegitimate child, nothing stood out." Tia smiled. "I'm pretty sure you're not adopted."

Only a few minutes passed before Kahlia came with their meals, Danny at her side. He bowed to both of them as he set the plates down. "Enjoy."

"Thanks, both of you." Tia smiled and picked up her fork. "It looks delicious." She took a bite. "Hmm, and it is."

Nance waited to start until Danny bowed again and left.

He ate in silence. Tia attempted a couple of times to start a conversation, but he was clearly mad about something and only offered one-word answers. He couldn't really be jealous, she thought, it had to be something more than that. To anyone watching, it looked like a romantic dinner, but it felt awkward and wrong to Tia. She was beginning to wonder why Nance had bothered to come. She was just about to ask him when Kahlia came back to take their plates. Nance ordered her another wine and a beer for himself, and once they had them, Tia finally spoke.

"Do you want to see what I've found so far?"

"Sure, why not?" Nance all but spit the words out.

"I don't know why you're being a jerk, but here's what I have so far." She pulled a file folder out of her bag.

"I'm not being a jerk," Nance protested. He took a deep breath. "I'm just... never mind. Am I getting the long version or the short version?" He was jealous, but he wasn't going to admit that.

Nance didn't act like he wanted the long version. Tia made a decision. "I can do the short version, I guess, if that's what you want." She took a breath.

"Your great-grandfather met a young woman named Elizabeth, they had a fling, he went off to war, then she found out she was pregnant. Her parents shipped her off to Ohio to have the baby, and made sure she gave it up for adoption. She got married, he came back from the war and married someone else. They both had families and then in 1929, she died."

"That's it?"

Tia wasn't sure why she was irritated, but she was. This was his idea, and she had spent the afternoon researching his family instead of sorting through totes. Now he acted like he could care less.

"In a nutshell."

"Well, how did they meet? What happened to the baby?"

Tia shrugged. "I don't know."

"Weren't there more letters?"

"One or two." Tia opened her file, relented. "I don't think they add much. The child aside, this chapter of John's life is pretty interesting, I think." She pushed a piece of paper towards him. "I put this together this afternoon."

Nance looked at it. It was a timeline of events.

"I think he met Elizabeth in the summer of 1917. She gets pregnant in December of 1917 and he leaves for Camp Fort Dodge near Des Moines, Iowa, in January of 1918."

She pointed to the paper. "He leaves for Camp Cody in New Mexico, March 1918. He has an accident of some sort and spends nine weeks in the hospital, eventually recovers and goes to France in October 1918, just before influenza breaks out at Camp Cody.

"He served as a quartermaster in the supply area and comes back to America in September of 1918."

Nance followed along as her finger skimmed down the list.

"I've added in the dates of Elizabeth's events, based on her letters." She paused. "There are some gaps I'd like to fill in, but if this is enough for you, then we can be done with the project."

Nance didn't look up. "I see you've put in when John got married and when Elizabeth died."

"I've also made pedigree charts for John and Elizabeth's families." She handed him two more pieces of paper. "I wouldn't mind going down to Henderson or LeSeur and taking a look at the old newspapers from those towns."

Nance finally looked up. "You can't find those online?"

Tia shrugged as she shook her head. "Not all of the old newspapers are available online, so sometimes, you have to take a road trip, and I love road trips."

He didn't say anything, so Tia continued. "Then there's Helen. I haven't found anything about her. Without a last name, it's almost impossible." She paused and thought for a minute.

"What?"

"Well, DNA might help." She waved her hand. "Never mind. We've found a bunch of information, so maybe that's enough for you."

Tia stopped talking and watched the expressions change on Nance's face. He clearly was bored with the project but seemed torn about quitting.

"You know, I could have just made dinner for us, or I could have come into Minneapolis to your house if you didn't want to come here." Tia could tell from the startled look on his face that neither of those options appealed to him. Fine, she thought, just fine.

"You can take this stuff with you, maybe talk to your mom, see what she wants to do." She gathered her things together and stood up before he could say anything.

"Wait." Nance caught her arm before she could move away and stood. "I'm pretty sure my mom will want to know who Helen was and what happened to her."

"It doesn't matter." Tia shrugged. "Just call me if you decide to pursue it more. The case, I mean, you can lose the jerk."

Nance sat back down and watched her go. He wasn't ready to be done with the project, he wanted to get to know Tia better, he admitted. Despite Reid's warnings, he was fairly certain Tia wasn't like Missy. And he could proceed with caution.

Nance continued to look at the door, even after she walked out. He had been a jerk, and maybe he was a little jealous. She shuddered every time he got near her and yet, she was perfectly comfortable with the attentions of a man twice her age. He didn't get it, and it made him angry.

He swallowed the last of his beer and signaled the waitress for the check. He silently groaned when Danny brought it instead and sat down across from him.

"Problems?"

"Not really, we just disagreed on a matter, and I think she may have lost her temper." Nance looked at the door.

Danny followed his gaze. "I've known Tia since she was little, and I don't think I've ever seen her lose her temper."

Nance raised his eyebrows. "Really? It seems to me that she's irritated with me most of the time."

Danny grinned. "How about that?"

Nance was confused. "How about what?"

Danny stood and offered his hand to Nance. "It's nice to meet you young man. We'll meet again."

He was gone before Nance could ask what he was talking about. The waitress brought his credit card back and Nance headed out the door, carrying the coffee can, and still wondering what the older man meant.

"Fine, fine." Tia decided she was awake and going back to sleep was not an option. She looked at the clock on her phone. Six-thirty. On a Sunday morning.

She used the bathroom, then padded into the kitchen. It was barely light out and looked like it could rain, maybe storm.

"So, no bike ride today," she said out loud as she scooped coffee into the coffeemaker. She got the coffee started and went back to her bedroom. She searched in her closet until she found an old Minnesota Vikings jersey that was her dad's. It probably should have been tossed out years ago, but she liked it, and it was comfortable. She added a pair of yoga pants and a pair of thick, purple socks. She shrugged as she brushed her hair and put it into a loose braid that hung down her back. She would shower later, before church, but this would work for now.

After pouring herself a cup of coffee, Tia wandered into the living room and turned on a lamp, surveyed the mess she called home. She shrugged again. It was as good as any time to tackle a few of the totes that still took up most of the room. The ladder still stood against one wall, waiting for the boxes from the attic. Neither Jamael nor Toby had time to help for a couple of weeks.

Tia sighed. It's not like they were going anywhere.

Armed with a box of garbage bags, and a couple of banker's boxes, Tia opened the first tote. The papers inside smelled faintly of perfume and reminded her of her mother. She wished she was still here, wished they could share a cup of coffee, go through these papers together.

Tia blinked away the tears that threatened to fall. She put her phone on to play rock music on her speakers to ward away the quiet and grabbed a tote and got to work. It wasn't until the room lit up from a flash of lightning, and a crack of thunder rattled the windows, that she realized she was hungry. She got up and stretched, checked the time. Dang. She had missed church. She would have to call Erica later to check in, since they were supposed to meet at church.

For now, though, she grabbed a granola bar and another cup of coffee and went back to work. Personal papers she would need for the estate settlement went into the cardboard box and family history and notes went in a tote. She was no longer trying to file things as she went, acknowledging that she would have to go back through them another time.

Tia picked up a piece of paper and threw it in the garbage bag after she skimmed through it. She hated to do it, but some of the random papers about other families had to go in the trash. So far, she had filled five more bags for the garbage pile in the garage. She had managed to whittle the pile down, but it wasn't gone completely. She would have to add these and start the whittling down again.

"Oh, well, better that than all of these totes taking up room in the house," she said out loud. "And you should be proud of yourself, Tia Carnes," she added, "you now have seven empty totes."

She had also discovered a tote that had a bunch of bound family histories in it. They were now in stacks on the coffee table, ready to be taken to her office and put on her shelves. Some of them were really old, and probably rare, but the information in them could be useful in her work.

Tia went back to work and was startled when she heard

a knock at the front door.

Tia looked up at the clock. "Crap, I forgot to call Erica. That's probably her now, making sure I'm alive."

She made her way to the door and opened it.

"Sorry, sorry, sorry. I was going to call." She looked up and automatically stopped back. Nance was standing there, rain drops glistening on his black hair and shoulders.

"You were going to call me?" he asked huskily as Tia opened the door wider so he could step inside.

"No, no, I was going to call my friend Erica, we usually check in with each other on Sundays if we don't have plans, but today we were going to meet at church. Then I got busy and forgot about church. And now it's raining." She shivered and rubbed her arms.

"It is," Nance observed as he shook the water out of his hair.

"I see that."

Nance was dressed in jeans and boots, with a plaid flannel shirt left open over a black t-shirt. Tia swore she could see the outline of his muscles through the taut fabric of his shirt. She could imagine what he looked like naked, and then she did.

She blinked and pulled herself back to the present. This was no time for lustful meanderings.

"Anyway, I came to say I'm sorry for last night." When Tia looked doubtful, he held up a bag. "I brought lunch."

"Well, okay then, you're forgiven," Tia laughed. She couldn't help it and was suddenly glad he had come. She would examine that later.

"The kitchen's that way." She gestured for him to go ahead of her. He weaved through the clutter in the living room, but stopped short when he got to the kitchen.

Tia, who was right behind him, ran into him. It was like running into a brick wall. "Ooomph."

"Sorry." Nance took a step into the kitchen. "What happened here?"

Tia followed. "Umm, nothing?" She looked around, didn't see anything out of the ordinary.

Nance set the bag of food on the counter and turned around. "It's clean."

"It's always clean."

Tia caught his glance into the other room.

"Oh, you mean the disaster that I call my living room."

Nance couldn't help the shudder.

"You think I'm a hoarder, don't you? That's why you always have that look of disapproval on your face when you're here." Tia laughed. "I should feel insulted, but I don't," she shrugged, still laughing. "I get it." Tia watched his expression change to apologetic again.

"You do?"

"All this stuff is my mom's." Tia walked into the living room, spread her hands. "Trust me, it was worse than this when I got here to take care of her. There wasn't much time for cleaning between that and work. Then, after she died, I had things to deal with, and still had to work. So, I've been working at it one room at a time." She looked around. "I consolidated it all in here."

Nance looked at the stacks of books, the boxes and totes, the filled garbage bags.

"I get it now." He noticed the pile of money on the coffee table. "What's with the money?"

"I've found about six hundred dollars today, and I think I'm up to almost twenty thousand now from around the house." Nance looked at her with surprise. "She had it stashed everywhere."

Nance whistled. "So, you literally have to go through everything."

Tia nodded. "Every paper, every book has to be looked at, and every paper needs to be looked at to make sure I don't need it to close the estate." She picked up a small stack of papers. "I've also found several thousand in savings bonds, so yeah, it's a mess, but I'm getting there."

She led him back to the kitchen.

"Are you going to sell the house?" he asked. "As part of the estate settlement? I'm guessing it's worth quite a bit of money." He wandered out to the sunroom and looked out through the rain at the river.

"Not selling," Tia replied. "I'm here now so I'm staying. Mom put the house in Marvi's name after dad died, but she's transferring it over to me as we speak."

"That's generous."

Tia shrugged. "It was part of the deal. I come home and I get the house for taking care of Mom." She shrugged again. "I would have done it anyway, I was happy to be able to and to spend her last days with her. Giving me the house made my sisters feel less guilty about not being able to do it themselves."

"Sure, I get that. I would do the same thing, I mean, taking care of my parents."

He didn't say anything more, so Tia turned back to the kitchen. "Did you say you brought food?"

They placed it all out on the wicker table in the sunroom. The dainty chair creaked when he sat on it, but it held. He brought enough Chinese food for six people, and it was still hot. Tia discovered she was starving.

"I don't have any beer, but I've got a couple of sodas."

"That'll work for me. I'd be okay with water."

After they were done eating and the leftovers were stored in the refrigerator, Nance stepped into the living room.

"Do you have cats?" He couldn't help himself.

Tia sniffed. "It doesn't smell, does it? Sometimes I walk in, and it smells like old people."

"No, it doesn't, I was just curious."

Tia was puzzled by the question, then realized she had suggested she might have six cats when she first talked to him.

"No, no cats here," she finally replied. "Why?"

"I thought you mentioned you had some." He shrugged. "It's nothing."

"I mean, I like cats and I've always wanted one," Tia said. "My mom was allergic to them, so we were never allowed to have one." She paused. "I finally got one when I was living in California." Her voice was sad. "Her name was Fetch."

"What happened to her?"

"I had to give her up to come back here." Tia sniffed. "I couldn't bring her back because, you know, Mom was allergic."

"Right," Nance replied, nodding. "I'm sorry about that. Well, maybe you can get one now."

"Maybe, but I'd like to get this mess cleaned up first." They both looked around the room, at the jumble of totes.

"What's that for?" Nance asked as he noticed the empty corner and the ladder standing next to a door.

Tia groaned and covered her face with her hands.

"Thanks for reminding me." She opened up her fingers to look at him. "There's an attic."

"Okay? Most houses have some sort of attic."

Tia watched the expression on Nance's face change. "You mean?"

Tia closed her fingers and nodded into her hands. "Yep."

"Let's see," Nance said. He picked up the ladder. "Which way?"

Tia dropped her hands and led him into her bedroom. He immediately spotted the opening and set up the ladder, climbed up and pushed aside the piece of wood.

Nance poked his head into the opening and used the flashlight on his phone to illuminate the area.

"I see what you mean." He pulled his head down to look at her. "Do you want me to help you get them down?"

Tia considered. She did want the boxes down so she could at least see what she was dealing with, but to have Nance help? She wasn't sure that was a good idea.

"I was going to hire a couple of guys to come help, but if you're willing, we could do it now," Tia finally said.

"Let's do it then," Nance replied and started to pull himself into the attic. Tia was momentarily distracted by his very nicely shaped backside and stood there admiring it until she realized he appeared to be stuck.

"What's wrong?"

He pulled himself out of the opening and stepped down a step on the ladder.

"I don't fit."

Tia should have anticipated that. His shoulders were just too broad. She studied the shoulders in question, and decided they were two of the things she liked about him.

"Well, that's that."

"No, wait, why don't you go up and get the boxes and hand them down to me? That would work."

They changed places and Tia, armed with a lantern she had found in the garage, crawled up. She was acutely aware that it was now her backside that was front and center for Nance to see. She squeezed her eyes shut and forced herself to ignore it.

Once up, she hauled boxes to the opening and handed them down to Nance, who carried them to the living room. It was cold up there, and she could hear the rain hitting on the room, but within minutes, Tia was sweating. By the time the last one was down, Tia was ready for a break. She looked at Nance, who looked like he had just stepped out of a sportsman's catalog, he wasn't even breathing hard.

"Are you okay?" he asked her as he put out a hand to help her step away from the ladder.

Tia took his hand without thinking. "Yeah," she replied. "That's my workout for the day."

"You did great," he replied as she dropped the hand. "Ready for a break?"

"Definitely." She led the way to the kitchen. "Water?"

He agreed to the water and wandered to the sunroom. "I would totally live in this room if I lived here. You should have your office out here."

Tia handed a glass of ice water to him and looked around. "That's not a bad idea, now that you mention it. It's a lot airier than the front bedroom."

"And you could watch the river."

She looked back at the sunroom as they walked to the living room and wondered why she hadn't thought of it. Well, it had been full of boxes to begin with, so there was that, but there wasn't any reason she couldn't make herself a little area, move her computer now and the desk later. It was something to consider.

The living room was considerably more crowded when they stepped into it, still carrying their water.

"What now?" he asked as he looked at his watch. "I can help with some of these too, if you want."

"I would love the company, but are you sure you want to help? You've already moved a whole room in boxes."

"Sure. That didn't take that long, just tell be what you want me to do."

He took the garbage bags to the garage, added to Tia's stack without judging, then carried a stack of books to her office. He finally sat down next to Tia on the couch.

She was suddenly aware that he was very close. She was sweaty and dirty, and just realized she was wearing the oldest thing she owned, her dad's jersey. She picked at the hem.

"You look fine," Nance assured her. It was if he had read her mind. "Are you a Fran Tarkenton fan?"

Tia looked down at her shirt. It was purple with the number ten in white, with the name famous quarterback's name on the back.

"My dad was, they were friends. This jersey was his."

"Tarkenton is a Vikings' legend. I'm a little jealous right now."

"It's seen better days, but it makes me feel close to my dad."

"I bet." He looked around the living room. "Is this where you grew up?"

Tia shook her head. "We lived in a little town near Rochester named Elgin. My dad was an insurance agent."

"Ah, the home of the Cheese Days."

"I haven't been back for a long time," Tia continued. "I went to the University of Minnesota after high school, then got the job in Sacramento."

"You went to the university?" He did the math in his head. "We would have been there at the same time. You would have studied science, right?"

Tia nodded. "Genetics. But I don't recall ever seeing you." She shrugged. "I didn't get out much."

"I don't recall seeing you either. Interesting."

"Anyway, Dad bought this place so we could spend summers by the river. It was the best childhood."

They went back to their chore, and they worked well together, which surprised Tia after the fiasco of the previous night. Tia chalked it up to a fleeting case of jealousy, however misguided. It was sweet, she decided.

When another storm kicked up, a flash of lightning and the accompanying crack of thunder made them both jump. The lights flickered and the room went dark.

"Well."

Nance stood up and stretched, then walked through the kitchen to the sunroom. Tia followed and found him standing at the windows, looking out at the river.

"Beautiful, isn't it?" His voice was husky. "I never get tired of it, and you've got a front-row seat."

Tia rubbed her arms. "As long as we don't have a tornado, or a flood, or get struck by lightning."

As if on cue, another crack of thunder followed a bright flash.

Nance surveyed the room. "We're probably safe enough, this property sits up high enough off the water to keep the flooding away." He paused. "Have you ever considered opening up the wall between this room and the kitchen? It would make a great space for entertaining."

"Actually, I have." Tia looked around and nodded. "I'd also like to update the bathroom, add a larger window in the front of the living room, and replace the siding so the house doesn't stick out like a sore thumb in this neighborhood."

"All good projects," Nance agreed. "It would be more comfortable living here, and I imagine it would make the neighbors happy."

"Maybe we'll find enough cash in our sorting to do all those projects, but seriously, this house used to be the only one on this street, built in the 1930's. The rest of them have just popped up in the last fifteen or twenty years."

"It would probably be very valuable to a developer." Nance continued to watch the storm as it moved across the river.

Tia nodded before she realized he couldn't see her in the darkened room. "I've been approached, and yeah, it would be pretty lucrative on my part to sell, but I have to have a place to live."

Nance glanced at her. "And?"

"And I choose here. Besides the memories of summer cookouts and playing in the river, the location suits me. I love this area and I'm starting to make friends here." She shrugged. "I like the history."

"And the house is nice."

"Or it will be, once I can get Mom's stuff gone through and organized."

The lights came back on as she finished speaking. Tia moved back to the living room.

'We've made some progress," Nance observed. "Do you want me to carry these boxes to your office?"

"That would be great." Tia picked up a box of her own and headed to the office. "I've been putting the stuff I need in here. It makes for another mess, but..."

"But it's necessary." He sat two boxes on the floor. "I get it now, but I'm still glad you're not a hoarder."

"Not in the true sense of the word anyway," Tia laughed. "That really bothered you, didn't it?"

"You have no idea." Nance looked off into space.

"Are you going to tell me about it?"

"Not today. Just know that I've been in a house that only had paths. One of the worst experiences of my life." Nance spoke seriously. "And just so you know, my mom says I have OCD and everything has to be in its place."

Nance didn't give her a chance to reply as he turned to the door. "I'd better get going. It's getting late."

"Don't you usually visit your parents on Sundays?"

"I do," Nance agreed, "but they had plans today, so here I am." He shrugged.

"I'm glad you came." Tia was surprised that was true, and she hadn't trembled every time he got close, at least, not visibly. Maybe she was getting used to him.

Nance started to open the front door, then stopped and turned around.

"Do you still want to do a road trip?"

Tia looked up at him in confusion. "A road trip?"

"Last night you said something about going to Henderson to look at old records. Are you still going to do that? I'd like to go along, if that's okay."

Tia had forgotten the conversation. She remembered now. "If we're going to continue the research, then yes, I'd like to go. And yes, I'd love to have you tag along, if you really want to." She paused. "I should warn you though, it can get boring."

"I doubt I'll be bored." He pulled the door open. "Let me know when." He leaned down like he was going to kiss her, and Tia resisted the urge to step back.

Nance gave her a little kiss on her nose and stepped out

the door. In a quick moment, he was getting in his SUV and driving away in the light rain.

Tia stood there for a moment. He kissed her. She touched her nose and shut the door, then shrugged.

"He probably does that to all the women he knows."

CHAPTER EIGHT

Tia was getting ready for bed when she realized she had never called Erica. She picked up her phone and hit the call button.

"Well, hello there, I thought maybe you ran off and eloped with your hunky weatherman."

"Ha, ha, very funny, Erica," Tia replied. "You know I've only met him three times."

"Three times?" Erica's voice carried curiosity with it. "I thought it was only twice." She paused. "Wait, you saw him today, didn't you? That's why you didn't call. Tell me all."

Tia laughed at Erica's hopeful tone.

"There's nothing to tell. He was crabby at dinner last night, so he came by today to apologize."

"Did he? And why was he crabby?"

"That's a story for another day, but he brought lunch, then stayed and helped me get all of the boxes out of the attic space."

"Wow, so he was there most of the day." Erica paused. "Interesting."

"It's not interesting at all," Tia groaned. She was beginning to regret telling Erica about it. "I just wanted to let you know we got all of the boxes down so the boys don't have to come do it."

"Oh right, well, that's good to know." Erica's voice held contriteness. "I'll let them know. But, back to the weatherman."

"Nance. His name is Nance and it's just business." Tia paused and asked herself why she had to keep telling people that.

"Right, just business."

"Anyway," Tia continued, laughing, "I'm going to bed now."

"Alone?"

"Goodnight, Erica."

Tia heard her friend laughing as she hit the end call button.

Tia spent the next three days focused on work but took the time before dinner each night to ride her bike. The weather had turned nice and Tia didn't want to waste it. She was able to sit outside for a little while each evening before she tackled a tote after dinner.

"And one tote a night means this is never getting done," she declared out loud as the looked at the offending stacks on Wednesday afternoon. It seemed that she was keeping more than she threw away right now, and that was frustrating. She didn't know where she was going to store it all.

She talked to Erica for a few minutes every day just to hear another voice besides her own, and she had taken Nance's suggestion and moved her work station to the sunroom. She was only using a card table for now while she saw how she liked it and how to make a permanent workspace while not turning the whole sunroom into an office. Her current desk wouldn't work since it had shelves above it that would block the window and the view of the river.

She finally called Erica, who offered to stop by after work.

"I don't know, Tia, I like the concept, but unless you buy a different desk, you'll have to have it against this wall."

The back wall of the sunroom butted up against Tia's bedroom, so there weren't any windows, but Tia didn't like the idea of sitting with her back to the rest of the world.

"Maybe an L-shaped desk," Erica suggested.

Tia nodded. "I like that idea, but I'm going to need some shelving and a file cabinet too. I've got to have some storage."

Erica walked around the sunroom, angling her head one way and then the other.

"If we make the north part of the room the office area, I could look out at the river and there'd be room for someone to sit on the other side of the counter part of the desk."

"You could put a tall bookshelf behind you and maybe you could find a short, long bookshelf to put on the north side so you have more storage, but it doesn't block the view that way either."

Tia's forehead burrowed. "Do you mean a credenza?"

"Something like that." Erica nodded.

"I can see it, but you know, I don't think I want new. Do you think we can find something antique?"

"Vintage? Or maybe mid-century modern?" Erica turned around in the space they had decided on. "Anything would be better than the card table."

"Right? Do you want to go shopping with me, maybe Saturday afternoon?" Tia asked.

"That would work," Erica replied. "Jamael isn't coming in until lunchtime so I'll have to work in the morning, but we could go after lunch. We could check out the antique shops in town for something."

"That's a great idea," Tia agreed. "It's a date."

A few minutes after Erica left, Tia's phone rang. It was Nance.

"Hi there," Tia answered. "I was hoping you'd call." She rolled her eyes and clapped her palm to her forehead. Talk about pathetic. She had as good as admitted that she missed him. She did, she just didn't want to admit it.

"Hi, yourself." Tia could hear the humor in his voice and silently groaned.

"So, are you calling to tell me a storm is on the way? Because I just watched the guy on TV tell us all it's supposed to be nice for the next week or so."

Nance laughed. "No, no storms, you can trust that guy on TV. I just called to see how the sorting and organizing are going."

Tia brushed her hair back. "Slowly, but I've been working on it in the evenings. At the rate I'm going, I'm never going to get done, and where am I going to store the stuff I want to keep?"

Nance laughed again. "I suggest not using the attic. Have you gone through any of those boxes yet?"

"I haven't, I'm afraid to see what's in them," she replied. "I thought maybe I could at least take everything out and put it in the empty totes I have now, just to get rid of the cardboard, but that's more work."

"I admit I would be tempted to do that just because of the cardboard, but I understand what you're saying," Nance agreed. "It's a conundrum."

"Oh, I took your advice and moved my workspace to the sunroom," Tia interjected. "It's just a card table for now, but I think it'll work."

"That's good, do you need help moving your desk? I

could stop by on Saturday morning."

"That would be helpful, but I'm thinking about getting a different desk. If I use the one I have, it has to be up against the wall and I'll be sitting with my back to the windows."

"That makes sense," he agreed. "Want me to help you shop for one?"

Tia was startled by the offer. Except for Sunday when he was helping her with the sorting, he was pretty focused on the coffee can and its contents. So far, he hadn't mentioned it.

"My friend Erica and I are going to hit some antique shops Saturday afternoon to see if we can find something that goes with the house."

"I like that idea, especially if you're going to make it your home. It should reflect your personality."

"Are you saying my personality is old?" Tia asked. There was no answer. "I'm kidding."

"You made a joke. How about that?" Tia could hear the surprise in his voice.

"I make jokes," she defended herself. "Anyway, I don't know if we can find anything, but we're going to give it a shot."

"Let me know if you find something," he said. "I'll be happy to help you get it home."

Tia wrinkled her forehead. He was being awfully helpful, then decided that he wanted to get her house in order as quickly as possible if he was going to have to come here. She bristled for just a moment, then exhaled. He was just trying to be helpful and she should appreciate that.

"I appreciate the offer and I'll let you know, but don't forget when you're lugging a heavy desk around that you offered."

"I'll remember and I'd better let you go." He paused. "Just call if you want the help."

Tia had barely hit the end call button when her phone rang again. It was Nance.

"Hello?"

"Hi, I forgot why I called before. I wanted you to know I have Friday off if you still want to take that road trip."

When Tia didn't answer, he continued. "The weather's supposed to be great."

"Sorry, I forgot what road trip you were talking about." Tia rolled her eyes at herself. She had forgotten. "Just a minute and I'll check my calendar." She walked to her work area and pulled up her calendar on the computer. "I've got an early online meeting, but I could probably leave by nine or nine-thirty.”

“I’m okay with that, it would be close to lunchtime by the time we got there, but we could have an early lunch before you get started.”

“Me? Oh no, L’Breck, you come on a road trip, you help with the research,” Tia laughed. “But that sounds good. I don’t think the library in Henderson opens until after lunch anyway.”

“You’ll have to show me what to do,” Nance warned. “Historical research isn’t something I do.”

“I can walk you through it.” Tia paused. “Should I meet you at your place at ten or so?”

There was a long silence before Nance spoke again. “I was thinking I would drive,” he finally said. “That way I could pick you up. It’ll be quicker if I come to you.”

“Okay, if that’s what you want.” Tia shrugged. She didn’t understand his hesitation, but maybe he liked to drive. “You know, you’ll have to bring me home when we get back.”

“No problem. I thought we could have dinner when we get back to Stillwater.”

“That sounds good,” Tia replied and after goodbyes again, she hit the end call button on her phone. Would that be considered a date? Did it really matter? She admitted she had liked him before she even knew him, liked him more now. He wouldn’t have had to stay and help sort through her mom’s things, but he did, and he was good company. She had been relaxed, for the most part, that day, so she could do this too. It would be fine.

It wasn’t fine.

The minute Tia opened her door to Nance Friday morning, her heart started thumping. He looked good, he smelled good, and it was all she could do to keep her knees from buckling. As it was, she stumbled as she backed up to let him inside.

And of course, Nance steadied her, bringing her up against his solid body. So, she backed up again and nearly fell over a tote. He grasped her arm to keep her from falling.

“I’m okay, really,” she answered without him having to ask. Tia picked up her bag and gestured him to go ahead of her. He waited on the porch while she locked the door, then guided her with his hand on her back down the step and to his waiting SUV. By the time Nance started the engine, Tia was in stimulus overdrive.

It took Tia more than thirty minutes to stop the internal shaking, and Nance must have been aware something was wrong, because he kept his eyes on the highway and didn't say anything until she relaxed.

"I brought you coffee."

Tia jumped. "Oh, yeah, right, thanks." She picked up the cup, took a sip. The movement settled her back down.

"I brought you a donut too," he continued when she replaced the cup in the cupholder. "It's right there." He gestured to a bag on the console.

"Thanks, I think I could use something to eat."

"Help yourself."

The donut and coffee helped calm her nerves and Tia was finally able to have a conversation. They talked about the weather... which was beautiful... and the countryside they were traveling through until Nance drove down a hill, around a curve, and across a bridge into the town of Henderson.

Tia hadn't been there before but immediately felt at home. Historic homes lined the streets and the business district was historic with quaint little shops lining the street. Nance pulled into the parking lot of the library and parked.

"Ready for lunch?"

Tia wasn't. The nerves were back and she wasn't sure she could eat anything, but she stepped out of the SUV when Nance opened her door. She immediately stumbled and nearly fell face first onto the pavement.

"Good grief," she muttered under her breath. "Get your act together."

"What was that?"

"Nothing." Tia was still silently lecturing herself as she stood up and started walking towards the cafe next door.

Nance guided her as she walked, which didn't help a bit, Tia decided.

"Are you okay? You seem a little off balance today."

Tia stepped away from him as soon as they were in the cafe, more than ready to put a little distance between them. A little off balance? Was he serious? She was in all kinds of trouble here. She should probably call it off and make him take her back home. It was just too much for her.

"I think so," she said instead. "I think I just need something to eat."

He searched her face, which made her even more uncomfortable, she could feel the heat fill her face.

"That's probably it."

They were shown to a table and with it between them, Tia started to relax again, was even able to eat a chicken salad sandwich served on a fresh croissant, and a bowl of beer cheese soup.

After Nance paid for the lunch... he insisted... they walked over to the library and introduced themselves to the librarian. Jane Howe led them downstairs to the research area and showed them how to use the microfilm machines. It was only when Tia was seated in front of an ancient microfilm machine reading old newspapers, that she was able to truly relax.

Within five minutes, Tia was immersed in the past and mostly able to ignore the man sitting next to her at his own microfilm machine. She had shown him how to run it and given him several reels of microfilm to read.

Two hours later, Nance sat back and stretched.

"What?"

"I need a break," he answered, standing up. "I don't know how you do this. We've been at it for hours and as far as I can see, we haven't found anything."

Tia flexed her shoulders. "I've found some references to the Beckwith family, but you're right, we haven't found much that's helpful. It's much easier to find information with the online newspapers because you can search a name, but this, it's old school and the real root of historical research."

"I suppose, but for now, I'm going next door to the cafe for something to drink," Nance replied. "Do you want something?"

Tia looked up. "Yes, please, if Jane says we can have drinks down here."

Nance winked. "I'll pour on the charm with our lovely librarian and see if I can make that happen."

He was true to his word and came back about thirty minutes later. He offered Tia a covered cup with a straw sticking out of it.

Tia took it and took a sip. "Umm, thanks." She sipped again. "It took you a long time. She must have been harder to convince than you thought."

Nance looked puzzled.

"Jane Howe? The librarian?"

"Oh yeah. No, that part was easy." He grinned. "She couldn't resist. She's really nice though, gave me a tour of the library. I made a donation."

Tia's jaw dropped. "You bribed her?"

He just laughed. "I made a donation because I like the

place and I like what they're doing here."

"Okay then. That was nice of you." She sat her cup down.

"There's more."

Tia looked back up at him. "More?"

He drew his hand out from behind his back. "Pie."

"Lemon meringue pie perhaps?"

"Cherry." He handed her a fork. "I didn't know what kind you like, so I got something I like."

Tia took a bite. "I like cherry, I like most pies." She paused. "Is it okay to have food in here?"

Nance laughed. "I got permission, but don't get crumbs anywhere."

Tia gobbled down the pie, didn't even worry about being polite. She was suddenly hungry and the pie was good.

She handed the empty plate back to Nance. "Ready to get back to work?"

He threw the paper plate into the trash and put his hands on his hips, just looked at her.

Tia licked her lips and wondered if she had cherry pie on her face.

"What?"

"I just realized something."

"Again, what?"

"You're a hard ass when it comes to work."

"I'm not," Tia protested.

Nance cocked his head to the side, never taking his eyes off her. "Seriously."

"Okay, maybe," Tia admitted. "But I take everything I do seriously."

"I believe that. Do you ever have any fun?"

"Fun?" She was confused, and it showed on her face. "I have fun."

"But you take it seriously."

Tia's voice faltered. "I suppose." She turned back to her machine.

"When was the last time you laughed just because something struck you as funny?" He sat down at the table.

Tia shrugged. "I guess I don't know, I don't keep track. How did we get on this subject anyway?" She was starting to get irritated. "We only have a little time left here unless we want to come back, so I want to make the most of it. Is that so bad?"

Nance shook his head. "Of course not." He turned to his machine. "Back to work then."

Tia tried to concentrate on the newspaper in front of

her, but his words stung. She could have fun, and she was having fun. This was her fun. Just because she wasn't laughing didn't mean it wasn't. She sighed and put it out of her mind.

"What was that?"

Nance's voice broke into Tia's concentration. She jumped.

"What was what?"

"That noise. You didn't hear it?" Nance looked up at the ceiling.

Tia followed his gaze and shook her head. She had been absorbed in the microfilm file of the local newspaper and quite frankly, had forgotten Nance was there. She stretched and leaned back in her chair. "What kind of noise?"

"It was a click." He looked at the ceiling again. "Above us somewhere. Maybe by the stairs."

"Hmm." Tia looked around and stretched again. "It's probably just the ladies upstairs. What time is it?"

"A little after six." Nance looked up from his watch. "Don't they close at six?"

"They do."

"It's really quiet now, do you think they left? Why would they do that if we're still here?"

"I think they probably did. I think they forgot we were down here and left for the day." She gathered up her things and looked longingly at the microfilm machine, then took the film out and turned it off. "That's too bad, I could have stayed here all night. These old newspapers are so interesting to read."

Nance started to disagree, but he knew she was being sincere. He had used the second machine, as old and ugly as the one Tia was using, but he hadn't found anything interesting and was a little bored, just like Tia had warned.

"We can just turn off the lights and let ourselves out."

Tia nodded and picked up her bag, followed Nance to the top of the stairs and the double doors that led to the main part of the library.

Nance pushed on the old doors. They rattled but didn't open.

Tia peered around him. "They're locked? From the outside?"

Nance tried again. "Damn, I think they are. With a padlock. Who does that in this day and age?" He examined the door, then turned to look at Tia, standing two steps down from him. "I could probably break it down." He looked hopeful, then sighed when Tia shook her head.

"I don't think that's a good idea. They probably wouldn't be happy if you broke their hundred-year-old doors."

"I suppose not." He looked at the doors again and back at Tia. "Maybe we can open a window in the basement and get out that way."

"That's a better option." Tia led the way back down the steps. They entered the large room and Tia stopped, her hands on her hips.

Nance, who wasn't prepared for the quick stop, nearly ran into the back of her. He put his hands on her shoulders to steady himself and Tia immediately moved away, so quickly the touch may have never happened.

"That might be a no go." Tia walked in a circle around the room.

"The windows?"

"There are windows, but as you can see…" she pointed to one. "They're the big glass tile type."

"I see that." Nance wandered around the room. "Maybe there's a coal chute."

Tia nodded in agreement. "It's an old building, so that's a possibility. Let's look."

They searched the main room, checked a small bathroom and a storage room, filled with cleaning supplies and old boxes of Christmas decorations.

"There's no coal chute." Tia sat back down at the table holding the microfilm machine. "I think we're stuck here until the librarian comes back in the morning."

"We can just call someone and have them come let us out," Nance suggested.

"Good idea." Tia picked up her phone off the table, while Nance pulled his out of his pocket.

"No signal." Tia sat her phone down.

Nance started pacing. "This is crazy. How could they forget we were down here?"

Tia shrugged, but Nance didn't wait for an answer.

"And how did they miss seeing my vehicle in the parking lot?" he continued.

"You have a point there, that thing is huge, but maybe they thought we left and walked down to the cafe or something." He started pacing again.

Nance stopped. "Well, it's big, yes, but I'm a big man. That's not the point."

"On the plus side, there's a bathroom." Tia's smile

brightened. "And I can keep looking for clues."

Nance sighed and sat on the chair next to her. Tia immediately scooted a few inches away.

Did he smell bad, or what? He almost sniffed himself. Nance knew she hadn't wanted to work with him on this project, but he thought she had changed her mind. She had loosened up a little, seemed more comfortable around him lately.

He sighed again.

"You know we could be murdered down here." Nance's statement was matter of fact.

CHAPTER NINE

T ia looked at him in alarm. "Do you really think we're going to be murdered in the basement of a library in a little town in the middle of Minnesota?" Her voice squeaked on the last word.

Nance smiled. "That's what happens in the movies."

"Be serious." Tia punched him in the arm.

As Nance rubbed his arm, he realized it was the first time she had actually touched him. His smile grew.

"I am serious. It happens, I'm sure of it."

"It does not, and why would anyone want to lock us in here and then murder us? Did you forget we're the only ones in the building? They all left." she looked up at the ceiling.

"Maybe they're coming back." Nance thought nothing of the sort, but it was fun to tease her a little.

Tia ignored him and sat back down at her microfilm reader, opened a new film box, and threaded it through the machine.

"I guess since we have more time, we can continue our research."

Nance groaned.

"What's wrong now?" Tia didn't look up from her machine.

"It's a little boring, don't you think?"

Tia looked up at him and shrugged her shoulders. "Never boring for me, but I suppose I understand. But," she drew the word out. "Are you interested in wars?"

"I like history in general," Nance replied, "but I don't know much about specific wars."

"Now's your chance to learn." She handed him a box of film. "Newspapers are a great resource for the day-to-day history and its effects on the everyday American. Maybe you can gain a little insight into your great-grandfather's life."

"Okay, okay." Nance threaded his machine like she had showed him. "I'll try looking at it with a new point of view, but I'll tell you, those Mr. and Mrs. So And So visited Mr. and Mrs. So And So on Sunday, or Mr. So And Mrs. So visited the village for business are enough to bring tears to my eyes."

Tia laughed, her eyes echoing the emotion, and Nance fell a little more as he turned to his machine.

"Just scan for the names we're looking for... Brownell, Olson and Beckwith. Skip the inside pages with the stories and national news," Tia suggested. "It'll go faster for you."

Nance went back to work. "Wait, what's this?" he asked a few minutes later.

Tia looked up from her machine.

"What's what? Did you find something?"

"This headline reads: 'Death By Defenestration.' What the hell is that?"

"Someone threw him out of a window?" Tia leaned over and read the first few lines of the news article. "Looks like it. You don't see that very often."

"How do you even know that?" Nance's voice was incredulous.

Tia shrugged. "I know a lot of things about death. It's not always useful, but sometimes it can be. Defenestration isn't common, but it happened more than you might think in the Middle Ages."

"Huh." Nance read on. "I've never heard of such a thing."

"And yet, according to your newspaper story, it happened in Minnesota in 1918." She leaned over again to read, taking care not to touch Nance's arm. "Was it anybody we know?"

Nance leaned forward. "No, it's a guy named Hubert Billingsly." He turned his head to look at Tia. "We don't know him, do we?"

Tia realized how close they were and leaned away, turned to her own newspaper. "We don't, so on we go."

Tia didn't know how much time had passed when Nance stood up and sighed.

"What?" Tia glanced toward him.

"Sorry, still bored. We've been at this for hours. It's dark outside and I'm getting hungry. Have we even found anything worthwhile?"

Tia turned to look at him. "Actually, I just did. Listen

to this. Mrs. Mildred Olson and children of Lexington visited the home of her aunt and uncle, Mr. and Mrs. Stephen Brownell and family for Sunday dinner. She and their
daughter Elizabeth Brownell spent the afternoon at the
church social."

"So?"

"These are Lizzie's parents."

"And what does that mean?"

"It means that Lizzie and Mildred not only knew each
other, they were cousins."

"You really didn't know that?"

"I suspected, but I didn't have Mildred's maiden name,
couldn't find it in the records."

"We found a piece of the puzzle?"

Tia nodded and raised an eyebrow. "A little piece. I don't
know if she's a niece of Mr. Brownell or Mrs. Brownell, so I
still don't have a maiden name, but I have a place to look.
Does that mean I can keep looking?"

"I suppose," Nance conceded, "but remind me next time
you want to go to a library to do research that I get bored
easily." He shrugged. "And I'm hungry."

Tia pushed her hair out of her eyes and smiled, a genuine smile this time that reached her eyes. "We have been at
it for a long time. I'm just used to it."

Nance realized it was the first time she had smiled like
this, just a real, sincere smile. He resisted putting a hand
to his heart to slow its beat back to normal.

Tia reached into the large bag she carried with her. "I
have granola bars." She handed two to him and reached
back in, brought out two bottles of water.

Nance took the bars and one of the bottles of water,
then tried to look into the bag. "What else do you have in
there? Cookies would be good. A steak would hold me over."

Tia laughed as she swatted his hand away. "As far as
food goes, this is it. It's my emergency supply, but it might
tide you over until we get rescued."

"What about you?" Nance held out the granola bars.
"Here, take one."

Tia shook her head. "It's not necessary. I'm not that
hungry, so the water will be fine." She twisted the cap of the
water bottle. "I admit to being a little thirsty."

"I'll eat one, so if you change your mind later, we'll still
have one."

Tia looked around the room. Nance's eyes followed hers.
All he saw were shadowy rows of old books.

"I know this kind of research can be boring, so why

don't you take a look at some of the books here? They're mostly local history books, so maybe you'll find something useful in one of them."

Nance looked at the rows and rows of books. This wasn't his idea of a fun Friday night, but he was stuck here, so why not? He wolfed down one of the granola bars and wandered around the shelves, looking for a place to start. He glanced back at Tia with her face glowing in the light of the microfilm machine. She had already forgotten he was there.

He selected several books and got to work, and for a while the only sound was the click of the machine as Tia moved the film through.

"Look, I found something!" Nance jumped out of his chair and held up a book.

Tia jumped, put her hand on her heart. She had forgotten he was there.

"What time is it?" She stretched and flexed her neck muscles.

"Eleven thirty." He checked his watch and held up the book. "Don't you want to know what I found? It's a biography."

He took the book to Tia and placed it in front of her. She was apparently intrigued enough that she didn't flinch away from him. Nance noticed but said nothing.

"This is the biography of Thomas Brownell, local pioneer."

"I see that," Tia said, reading. "Born in 1845, in Knox County, Ohio, and married Phoebe Carnes. They came here in 1880, with children Stephen, Edith, Louis and Thomas. He was a prominent banker at the City Bank."

"Hey, wait, Carnes is your last name. Are you related?"

"I don't think so," Tia replied, thinking. "The name doesn't sound familiar. I think I would have already recognized the name Brownell. She could be a distant cousin, I suppose. Some of the Carnes did come from Ohio, so maybe I'll have to look into that."

"And look, he was a banker, very prominent. There's even a picture."

Tia ignored him and kept reading. "His son, Stephen, married Alice Hamilton and joined his father in the banking business. His son Louis is a respected pastor at the St. Helen's Episcopal Church and son Thomas has just completed his law degree in Chicago."

"Very prominent," Nance repeated, still looking over her shoulder. "How did I do?"

Tia looked up and found him very close to her, she

quickly looked back down at the book.

"Good," she stuttered. "This is good."

"Shh." Nance put his finger on his lips. "Do you hear that?"

Tia listened. Footsteps. Slow and light, upstairs, maybe two people. Her eyes widened. "You don't mean..." she whispered.

"Someone is coming to murder us?" Nance gestured to a spot by the bottom of the steps, out of sight of the doors above. The footsteps stopped at the basement doors. They rattled. Tia sucked in her breath and held it for seemed like hours.

"Hello, anyone down there?"

Tia let her breath out and called out. Jane Howe clattered down the steps, clad in pajama pants and a t-shirt, followed by an older man in uniform.

"There you are." Jane hurried over to Tia. "I'm so sorry," she exclaimed. "I forgot all about the two of you when I locked up. One of the others mentioned your car was still parked in the parking lot. I just thought you were getting a bite to eat or something. I'm so sorry."

"It's no problem," Nance replied for Tia. "We lost track of time."

"How did you find us?" Tia pushed her hair back.

"Oh, Deputy Schultz saw the basement lights on when he was patrolling through town." Jane turned to the man next to her. "He saw the vehicle too and called me to see if anything was wrong. All of a sudden, I realized you two were down here, so here we are." She spread her hands out.

"We're glad to see you, although Tia was perfectly happy reading old newspapers all night." He smiled at Tia.

"Guilty as charged," she laughed, "but we're ready to go. And we thank you for rescuing us. We'll just be a minute." Tia turned to get her belongings. She took a picture of the page in the book and handed the book to Jane, then started to shut down the microfilm machine.

"Oh, leave that, I'll take care of it in the morning. I'm sure you're more than ready to get home."

"As fun as it was, you're right, we're ready to get out of here." Nance waited for Tia to gather the rest of her things, then carried them up the stairs for her and to the SUV.

"Thanks again for rescuing us," Nance told Jane as he shook her hand. He turned to Deputy Schultz and offered his hand. "I'm Nance L'Breck, by the way."

The deputy shook his hand. "Dean Schultz, and we know who you are."

"And thanks for noticing something was off. We appreciate it."

"Well, we didn't want our favorite weatherman dying in our basement," Jane said nervously. "It could be bad for business."

Dean nodded and agreed, then shrugged. "After I ran your car's plates, I realized we had a celebrity in town. And then I saw the lights. I hadn't put two and two together yet. You know, we don't get many famous people here, so this is actually an honor."

"Part of it is my fault," Tia said. "I wasn't watching the time like I should have."

Nance nodded. "Me either, I'm afraid. So, how about we keep this quiet for all our sakes?" He grinned and the other three laughed.

"It is a little funny though, you have to admit," Jane said.

"We'd better get out of here, so you guys can get on with your night," Nance said, looking around. "Tia? Do you have everything?"

They all trudged up the stairs and after saying goodnights and more thanks, Nance drove off into the night.

To Nance's surprise, Tia laughed for the first ten minutes. "Oh my God, I thought for a moment we really were going to be murdered down there." She wiped her eyes. "And you, sending my imagination into overdrive." She punched him on the arm for the second time that night.

Nance found himself joining in her laughter. "I bet the looks on our faces was priceless. I had almost convinced myself that we were actually going to be murdered too."

"Murdered in the basement of a library in a small town." Tia laughed harder and wiped tears away.

When they finally calmed down, Nance pulled into an all-night convenience store.

"Hungry?"

"Starved, now that you mention it," Tia replied as they got out.

They loaded up on snacks and soft drinks and set off again, the rest of the ride back to Stillwater going quickly.

When they were back at Tia's, she got her bag and started to get out.

"Let me help you." Nance got out and came around to Tia's side of the SUV.

"I've got it." She dug her keys out as he followed her up the sidewalk to the front door. "Really. I've got it." She set the bag down to unlock the door and when she turned around to say goodnight, Nance was right there.

His lips met hers before she could protest and his hands grasped her shoulders. It was over before Tia could react and he was helping her through the door.

Before she could say anything, Nance dropped her bag and turned away, closing the door behind him.

"Goodnight," she heard him say from the other side of the door.

Despite the lack of sleep, Tia was up and dressed early the next morning. She started her laundry and dusted the floors in the kitchen and sunroom, scrubbed the bathroom, then swept the patio and steps to the little beach on the river. The day was just as nice as the previous day, Tia decided. It was sunny and warm with no wind. She breathed in deep and looked at the river, always the same, but always different. The water never stopped moving and from one moment to the next, it had changed completely.

She breathed in deep one more time, then turned back to the house. She still needed to shower and change so she could have lunch before meeting Erica to go shopping.

The great thing about Stillwater, Tia decided as she drove into town, was that everything was close by. She and Erica would be able to walk to the various antique shops. She parked at the bookstore and the two women walked across the street to the first shop.

Tia had chosen to wear blue jeans and an olive-green sweater with tennis shoes since they were walking. Erica had worn tennis shoes as well, but they were bright pink to match her leggings. She was wearing a flowery, flowing long blouse in magenta and orange and wouldn't be blending into the background. Tia envied the older woman, wished she could be comfortable wearing bold colors and clothes that made a statement.

They found an antique wood file cabinet in the first shop, but nothing else Tia thought would work.

They moved on to the second shop and finally found a desk. It wasn't mid-century, in fact, if Tia had to guess, she would say it was an attorney's desk from the early 1900s, made of oak, and heavy. It took some searching, but they found a small library table that mostly matched the desk. It would help with the L-shape Tia was going for.

They walked to the third shop to see if they could find a bookshelf, but after combing the store, Tia couldn't find one she liked. She was just ready to call it quits when Erica called out.

"Oh, look at this," Erica exclaimed. "It's an attorney's bookshelf. This would be perfect."

Tia wandered back to her friend and examined the bookshelf in question. It was built in sections and each shelf had a glass front that opened and closed.

"I love it," Tia exclaimed. She looked at the price. "Ouch."

Erica laughed. "I didn't say it was cheap."

"No, you didn't." Tia studied the tag. "Do you think it's worth it?"

Erica nodded. "I did a little research on office furniture this morning and it's all expensive, but not nearly as well made as these."

Tia nodded. Erica was right, and on top on that, Tia loved the bookcase. "I do love it, and I feel like this is an investment in my career. I don't think I can work in the spare bedroom forever."

"Did you consider taking out the bed and making it a full office?"

"I did," Tia replied, "and I was seriously considering it, but Nance is right. Why not take advantage of the light and the view the sunroom offers?"

Tia paid for the bookcase and asked the store owner if she could pick it up the next day. They stepped out and walked to the next shop.

"I was just thinking," Tia said as they walked. "Would it be smart to get an area rug to put in that area?"

"Hmm." Erica considered the question. "Actually, you could have two, one for your area and one for the sitting area in the sunroom. They would make the whole space feel more homey."

"I like that idea. We'd better find a couple now so they can be moved with the rest of the furniture."

"There's a store a little farther down the street that has new furniture," Erica said. "I think they have area rugs. We'll go look when we're done here."

"It's a plan."

"So, Nance L'Breck is going to help you get this all home." She raised an eyebrow.

"He said he would," Tia replied as they walked. She ignored the eyebrow. "I decided to take him up on it. He said he was bringing a friend to help."

"That's handy."

"So, on to another subject. What am I going to do about shelving on the north side of my little space? I think I'm going to need more than just one bookcase."

"Hmm, I'm not sure." Erica pictured the space in her mind.

"It can't be very tall, or it'll obstruct the windows."

"Right," Erica agreed. "You might have to build one, but we can look and see if we find something."

"You're right, I might have to build something. It would work well and I could build one on the opposite wall by the wicker table."

"I like that." Erica paused. "Do you think you could actually build something like that?" She stopped while Tia opened the door of the shop.

"Absolutely not. Do you know a good carpenter?"

They both laughed at Tia's admission, making other customers in the store look up.

They didn't find any shelves that would work, but Tia fell in love with a very old brass nautical clock that could sit on her desk.

The trip to the home decor store yielded two blue and gray area rugs. Again, Tia asked if they could be picked up the next day and was told that was fine.

"You're going to be busy," Erica told Tia as they walked back to the bookstore. Tia carried three bags with her, in addition to the clock, she also found an old wooden paper stacker and a unique desk set that included a pencil holder and a container for paper clips. She also bought a couple of beach-themed items to hang in the sunroom. She was going to love working out there, Tia decided.

Right now, the walls in the whole house were pretty bare. Esther had a few pictures on the walls, but they were prints from the 1980s and not very inspiring. There also weren't many knickknacks sitting around. Tia had never questioned it before, but even as a child, there weren't many decorations in their home.

It seemed like an oxymoron to Tia, given all the clutter in papers and books, but looking at it now, it came off as odd.

Tia decided this was her home now, as Nance had pointed out, so she was going to redecorate and make it hers.

When she got home, Tia kicked off her shoes and poured a glass of wine. She padded out to the patio to watch the water. It was starting to cool down, but Tia didn't mind. How nice it would be to have someone to share the quiet with, she thought, then sighed.

She apparently couldn't even be close to a man, let alone be in a relationship. She wondered how she had managed it with Brock, the only man she had a long relationship with, but then they hadn't ever gotten to the part where he moved in. Of course, there was a reason for that, Tia admitted. The man had a wife, a wife she knew nothing about for three years. When she found out, courtesy of the wife, Tia immediately broke off the relationship.

She shook herself out of those thoughts and turned back to the house just as her phone rang.

"Hello, Nance," she answered. "I was just going to call you."

"Did you find some furniture?"

"I did," Tia replied. "Is your offer to help still good?"

"Definitely," was the quick reply.

He almost sounded excited about it, Tia thought, and decided he had no idea what he was in for.

"I hope your muscles are up to it."

His chuckle was low and husky, and Tia shivered and sat down in one of the patio chairs. She wished she hadn't said anything.

"I try to work out most days," he explained, even though she hadn't actually asked. "It makes me feel better about life."

"I get that," Tia admitted. "I don't do weights or anything, but I do try to get a couple of bike rides each week, when the weather's decent."

"I like to cycle too, and before I forget, the station is sponsoring a fun ride to raise money for the food bank. Do you want to come?"

"Umm, sure, I suppose?"

Even to her ears, that sounded lame, but he continued as if he hadn't heard the hesitation in her voice.

"It starts downtown and ends up at one of the parks," he explained, "You can loop off of the trail, so you can choose how far you want to ride. Trust me, it's fun. There's food and a dance afterward."

Tia screwed up her nose. "Is that mandatory?"

Nance paused for a moment. "No, of course not, but it's pretty casual and a lot of fun."

Tia remembered his comment in the library about not having fun and found it still stung.

"I'm sure it is," Tia finally replied as she stood up. "Let me think about it."

They made plans to meet at the first antique store the next day and Tia wandered back inside. She wasn't hungry, but she supposed she should eat something.

She opened the refrigerator, spied the bottle of wine and poured herself another glass. She took a sip and sighed, pulled out a container of chicken left over from her trip to the See-Food Inn a couple of nights ago. She heated it up in the microwave and stood with her back against the counter to eat.

Tia was certain going to any event with Nance would be a mistake, their trip to Henderson had proved that. She eventually had gotten used to him, and a bike ride might not be that bad. If fact, she was certain she could do a bike ride, even if Nance was a part of it. They wouldn't be in close quarters like yesterday, she reasoned, and it was for a good cause.

She took another sip of wine, wandered into the living room.

"Why does he have to be so good looking? And smart?" she asked out loud. "Because he is and all the other stuff you like, and he is fun, and he makes your heart race."

After another sip of wine, Tia crashed on the couch, put her feet on the armrest. Before she lost her courage, Tia picked up her phone and texted Nance that she would go to the bike ride fundraiser.

He immediately texted 'OK' and nothing else.

"Well, okay then," she said, strangely disappointed. "Maybe he doesn't do texts. Fine then."

Tia gulped down the last of the wine, stood up and walked into the kitchen. She rinsed the empty glass and padded back to the living room, looked around and decided she was tired of totes and boxes, and papers.

She looked at the huge pile of boxes in the corner and sighed. She hadn't looked in one of the attic boxes since she and Nance brought them down.

That brought her thoughts back to the man whose voice made her toes curl, and for some reason, that made her mad.

She stomped over to the boxes and took one off the top, took it over to the couch and opened it. Her hand stilled. It wasn't a stack of papers. Tia reached in and pulled out an object wrapped in newspaper. She unwrapped it and held up a very old plaster pelican. The paint was faded and chipped in a couple of places, Tia noted, but it was still cool. She sat it down and unwrapped another. This one was a wood-carved pelican, dainty, smooth and obviously original work.

The third pelican was delicate blown glass in oranges and reds. Tia held it up to the lamplight and watched the colors glow. Beautiful, she thought, just beautiful. She set it aside and looked back in the box, drew out another carved pelican, similar but not the same as the first one. In all, there were eight pelicans, two of tarnished brass, a cast-iron pelican and a set of salt-and-pepper shakers of two pelicans.

Tia rubbed her eyes. Where had they come from? she wondered. They were beautiful and unique and yet, they were all stuck in the attic. She would take pictures and send them to Marvi and Dawn to see if they knew anything about them. She took them to her bedroom and placed them on her dresser.

The pelicans were the first things she saw the next morning. She was still curious about them, and now she was curious about the rest of the boxes. She wanted to go out and go through them all right now but resisted. She had things to do before Nance got there and this would have to wait.

CHAPTER TEN

"Why are we doing this again?" Reid asked as he drove towards Stillwater. His boys were chatting happily in the backseat of their dad's pickup. They had stopped at McDonald's for lunch and Trey and Benny were playing with the toys that came with their meals.

"Because I thought it would be nice to do something for her," Nance explained for the third time.

"I'm still not buying the nice thing," Reid said. "I think this Tia is prettier than you're letting on."

"Did I say she was pretty?" Nance retorted. "I don't think so. Anyway, we're here now."

Tia was waiting outside the shop and directed them where to park.

"Well, about that?" Reid grinned. "She is pretty."

"Shut up, Denning."

By the time they picked up the area rugs at their last shop, the back of Reid's pickup was full, and even so, they had put the sections of the bookcase in Tia's car to transport them.

The men followed her and parked on the street.

The boys were happy to be free since they had to stay in the pickup while the grownups were loading furniture. Now, they were running around the yard. Tia got out of her car and watched them. She didn't know there would be kids, she wasn't sure she was ready for that, or at least her house wasn't. She assumed Nance had told his friend about the mess in the house, still preferred he didn't see it, but she really had no choice at this point.

Reid Denning was a surprise. He was good looking,

nearly as good looking as Nance, and they shared the same body type, strong and muscular. He was friendly and his eyes lit up when he smiled. Tia was immediately at ease in his presence. He didn't affect her the same way Nance did, she decided. Interesting, and definitely telling. She might have to admit that the feelings she had for Nance weren't just lust.

No time for that, Tia thought, there was furniture to be moved.

She showed Reid and Nance the easiest route in, across the patio and through the back door, so they didn't have to negotiate the totes.

The two little boys tagged along, but the minute they saw the river and the steps leading down to the little beach, they ran to their dad.

"Can we go down to the water?" Trey asked.

"How cool is this?" Benny added. "This house has its own beach."

Reid looked at the river and back at the boys. "I don't think so," he finally said. "Maybe when we get done here."

Their faces fell, but they didn't argue.

Tia stepped in. "If you guys can deal with the furniture, I'll take them down to the beach."

Nance looked at Reid and gave him a slight nod. He had no idea if Tia even liked kids, didn't know if she had any experience with them. They'd never talked about it, but he knew she was a good person and wouldn't let any harm come to them.

"Okay, boys, if Tia's sure," Reid finally said.

"I'm totally fine with it, but I go first, okay?"

They were still down there when Nance and Reid finished with the furniture. Reid went to the truck and brought back a cooler filled with ice and beer, and juice boxes for the boys.

Nance stood at the edge of the patio that was trimmed with a low rock fence. Reid handed him a beer and together they watched the woman interact with the boys.

Tia was watching the boys try to skip rocks. She laughed and clapped when Benny got a rock to skip, praised Trey on his technique.

"She's good with them," Reid noted. "They're not even wet."

"I see that," Nance replied. "I wasn't sure, I haven't seen her with kids before, but I knew she would keep them safe."

"But, Nance, what's with the house? I made the mistake of looking into the living room. It's a disaster."

"Yeah, that's a long story." Nance ran his fingers through his hair. "We'll save it for the ride home. But," he paused, "she's working on it. That's what we were doing last weekend."

Tia said something to the boys and they cheered, ran up the stairs to their dad.

"Tia says she has cookies," Trey shouted. "Can we have some?"

"Absolutely," Reid answered. "Bring them out here and you can have some juice too."

Tia held the door as they ran into the house. She paused for a moment to admire her new workspace. Nance and Reid had it set up exactly as she had envisioned. The boys ran back to her and pulled her into the kitchen.

She gave them each three cookies out of a basket lined with a napkin, then followed them back out to the patio. Reid and Nance took a couple each.

"You should know I never pass up food," Reid said before he bit into the first one.

"Same here." Nance took two as well. "She's made me very happy with just a granola bar."

Tia laughed. "I thought I'd get out the company snacks today. I really appreciate the help. I could never have done it alone."

"We were happy to help," Reid replied. "Do you want to see if we got everything where you wanted it?"

"It's perfect," Tia replied, but they both had turned to go in the house.

Reid turned to Trey and Benny.

"Boys, stay right there."

They nodded and apparently were happy sitting at the table eating cookies and watching the boats go up and down the river.

Tia looked at her little workspace. "Really, it's perfect," she repeated. "I'd like to add some shelves under that window, but we didn't find anything that would work." She turned around to show them the other end.

Nance and Reid looked at the spaces and consulted. They turned to Tia.

"We could probably build some shelves for you in a morning or an afternoon," Nance said.

"No, I couldn't possibly ask you to do that." Tia backed up. "I'm going to hire a carpenter."

Both men just grinned.

"We're carpenters," Reid stated.

"Well, sure, most guys can do DIY projects, but I think

I should hire a professional." She paused. "No offense."

"None taken," Reid replied. "But we are professionals."

"You're a carpenter?" she asked Reid.

Reid laughed. "Well, actually, I'm a high school science teacher and football coach but Nance and I spent our summers during college doing construction. We still dabble in it occasionally."

"Really?" Tia looked at Nance. "You never said that."

"The subject didn't come up." He shrugged.

"Well, okay, I'm happy to pay you."

"Not necessary," Reid replied. "Maybe you treat us to steaks on the patio?"

"Done."

"It'll be a couple of weeks before we can get to it," Reid continued. "We have a fundraiser next weekend."

"She's coming to that too, right, Tia?"

"I am? I mean, I am." She looked up at Nance. "I may have forgotten about that. Never mind, I said I'd come, so I'll be there."

Nance went to the garage to find a tape measure and the men measured the spaces for the shelves, while Tia went outside to keep the boys company.

They were all three laughing when the men came back out. Nance and Reid shared a surprised look, then both shrugged.

Tia helped the little boys gather up their things and watched as all four disappeared around the side of the house, Trey and Benny running ahead. She started to turn around when she spotted Nance out of the corner of her eye. He loped up to her and before she could ask if he had forgotten something, he put his hands on her cheeks and kissed her. It was over before she could react, and he was jogging away before she could let out the breath she didn't know she was holding.

"It's just the way he is," Tia said out loud. "Just Nance being Nance."

She went back in the house, stopped and sat down at her new desk. She had pulled her old chair from the other bedroom and would be using it for now. She tried pushing herself up to the desk and decided she would have to get the floor pad from the other bedroom as well.

She loved it, absolutely loved it, she decided. After doing a little happy dance, Tia started setting up her new office. It took several trips with a tote to move the office supplies she would need the next morning for work.

On a whim, Tia collected the pelicans from her dresser,

put five on top of the bookcase and the other three on her desk. She ran her hand over the smooth wood of the desk and marveled at its smoothness. She would have to get a blotter for it, but for now she would appreciate the feel of the wood beneath her hand.

It had been her intention to walk down to the See-Food Inn for dinner, but decided she was too lazy and settled for popcorn and wine instead. It had been a busy couple of days and she was ready to relax.

She turned the television on, sat down on the couch with her popcorn and tried to watch a movie. The boxes in the corner mocked her, and she finally hauled two over to the coffee table and opened the first one. It was full of old books.

"Wait, these aren't just ordinary books," Tia exclaimed to the room. "This is a first edition of 'Anne of Green Gables.' And a first edition of 'Gulliver's Travels'."

She carefully removed them all from the box and stacked them on the coffee table. There were twelve books in all, all very old and all first editions.

"They must be worth a fortune."

She picked up her phone and typed a title into the search engine, scrolled down and stopped and stared at the screen.

"It is worth a fortune." She started to text Nance about the books, then decided she wanted to see what else was in the boxes.

Tia had texted the pictures of the pelicans to her sisters, and both texted back that they had never seen them, never knew anything was in the attic space, but Tia was welcome to whatever was up there.

She gently dusted the books, checked for bugs, and finding none, carried them to the new bookcase and lined them up inside. She supposed she could sell them, but for now, she was keeping them.

Tia was excited to see what the next box held. She peeled back the flaps and peeked in. It wasn't books and it wasn't pelicans. Tia reached in and pulled out a very old and fragile beaded purse. Reticule. They would have called it a reticule. She held it up to examine the beads, thousands of them shimmered in the light. It was unusually heavy, Tia decided. She hefted it a bit and decided there was something inside.

She gently opened it and looked inside, her eyes widened. It was full of coins. She carefully poured them onto the coffee table.

There were probably fifty or sixty coins inside, some gold, some silver, all old. She picked one up and examined it carefully. It was a twenty-dollar coin, dated 1895.

"I think it's gold." She picked up another coin, also gold. They must be worth a lot of money. She took a picture of the first one and searched online. "Oh my God, it is worth a lot of money." She stood up and did her happy dance, then sat back down and counted them. There were fifty-five total, and twenty-three were the same twenty-dollar gold coin.

She went to the kitchen, came back with a mixing bowl and put all the coins inside.

She peeked back into the box, pulled out three purses, all old and beautiful in their own right, but also filled with money. She poured them all out, counted them and put them in the bowl.

"I could have paid for college with what's here." She shook her head. "Why would someone put these in an attic and leave them there?"

At the bottom of the box was a wooden box with a tapestry cover. It was beautiful, Tia thought as she ran her fingers over the fabric. It was also heavy. She sat it on the coffee table and opened it slowly, holding her breath. She exhaled as she looked at the array of jewelry inside.

Tia picked out several pieces and studied them. An art deco bracelet with chunky, red stones. The gold looked real, but Tia was pretty certain the stones were glass. "They have to be, right?" She held up a pearl necklace. "Pretty." Next was another bracelet, this time with green stones. She put it on her wrist. "Probably not worth much, but I like it."

She took a picture of the box's interior, immediately thought of texting it to Nance to see what he thought, then looked at the time. It was after ten.

"My own little treasure, and a mystery as well." She clenched her fists and did several air punches. "Woohoo! He's going to be so jealous."

She would have to take it all to a jeweler or someone to get an assessment on what they were worth, but for now, she sat the wooden box of jewelry under the coffee table.

She went and got more boxes, opened them all, and sat the contents on whatever surface she could find, from the totes and couch to the floor. It looked like a garage sale had exploded in her living room.

There were old cookie jars, a box of shells collected from faraway beaches, vintage dresses from the 1920s, two boxes of fancy clocks. There were several boxes of papers, Tia set them aside to look at later, and there was one box that was full of journals and diaries. She glanced at them, they didn't belong to either of her parents, but to a Sally Baldwin. It wasn't a name she was familiar with, so she put them back in the box for another day as well.

Tia stood up and looked around in disbelief. This was someone's life, all their possessions, just left behind and forgotten. It was a little sad, Tia decided, but certainly interesting to her.

She looked around at the mess she'd made, then looked at her phone. It was after two, and how did it get that late? she wondered.

Tia decided to deal with it all later and after washing her face and putting on a pair of soft pajamas, all but fell into bed.

Later didn't come. Tia had been given three cold cases to look at and had spent most of every day working on them. She ate when she needed to, meals that were quick and easy. She tried to ride her bike every day, but two days were rainy, so she went out, but cycling in the rain wasn't her idea of fun, so those rides were cut short. Still, it was necessary if she was going to ride any distance on Saturday.

Now it was Friday and Tia couldn't stand it anymore. The living room was a disaster, worse than it had been. She made a decision and quickly broke down all the old cardboard attic boxes and hauled them to the garage for recycling. She gathered her empty totes and put everything from the attic in them. There was a tote for things she wanted to keep and left that one by the couch. All the others went back against the wall. She would have to re-sort later and figure out what to do with it all, but not today.

She had already taken the box of jewelry and the coins to her bedroom, had actually found one box that had old stationery boxes full of coins. She hadn't counted them, just put them with the others. It was probably time to go to the bank and find someone who could tell her more about the jewelry.

Okay, she thought, looking around the living room. It was livable again. Not great, but livable. She pushed her hair off her face and went to the kitchen. She had earned a glass of wine and was going to make something substantial for dinner. She needed to eat.

"You know you're just postponing the work of getting

rid of all of this," she scolded herself as she made herself a salad and put a chicken breast in the oven with some garlic and lemon. "You can't keep it all, and you don't need it all." As it was, she wasn't sure she had enough storage for her mom's stuff.

Saying it didn't make it happen, Tia knew, but it was out of sight for now. The bike ride was tomorrow and she had to get up early to be in the city before it started.

Tia woke up just before her alarm went off.

I can't do it, she thought, and then gave herself a pep talk while she got dressed. She put on long pants over her yoga pants and a blue t-shirt. She didn't own any fancy cycling clothes, so this would have to do. She added a jacket over the t-shirt since it was chilly out, but she wasn't trying to impress anyone. On the other hand, Nance would be there, and so would his co-workers, Reid too, and lots of people she didn't know, so she went to the bathroom and added a touch of makeup.

The thought of being around a bunch of strangers almost made her change her mind again. She put her water bottle in her backpack and stood still. She shouldn't go, suddenly didn't want to. Why had she agreed to it? There would be too many people.

Tia glanced around as if looking for an escape route.

"Stop that now," she admonished herself. "You agreed to go and you're going."

Tia gathered her gear and courage, squared her shoulders and drove to the Minneapolis park where the ride was starting. After she parked and removed her bike from the rack on the back of her SUV, she grabbed her helmet and backpack. She looked around as she walked her bike to the big tent labeled registration. There were so many people here, she thought, many more than she had expected.

"There's still time to turn around and go home," she told herself, then stopped and stood for a moment thinking about doing that very thing. No one would notice if she wasn't here.

"Hey, Tia, come over here." Nance waved at her from the crowd near the tent.

"Rats, too late." She waved back and pushed her bike over to him.

"There you are," he greeted her.

The crowd faded away and all she could see was the big,

handsome man standing in front of her, wearing cycling shorts and a tight... very tight... cycling shirt. He wore the shoes as well, making him look like he just stepped out of a cycling magazine photo.

And of course, the reality of him now standing next to her sent Tia into shivers. She forgot to pay attention to her feet and stumbled as she stepped back.

She caught herself before he could catch her, but he put his hand on her arm anyway to steady her. Tia felt the tingling all the way to her shoulder and jerked her arm away. She saw him frown and pasted a smile on her face.

"I'm here," she said, hoping she sounded cheerful.

"Good morning." Nance smiled, and that very nearly ended her.

Crap, crap, crap, she couldn't do this, Tia immediately thought. She needed to leave. She started to turn around to do just that, but Nance caught her arm again.

"You just need to get your registration packet," he stated, "and then we'll be on our way."

Tia looked at the large crowd of cyclists gathered at the start line and shuddered. She wasn't sure she could do it.

She didn't have a chance to change her mind before Nance was handing her a packet and a t-shirt. He led her to his bike, where Reid waited.

"Hi, Tia, I'm glad you came." Reid greeted her with a smile.

"Good morning, Reid." She looked around. "The boys didn't come?"

"No, they're with my mom, but she's bringing them by afterward for the festivities. Benny's just too young to ride this far."

"Although he would try," Nance added with a smile.

"They both would," Reid added with his own smile.

Nance turned as an older couple approached.

"Tia, these are my parents, Allen and Paula. Mom, Dad, this is Tia."

"The genealogist," Paula stated as she offered her hand. They shook, then Allen did the same.

"How's the puzzle solving going?" Paula asked.

"Good," Tia answered, glad to be talking about something that would take her mind off the ride. "I haven't had much time to work on it since we went to Henderson, but hopefully, I can get back to it tomorrow."

"Well, we really appreciate your help and expertise, and there isn't any hurry. We're just grateful you agreed to help Nance with this."

"I'm having fun," Tia replied and knew it was true. "It's kind of nice not having to deal with a murder investigation."

"I imagine so," Paula agreed with a friendly smile. "Are you ready for today?"

Tia smiled. "As ready as I'll ever be."

Allen and Paula left to get their bikes, and the two men and Tia pushed their bikes to the starting line.

"Hey, Tia, we didn't know you were riding today." Tia turned to see Micah and Danny striding towards her.

Tia grinned at them. "Likewise, I didn't know you were riding either. You never mentioned it."

Danny engulfed her in a hug, Micah followed, and Tia's nerves immediately calmed. They were her friends, her family, and Tia was grateful for them both, even more so today.

"Tia." Nance's voice interrupted her thoughts and she turned towards him.

"Nance, look who's here."

"Danny." Nance shook the older man's hand. "Micah. I didn't know you cycled."

Danny smiled. "We have since Micah was young," he explained. "We try to get out on a trail every chance we get. And it's a beautiful day, and for a good cause."

Reid stepped up to the group and Tia introduced him.

"It's good to meet friends of Tia's," he responded in his easy way, and shook their hands. "Are you planning on riding with us?"

Danny shook his head. "We're riding with a couple of friends from Stillwater, but we'll likely see you later."

"Sounds good." Tia nodded. "Have fun."

"Same to you," Micah replied.

"They seem nice," Reid said as they walked away. Nance said nothing.

"They are nice." Tia smiled. "I'm not sure I'd be here without them."

Reid looked at her in surprise. "Really?"

Nance stepped up to them. "Ready to go?"

"Yeah, man, just a minute. Tia?"

"They run a restaurant near my house and make sure I eat good food on a regular basis, provide moral support, you name it."

"Really good friends, then."

He looked up to see Nance scowling. "What's wrong?"

The scowl was gone in an instant as Tia looked up at him as well.

"Nothing," Nance replied, smiling. "We should get going."

Tia took off her long pants and put her helmet on. She

would have preferred to leave the pants on since it was still chilly, but knew that once she got started, they would be too hot.

She knew the men were watching, tried to ignore them both. Once the pants were folded and stored in her backpack with the t-shirt Nance had given her, Tia declared herself ready to go.

They set off at a nice pace, Tia thought, and she finally relaxed. The route would take them along a path from the park over towards the Mississippi River, along the river and back around to the park.

This was nice, Tia decided, riding along in the sunshine. The north wind was brisk, but she didn't mind. She breathed deep and listened to Nance and Reid chat about their week. Tia had never ridden in the city, was content with her own river rides, but this was definitely worth getting up early for.

"What do you think, Tia?" Nance's deep voice startled Tia out of her thoughts, and she pulled on the handlebars of her bike. That caused her to nearly run into Nance, so she jerked the bike back and went tumbling off the path. She skidded on a patch of rocky ground before collapsing on the ground.

Tia untangled herself from the bike and rolled to her butt, sat there to catch her breath.

"Are you okay?" Reid asked as he knelt beside her. Both he and Nance had bolted off their bikes as soon as Tia went down.

Tia nodded. "Mostly, but I think I skinned my knees and my left hand." She held it out. It was red and raw.

"Definitely skinned," Reid agreed.

"Let's look at your knees." Nance knelt next to Reid.

Tia pulled up her pant legs for examination. Blood ran down both of her legs.

Reid whistled. "Those look bad."

Tia shrugged. "I'm fine, really."

"Just wait a minute, I have a first aid kit on my bike." Nance turned away and Reid leaned in close.

"What happened?" Reid whispered. "One minute you were riding along and the next you were veering off the path."

Tia glanced at Nance, nodded. "He distracted me," she whispered back. "I can't help it, he just does something to me. I get all nervous around him and stumble and bumble like an idiot."

Reid grinned over her head at Nance, who was getting the first-aid kit, then leaned back to Tia. "It'll be our secret."

CHAPTER ELEVEN

"What? What secret?"

"You're in love with him."

"Nooo, I'm not." Tia shook her head in denial. "He just distracts me."

"Really, it's okay. I won't say anything to him." He winked at her as Nance approached with some antiseptic wipes and adhesive bandages.

Tia looked at Nance, then back at Reid with a stunned look on her face. He winked again and Tia closed her eyes.

"Dear God, no," she muttered.

"What was that?" Nance asked as he knelt down.

"Nothing." Tia shook her head and sat still while he cleaned her knees and hand, then applied the bandages.

"That'll have to do for now," Nance announced as he finished and stood up. "Do you think you can ride?"

Reid reached in to help Tia stand. She tested her legs, flexed her shoulders. She was pretty sure she had scraped and bruised her left elbow as well, but she wasn't going to say anything to the men. She could deal with it when she got home.

"I can ride," she finally said as Nance stood her bike on its wheels.

Reid examined it and declared it good to go. "There's a bit of paint scraped off, but everything else looks good." Nance held the bike while Tia got on.

"You sure you can ride? I can send Reid on, and we can

walk back."

"I'm fine, really. I've fallen before, you know."

The three rode in silence. Tia kept her eyes straight ahead. Her hand and knees stung, as did her left elbow. Her left knee was throbbing, and Tia was pretty sure it was swelling. She just wanted to get the ride done and go home.

When they finally reached the finish line, Tia stopped her bike and just stood there.

"You okay?" Nance got off his bike and stepped over to her. Reid followed.

"I think I'm stiffening up a bit, that's all. I think I should call it a day."

Danny noticed the group talking and strolled over to them. "You okay, baby girl?"

"She took a spill a ways back." Nance answered for her.

"I'm fine," Tia added with a scowl. "I just think I'm ready to go home."

"Do you want one of us to drive you?" Danny touched her arm.

Tia looked up at him. "That would be great, but are you sure?"

"You know, I could take you," Nance interjected.

"Man, you need to stay here," Reid replied. "Sponsor, and all that."

Nance frowned but couldn't dispute Reid's words. He absolutely had to stay, didn't want Tia to leave, but he felt outnumbered.

After a few minutes of discussion between the men that left Tia tapping her foot, it was decided that Micah would drive her home in her car, so it wouldn't be left in the city.

As Tia hobbled off with Danny and Micah in tow, Nance stood and watched.

Reid smacked him on the shoulder. "You okay, man?"

Nance shook his head. "I'm not sure what just happened."

Reid turned his friend and guided Nance to the food tent.

"I think Tia's hurt more than she was letting on, for one thing, but didn't want us to know that."

Nance looked up at his friend. "You think?" He started to turn to go after her, but Reid grabbed his arm.

"Leave it. She just needs some space. You can always call her later to check on her."

Nance let Reid lead him over to his parents.

"What even happened to make her fall?" Nance asked Reid as they walked. "One minute she was riding along and the next she was on the ground.”

“I’m not sure,” Reid lied. “She said something startled her.”

“Startled her? What would have startled her? I didn’t see anything out of the ordinary.”

“There must have been something.” Reid wasn’t sure Nance was buying it, but it was the best he could do. They met Paula and Allen in the food line.

Paula looked around. “Where’s Tia? I saw her just a little while ago with you.”

“She crashed and burned earlier,” Reid replied. “She was getting stiff, so she headed home.”

He watched Nance’s expression, knew his friend was frustrated, but there was nothing to be done about it now. He had promised Tia.

“That’s too bad,” Paula said. “I really liked her and I wanted to talk to her more about my grandfather and what you’ve both discovered.”

“Maybe another day, dear,” Allen told her. “There’ll be another day.”

“Are you going to check on her?” Paula asked Nance.

Nance ran his fingers through his hair. “I’ll give her a call later, okay?”

“She’s in good hands,” Reid said. “A friend took her home.”

“Well, that’s good then, that she didn’t have to drive.”

They turned their attention to the food that was now in front of them. Reid picked up a plate and followed Nance. He shook his head and grinned. Those two were in for a ride, and he had a front-row seat. This was going to be fun to watch, he thought as he chose a turkey sandwich and put it on his plate.

After Micah dropped her off, Tia assured both him and Danny that she was fine. It might have been an exaggeration, Tia thought as she limped into the house. She dropped her gear by the front door and walked straight to the bathroom, where she peeled off the yoga pants and inspected her knees. They were both scraped but the bandages Nance had applied hid most of them. She took them off and looked again. They would heal, but her bigger concern was the bruising and swelling of her left knee.

It definitely needed ice, she thought as she took off her shirt and examined her left elbow. It was scraped as well, with a pretty good bruise forming, but it wasn’t swollen, so a good cleaning was all that was needed.

Tia craved a hot bath, but decided on a shower, just to save her knee. Her hand hurt as much as the other scrapes when the water hit them, but she washed them all and then washed her hair. She dried her hair and re-bandaged everything, then padded to her bedroom for a pair of sweats and a t-shirt.

Twenty minutes later, Tia was reclining on the couch with an ice pack on her knee. In another ten minutes, she was sound asleep and never heard the ping of her phone in the bedroom, or the ring several minutes later.

Nance paced around his apartment. Why wasn't Tia answering? He was sure something was wrong. They didn't check for a concussion, he didn't think she hit her head, but it all happened very quickly.

He stopped and looked out past the patio at the city. He didn't see the bright lights as he went back over the events of the day.

How had everything gone so wrong? Tia had acted like she didn't want to be there, which was in keeping with the way she usually acted around him. But she looked like she was enjoying the ride once they got started. After she fell, Tia and Reid acted like they were old friends. He saw them whispering to each other while he was getting the first-aid kit but couldn't hear what they said.

Were they seeing each other behind his back?

Nance discarded that thought as quickly as it came to him. Reid was his best friend, he trusted him with his life, and knew without a doubt that was something he would never do.

And Tia? Tia wasn't like any woman he had ever met. She didn't seem to want anything from him, she certainly didn't flirt with him or fawn over him. He snorted. Most days she acted like she couldn't stand him. And God forbid that he touched her.

The only times she had been semi-comfortable with him had been after they got locked in the library in Henderson, and when they were sorting her mother's things. He turned back to the window. So, she didn't hate him, he thought, but she certainly was hiding something. And despite it all, he decided, he liked her.

Now, though, Tia wasn't answering her phone. What if she did have a concussion? He started toward the door, planning to drive to her house and check on her, then turned and went back to the patio door, made a decision. If he didn't hear from her in the morning, he would pick up some lunch and check on her in person.

Tia woke up the next morning feeling a little disoriented.

"Why am I on the couch?" She held up her scraped hand. "Oh, yeah, the cycling accident."

She stretched, felt the pull in every one of her muscles, then checked her elbow and knees. The swelling on her knee wasn't as bad as it had been the night before, but the angry bruises hurt to touch. She stood up and gingerly walked to the bathroom, limping just a little.

"It'll be fine," she assured herself. "But maybe I won't ride my bike to the bookstore this afternoon. I think I'll drive." Earlier in the week, she and Erica had made plans to meet today for nothing more than a visit, and since it was even nicer outside today than yesterday, Tia was looking forward to a glass of iced tea and watching the river go by while catching up with her friend.

Having made that decision, Tia hobbled to the bedroom and dressed in a pair of loose black pants and a knit, pale-blue, long-sleeved shirt. She would have to wear tennis shoes, but she didn't care about that.

She turned to go find something to eat and noticed her phone on the dresser. She picked it up and turned to leave again, then noticed a missed call notification.

"Crap." She counted five missed calls, one text and three voicemails, all from Nance last night.

Tia listened to the voicemails, then sat down on the bed. His voice. She loved his voice, loved the deep tones that held concern as he asked if she was okay. How could a voice make her weak in the knees? she wondered. Lust, Tia told herself. His voice turned her on, that was all.

Then she recalled yesterday's conversation with Reid. He seemed to think Tia was in love with Nance and that was what caused her accident.

"So, you're saying that he makes me so nervous that I stumble and fall because I'm in love with him?" she asked the absent Reid. She thought about it, then shook her head. "Nah, that can't be it. Love makes you clumsy, said no one ever."

Tia chuckled as she took the phone to the kitchen. She was starving and needed a cup of coffee. She carried that and a bagel back to the living room and after eating, she felt better, well enough to work on Nance's family history, but she wanted to put her knee up.

She retrieved Nance's file and reread all the letters, including one they hadn't paid much attention to.

John Beckwith

Minnie
Stevens Thomas
Henderson, Minn.
        Chicago, Illinois

Dear John,

It has been so long since we talked. I hope you are well and your business is doing well. It seems so very long ago that I helped nurse you to back to health in what we called home for so many months. It always makes me smile to remember how you, a blacksmith, was kicked by a horse, but of course, the resulting injury was no laughing matter. So many men died of pneumonia in those times, and I for one, am so glad you were able to survive it. We had so many good times talking and reading while you were in the hospital and getting well. Nine weeks was a long time. I'm also glad that you were well and healthy when you came home from the war.

I think of you often and wonder what my life would have been like if I had come back to Minnesota instead of coming to Chicago to work. As you know, I met my husband here and we have had nine happy years together.

I finally get to the point of this letter, the sad news that my Theodore has passed away. He was badly injured in a train accident and did not recover. I weep for him daily, it's all I can do these days. For a long time you were my best friend and I regret that we went our separate ways without staying in touch.

I would like very much to visit you sometime and we could remember old times. I haven't heard if you married or not, but I shouldn't let that discourage me from rekindling our friendship.

I should be going now, I look forward to hearing from you.

Your nurse and friend,

Minnie

The letter explained what happened to John Beckwith when he was in New Mexico before he shipped off to France, but all it told Tia was that another woman was in love with him. Tia sorted through the pieces of paper in front of her, realized she didn't have a picture of him. Did Nance resemble him? Did he have the same charm?

Tia went and got her laptop, brought it back to the couch and searched for John Beckwith. No pictures, but she found his draft registration from 1917. Six-foot tall, blue eyes and black hair. She imagined he did look like Nance.

She reread John's obituary. There was nothing out of the ordinary. They had only found a few references for him in the newspapers so there was nothing there.

A deeper search yielded the military unit he was associated with and she was able to piece together a timeline from the time he left Minnesota to the time he came home from France, well after Elizabeth had her baby and gotten married. She wondered if he ever tried to contact her.

Tia held up the copy of the letter sent to John from Silas Perkins. How strange. It was the odd letter out, and she could see John keeping it and the obituary, even the picture, but how did he get the rest of the letters? There was no evidence that John ever had any contact with Mildred.

Mildred Olson, cousin of Elizabeth. Tia tapped the paper against her forehead. Maybe she needed to look at Mildred again. Tia set the paper down and rubbed her forehead. Her knee throbbed and she was getting a headache. She looked at her phone and decided some ibuprofen would help. She realized she should have taken some last night, but better late than never. She would get a new ice pack and a snack, and then she needed to call Nance back.

Tia had just gotten a soda, a granola bar, and the ice pack and was putting it all on the coffee table when there was a knock at the door.

"Coming," she shouted, when the knock came again. She opened the door and stepped back when she saw it was Nance standing there, looking good and holding two plastic bags.

"Oh, hi," she stammered. "What are you doing here?"

He just raised his eyebrows.

"Oh, yeah, I forgot to call you back. I was just going to."

"You didn't," he replied as he stepped inside, "so I came to see for myself how you are."

Tia moved aside to let him by, then followed him to the kitchen, trying not to limp.

"I brought food too, in case you're not eating."

"I ate," Tia protested. "In fact, I was just going to have a granola bar." She limped back to the living room and picked up the bar. "See? And I'm fine."

He stood in the door of the kitchen, not moving.

"What?" She looked around, "I know it's a mess, but you knew that."

"You're limping," he pointed out. "You are hurt."

"My knees are just a little sore, that's all."

"Sit down and let me look."

"That's not necessary," Tia protested. "I'm an adult you know, and you're being bossy."

"I think it's more than scraped knees, so show me."

Tia would have stomped to the couch if she could have. Instead, she limped over and plunked down, pulled up her pant leg in a huff.

"See, it's nothing."

"Other knee."

She complied with pursed lips.

Nance moved the low table out of the way and knelt next to the couch, gently touched the swollen area.

"It's not nothing." Nance looked up at Tia with concern in his expression. "It's bruised and swollen, and it hurts, doesn't it?"

Tia bit her lip and tried not to focus on anything but the touch of his hand on her leg and his husky voice.

"It does hurt a little bit, but I've had ice on it, and I've had it elevated." Before he could speak, Tia continued. "I took a couple of pain relievers and I'm resting it. Look, I have the ice pack I was just going to put back on. I just banged it when I fell."

Nance pulled Tia's pant leg down and looked into her eyes. "You're sure?"

"I'm sure." Tia nodded. "It'll take a few days to get back to normal, and if it doesn't, I'll go to the doctor. And seriously, I've been resting it." She pushed her hair out of her face. "I didn't call you back because I was sleeping."

"Sleeping? Do you have a concussion?"

Tia supposed that was the football player in him talking, so she tried not to be offended.

"No concussion." She sighed. "I was just tired. Yesterday was farther than I usually bike."

"Okay, then. Are you hungry?"

Tia nodded and pointed to the soda and the granola bar "I was just getting something to eat, and then I'm going to put more ice on my knee."

Nance stood up. "You put the ice on, and I'll get the food."

"You brought food, oh, you said that, didn't you?"

"Burgers and fries, and a six-pack of beer."

Tia's mouth watered. "I'm all in on the burgers and fries, but I'll pass on the beer for now."

She adjusted herself on the couch so Nance could sit at the other end. She probably could use a couple more comfortable chairs, but for now, the couch had to do.

Nance came back in with two containers and a beer, handed one container to Tia.

"Smells good." She opened the container and took out the sandwich. "Hmm, it is good."

They ate in a comfortable silence and when they were done, Nance took the empty containers back to the kitchen. He came back with a second beer and sat back down by her feet.

"So, what have you been doing while sitting here?" He gestured towards her laptop.

"I was rereading all John's letters, just trying to put it all together."

"And?"

"Nothing more than we already knew, but I made a timeline for John's time in the Army. Here, look."

She tilted the computer screen so he could see it and they were both quiet while he read.

"Wow. You found out all this."

Tia nodded. "Yeah, but none of it tells us how John got the letter from Silas Perkins or the letters from Mildred. I can only think that Mildred met up with John at some point and gave them to him. Oh, and do you have a picture of John?"

Nance shrugged. "I don't know, but I would think Mom would have one." He stood up. "Hang on, and I'll call her and ask. I need to let her know I'm not coming for lunch."

He walked to the sunroom, and Tia could hear him talking to Paula. She yawned. Now that she had eaten, Tia was tired again. She closed her eyes, decided to rest them until Nance came back.

CHAPTER TWELVE

Nance looked at the woman curled up and sleeping on the couch. She looked very fragile, he thought, so unlike the woman he was used to. He wanted to protect her, and he was feeling bad about yesterday. He knew Tia hadn't been excited about going to the fundraiser, knew she was a solitary person and didn't really like crowds.

He had actually thought she would back out at the last minute, but she didn't. He didn't understand the solitary thing, and he didn't understand why she crashed. He didn't buy Reid's story that something, apparently invisible, startled her so badly that she rode right off the path and crashed. There was nothing out of the ordinary, no birds, no one passing them, nothing.

And now she was sleeping, after, according to Tia, she had slept all night. She didn't have any makeup on that he could tell, a sharp contrast to Missy. She had to look perfect all the time, spent hours getting ready for an evening out.

If he thought she would let him, Nance would take Tia to urgent care or the emergency room just for a checkup.

His phone pinged and Nance reached to get it off the coffee table. Tia roused and looked at him, looking surprised he was there.

"Sorry, I was just getting my phone." He turned it to show Tia. "Mom sent me a photo of Grandpa Beckwith." He handed her the phone.

"Hmm," Tia yawned. "Sorry, I'm not sure why I fell asleep. You didn't have to stay." She looked at his phone, and a young John Beckwith looked back at her. He was slim and tall with the same black hair that Nance had, worn almost identical, shorter and parted on one side with the hair on top combed off to the side. His grin was identical to Nance's, a little off centered.

"Mom says I look like him, and according to her, I act like him."

"I can see that, the looking like him. He has a slimmer, smaller build than you, but looks very charming as well."

Nance nodded. "Jill and Jan have bright red hair and green eyes, from my dad's side. They're almost as tall as I am, and they're amazing."

Tia smiled as she handed his phone back. "Spoken like a true brother, I can tell you love them."

Nance took the phone back. "I'm going to send this to you." He did that, then pulled up another picture, this one of two stunning redheads.

"Wow," Tia breathed, "they're gorgeous."

Nance nodded and put his phone away. "They look identical, but they're a year apart."

"Older than you?"

Nance nodded again.

Tia swiped at her hair. "I feel a little inferior."

Nance looked at her again, puzzled. "Why?"

"Tall, red hair, beautiful bone structure, and those green eyes, I mean, they're the color of emeralds."

Nance laughed and examined her face. "There's nothing wrong with your face."

He watched that face flush. "I mean it, I like your face."

Tia, clearly uncomfortable, untangled herself from the couch and stood, tested her knee.

"How's it feel?" He rose to stand next to her.

"Good, I think, which is great, because it's too nice of a day to spend it inside. Thanks for that, by the way."

"No thanks needed." He cocked his head. "What did you have in mind?"

"Well, I was going to ride my bike downtown, but," she amended when Nance frowned, "it would be better if I drove."

"Can I tag along?" Nance didn't know why he asked, but he knew he wasn't ready to leave.

Tia only considered it for a moment. "Sure, I'd like that. I'm not doing anything special, I was just going to stop in at my friend's bookstore, maybe walk along the river and get some ice cream."

"I like ice cream."

"Let me get some shoes on and take a brush to my hair and I'll be ready."

Nance wandered around the living room while he waited

for her, noticed the boxes from the attic were gone. He won-dered what she did with them.

He asked her when she came back, she pointed to the corner of totes.

"You just unpacked them all, and put them into totes? Why would you do that?"

Tia grinned. "Two reasons. One, I couldn't stand looking at the dirty cardboard boxes and imagining what critters might be living in them, and two, I finally got curious as to what they held. So, I unpacked them all and everything that was in them was all over the living room." She giggled and Nance felt his heart fall a little more. "You would have hated it, I couldn't even sit on the couch."

"So, what was in them?" He couldn't help himself. "Do I get to see?"

"You can and you should, but I'll show you when we come back if you have time."

Nance followed her to the front door. "You could show me now." He had actually been curious about their con-tents since they brought them down from the attic.

"Nope, not until I get ice cream," she quipped. "And you're driving, right?"

"Sure." Nance wasn't sure what was going on. She was teasing and joking with him, something he seldom saw, in fact, hadn't seen except the night they got locked inside the library at Henderson. She didn't appear to be scared of him, or act like she hated him, which made him wonder what was different.

He liked this Tia, grinned, as she opened the car door and stepped in, mindful of her knee.

"To the bookstore?" Nance asked as he pulled out of the driveway.

"To the bookstore!" She giggled again and made him wonder what was in that pain reliever she took.

"Are we buying books?"

"We could, but really, I just wanted to visit with my friend Erica. We usually get together on Friday nights, but I didn't have time then, so we decided I'd stop in today and have a glass of iced tea, if she's not too busy. A walk after that. Actually, I was going to ride across the river today to loosen up my muscles from yesterday, but now, definitely just a walk along the river."

"Are you sure your knee is up to a walk?" Nance asked doubtfully.

Tia flexed it. "I think it'll be fine." She turned to him. "We won't walk very fast, and if it acts up, we can stop and rest. How's that?"

"Fair enough." He parked in the lot next to Pages, went around to open Tia's door. She allowed him to balance her as she stood, and again, he noticed the shuddering she usually did when he touched her was absent.

Nance wondered at the difference for just a moment, then forgot it as he followed her into the store.

He waited while she hugged a tall, thin young man with rich black braids tied back into a ponytail that trailed down his back.

"Jamael, meet Nance L'Breck. Nance, this is my friend Jamael Taylor."

Nance and Jamael shook hands as Erica walked up to the counter.

"Tia, dear, why are you limping?"

Tia waved her hand in dismissal. "Just a small bicycling accident, it's nothing to worry about."

Erica appeared to accept Tia's explanation and moved her gaze to Nance. "And this is your weatherman." She looked him over and it took everything Nance had not to blush.

She was a small, feisty woman, he decided, wearing an orange dress with yellow flowers, with a chunky yellow necklace and dangling earrings to match. Even with the four-inch yellow heels, Erica only came up to Nance's chest.

"This is Nance, he brought me some lunch and decided to come with me this afternoon."

Nance gently grasped the older woman's hand and gently kissed its back.

"And I'm Erica." Her voice was friendly, and her eyes sparkled when she looked at him. "It's nice to finally meet you. Tia's told me all about you."

Nance turned to Tia. "You told her about me."

Tia rolled her eyes and ignored him. "Traitor."

Erica's laughter rang out in the shop. "Let's go outside and sit, go on and I'll bring our tea."

"I'll get it," Jamael offered. "You go ahead."

"I'll help you, Jamael," Tia added. She turned to Nance and Erica. "I'll be out in a minute. Is iced tea okay for you, Nance?"

He nodded and escorted Erica out to the patio.

"This is nice," Nance said when they were seated. He looked out at the river and then back to the window where Tia and Jamael worked together getting their drinks.

Erica sat and watched Nance watch Tia, smiled before she spoke.

"She's something, isn't she?"

Nance nodded. "That she is. She hasn't always been very friendly, but today, I don't know, it's like she's a different person." He glanced at Erica.

She raised her perfectly shaped eyebrows at him.

"I'm worried she has a concussion and doesn't realize it."

Erica could see he was serious. "She's usually like this, you know, around me."

"Really?"

"Yes."

Oh, he had it bad, Erica thought, and he didn't even know it.

"I've hardly seen it, she acts like she doesn't like me most of the time." Interesting, but I think you trust that she knows her body best." Erica's voice was gentle. "If she's not feeling well, she'll tell us."

"That's what she said," Nance murmured, "but I'm not sure she would tell me."

Erica patted his arm. "I say you stop worrying and just enjoy the day."

"I will, thanks." Nance smiled at Erica, then stood up as Tia came out the door carrying a tray with their drinks and a plate of blueberry scones.

Tia was glad that Nance and Erica were getting along, but she noticed he didn't contribute much to the conversation as they caught up on their week. Erica was planning a book-signing event in a couple of weeks, and Tia was happy for her. An event like that could bring in a lot of readers and a lot of business.

"Are you helping Erica with it?" Nance unexpectedly asked Tia.

"Umm, no, I wasn't planning on it," Tia replied as Erica shook her head.

"Why not?"

"It's not really her thing," Erica answered.

"And I'm going to be out of town," Tia added. Now why had she said that? She could only blame panic for the lie. She supposed it didn't have to be a lie, she could go somewhere. She had no idea where, but she could go somewhere.

"She's planning a trip to the state archives," Erica explained. "I mean, it's only in Minneapolis, but she's had the day planned for a while."

Nance shrugged. "Maybe you could reschedule so you

could help your friend."

Tia and Erica looked at each other. Tia appreciated the lie on her part, Erica knew she didn't do crowds, but Tia was sure she'd just been trapped. Erica shrugged.

"Well?" Nance finally asked.

"Sure, of course, I can reschedule and help Erica." Tia nodded to her friend. "I'd be happy to help you at the book signing." They both knew that wasn't going to happen, Tia thought.

"There you go."

Nance looked pretty happy with himself, Tia thought, and maybe she could do it, after all, she went to Nance's fundraiser. It might be okay, the bookstore was small, so how many people could attend? The bottom line was, she would like to help Erica. She would think about it.

"Yeah, it'll be fun." Tia smiled at Erica, but she admitted to herself she was a little irritated with Nance for forcing her into a situation that she knew she wouldn't be comfortable in.

Tia and Erica shrugged at the same time and their eyes met, Erica's shining with laughter now. Tia's mood lightened and she laughed. Erica joined in, and Nance looked at them, clearly confused by the laughing,

The door to the bookstore opened and Jamael stuck his head out.

"Erica, I've got a lady with a couple of questions. She asked to talk to you."

"Okay, thanks Jamael. I'll be right in." She turned to Nance. "Duty calls, but it was nice to meet you, come by again." Erica waved as she walked away.

"I like her." Nance said he watched Erica go inside.

Tia grinned. "Everyone likes Erica, and I'm fortunate to have her as a friend. We've only known each other since I came back, but she got me through some dark days, made sure I ate." She changed the subject. "Ready for that walk?"

"Lead the way."

They walked along the river's edge, past the gazebo in the park that sat at the edge of the water, and the huge, historic lift bridge that spanned the St. Croix River and led to Wisconsin on the other side. It was limited to walking and cycling since they built the new bridge farther down on the river.

Tia led Nance to the ice cream shop and ordered a double scoop of chocolate. It was something they agreed on, and once they had their cones, Tia and Nance walked back to a bench by the river to eat them.

"So, what were you like as a little girl?" Nance asked as he bit into his cone with a crunch.

"I don't know. I liked to read, I liked to play with dolls, all the usual stuff. How about you?" They were sitting side by side, but Nance wasn't touching her, hadn't gotten too close all day, and it had made a huge difference, Tia realized. But maybe she missed the attention, she mused, then told herself she was being ridiculous.

"I played a lot of sports, tried to keep up with Jan and Jill. They used to dress me up as a princess, I remember that."

Tia laughed. "Not a prince?"

"Nope, but I went along with it because, you know, I wanted to be included in the big kids' activities.

"Worst thing that ever happened to you?"

"Like falling out of a tree and breaking my arm, or most traumatic?"

"Most traumatic."

Nance shook his head. "We don't know each other well enough to tell you that, so we'll save it for another day. What about you?"

"I think that we all have things that are traumatic, like losing a parent, and while that was traumatic for me, I think it's the things that we think are trauma and affect the rest of our lives happen when we're little."

"So, what was it for you?"

"I got a 'D' on a health test in fifth grade."

Nance laughed. "Was that the most traumatic or worst day?"

"One and the same. I was good in all my classes, proud of my grades, so that was a huge blow to my pride."

"But it was just a test, not a report card grade, right?"

"Well, yes, but I was appalled, and I think that carried through to now. I buckled down and studied, got the good grades, all the way through college. Even now, I push to make sure everything I do is done well."

"I can see that." Nance nodded. "I studied because I couldn't play sports without the grades, but I wanted to have a good time too. I wanted to go out with my friends, have fun."

Tia didn't want to have another argument about having fun, so she didn't answer.

"Okay, best date," she said instead.

"April 25th," they said in unison.

"Because it's not too hot, not too cold," Tia quoted.

"Are you a Sandra Bullock fan?"

"I am," Tia replied. She munched on the last of her cone. ""Miss Congeniality,' 'The Proposal,' all of them."

"Well, how about that? Me too."

Tia wiped her hands on the napkin that came with her ice cream and shoved it in her pocket, looked around the park. "I suppose we should start back if you want to see what's in my totes."

Nance stood as well. "I do want to see what's in your totes." He wiggled his eyebrows, but got no reaction from Tia. They started walking. "How's your knee?"

"Sore, but the walking isn't bothering it." She rubbed her leg. "I'll take some more pain reliever before I go to bed, just in case."

"Good idea."

Tia was true to her word and as soon as they got back to the house, she led Nance to the totes in the corner. They opened one at a time, taking things out and looking at them.

"I love the clocks," Tia said, picking up an old alarm clock. "It's like whoever owned this stuff collected it through-out their life, then just left it all here to rot."

Nance picked up a little toothpick holder that was en-graved with the date from the World's Fair in Chicago. "What are you going to do with of all of it?" He lifted a hand-blown blue vase out of a tote.

"I've been thinking about it and some of it I'm going to use to decorate the house. I've realized that once I get rid of all the totes stashed in here, there's not much for homey decor."

Nance looked around the room, wandered to the fire-place and over towards the front window, looked behind the remaining totes.

"I think you're right. I hadn't noticed before, but it's pretty sparse in here, or will be once you move the totes out."

"I don't even have a place for anyone to sit except for the couch."

"So, that will take care of some of it, but what about the rest?"

"I'll donate it, I suppose." She picked up an old cookie jar, probably from the 1920s, that was in the shape of a bear.

"All of this is old, probably worth some money. You could sell it." He paused. "Is it part of your mom's estate?"

Tia shook her head. "Since the house is in Marvi's name, well, my name now, since the paperwork is finally done, none of this goes into the estate. Speaking of which, I meet with Mom's attorney this week to finish things up."

"That's great. Congratulations. I know it's a lot of work to settle an estate."

"Thanks, anyway, it's supposed to rain all week, so..."

"Not until Tuesday," Nance interrupted, "so tomorrow should still be nice."

"Right. So, I'm hoping to put the spare bedroom into some semblance of order. I want to make it a bedroom again."

Nance walked to the door of the bedroom, stopped and whistled. "That's going to take a lot of work."

"I know, but I need the closet space to store Mom's family histories and stuff. I want to get rid of the rest now that I have my own."

"I can see it, but what about the totes in the living room?"

Tia noticed he didn't look like he wanted to run screaming from the clutter like he did the first time he came here. "I still have some sorting to do, but I'll decide what I want to keep from the attic and get rid of the rest."

Nance nodded. "It's hard to do, I know, but I'm impressed that you have a plan."

Tia laughed. "I always have a plan, but thanks." She walked back to the couch, only limping slightly. "Oh, I almost forgot, I found a couple of other things. Wait here."

Tia went into the bedroom and returned a few moments later a small cedar box, two old cigar boxes, and a plastic mixing bowl balanced on top of the stack.

She sat them down on the coffee table. Nance stood and looked down at the bowl, filled with old coins.

Tia picked up two and gave them to Nance, who turned them over and examined them.

"I found them in several boxes. They're all older than 1938. I found some old journals and diaries that belonged to a Sally Baldwin. She lived here and died in 1938."

"These were in the attic?" Nance put the coins back and picked up several more. "They must be worth a fortune."

"I hope so." Tia sat down and handed him the wooden box full of jewelry.

He picked up a pocket watch. "I'm a little jealous that I wasn't here to find all this stuff with you." He examined the pocket watch, put it back and plucked out a woman's ring with a huge diamond surrounded by tiny sapphires. "Real, do you think?"

"I doubt it." Tia picked up the bracelet she liked. "Who

would put all this valuable jewelry in the attic and leave it?"

Nance looked at her and grinned. "The same person who left all this money up there?"

"True, true." She put the bracelet back. "I'm going to take it all to have it appraised, but I'm not very hopeful about the jewelry." Tia closed the box and set it aside. "But wait, there's more."

"More?"

"Yep." Tia picked up the cigar boxes, gave them to Nance. "Pretend I don't know what's in them and we can be surprised together."

CHAPTER THIRTEEN

Nance opened the first box and peered inside. He didn't say anything, just carefully set it on the low table and opened the other box, looked up at Tia with a shocked look on his face.

She shrugged and sighed in disappointment. "How about that? I was hoping for more jewelry." She started to reach in but Nance took her hand and held it in the air.

A jolt of electricity shot through Tia's arm, and she shivered. Nance dropped it immediately. "Tia, do you know what these are?"

"Old baseball cards," she replied. "I would rather have jewelry."

"They're old baseball cards." He looked into the box, but didn't touch anything, didn't pick one up like she thought he would.

"What?" She started to pick one up and he moved the box out of her reach.

"Do you have any gloves?"

"Umm, like glove gloves?"

"No, like those white gloves you wear with a tux, or at least a pair of latex gloves."

She looked at his big hands and knew already that she had no gloves that would fit those big, warm hands. "Oh, ohh, I get it, I see where you're going with this. The answer is no, but give me a minute.”

When she came back from her bedroom, Nance was still staring at the boxes.

“No gloves, but I have a couple of my mom’s hankies. Here.”

He took the handkerchiefs but still didn’t move.

“I thought you’d be excited.”

Nance looked at Tia, then back at the boxes. He still didn’t move.

“Do you know what you have here?”

“Umm, a bunch of old baseball cards. So?”

Nance used a hankie to gingerly pick one up. “They’re old baseball cards,” he repeated.

Tia giggled. “I just said that. Probably from before 1938, like all the other stuff.”

“Yeah.” Nance held up the card. “These are amazing.” He took several more out, looked at each one before putting it into the stack he was making.

“I have a confession to make.”

Nance stopped with a card in his hand and looked at Tia. “A confession?”

“Yes.” She wanted to flinch under his intense gaze. “I touched them with my fingers.”

“I figured.” He turned back to the card and examined it. It had a picture of a man pitching a baseball and was labeled Ty Cobb.

“I thought you would be excited about them.” Tia was strangely disappointed by his reaction. It was like giving someone a cherry lollipop, only to have them give it back because they only liked orange lollipops.

Nance replaced his pile of cards and stood up, pulled Tia up with him.

“You have no idea how excited I am.”

“You don’t look excited. You look grumpy.”

To her surprise, he scooped her up and swung her around, kissed her and then kissed her again. All Tia could do was hang on.

“You found baseball cards, I mean, really old baseball cards, the collectible kind. It’s amazing.”

Tia laughed, let him swing her around again before he set her down and kissed her again. In the next second he deepened the kiss. Tia was caught off guard and forgot to be nervous, just enjoyed the sensations. When he finally let her go, Tia nearly melted to the floor. As it was, she plunked down on the couch.

Nance sat down again and looked at the two little boxes

of cards.

"These are so cool. And they were in the attic."

Tia nodded, "I thought maybe you would like them."

Nance looked at her in surprise. "You're giving them to me?" He placed a card back in the box. "Why would you do that? They're worth a lot of money."

Tia shrugged. "I don't know. I don't need the money, and I thought you might enjoy them."

Nance closed the lids on both boxes and stood.

"I've got to get going." He strode to the door and left so quickly that Tia could only stand and watch.

"What the hell was that?" She looked at the cigar boxes still sitting on the coffee table. "I guess he didn't want them."

She picked them up and stood there for a moment, disappointed, and if she admitted it, her feelings were hurt. She hadn't given them as a gift lightly, and why wouldn't he have accepted them?

Tia carried them to the bedroom and slid the boxes under her bed, then gathered up the boxes with the jewelry and coins and took them to the bedroom as well. She had to meet with the attorney later in the week, so she would take them along and see about getting them appraised. Not the baseball cards, though, she thought. They were Nance's if he changed his mind.

The man was a puzzle, Tia decided, and sighed. She had really thought Nance would like them, and he said he did, but why didn't he take them. And why had he left so quickly?

"You were wrong about that, now, weren't you?" she asked herself out loud. "They're just a bunch of baseball cards, and I can give them away if I want."

The minute Nance shut the door behind him, he cursed. He had behaved badly, just walked out. He should go back in, accept the cards gracefully, but a nagging voice inside told him to go home.

No woman had ever given him a gift, except for Missy. He grimaced as he remembered. It took him a long time to realize that every time Missy gave him a gift, she wanted something from him, expected something from him. Usually, it involved a very expensive piece of jewelry, or a very expensive trip she wanted him to take her on.

It was her form of bribery, and he fell for it every time. It had taken Reid to show him what was going on.

Nance got in his SUV and drummed his fingers on the steering wheel. He didn't think Tia was like Missy, and the more he thought about it, the more he was convinced the cards were just something nice she wanted to do.

There was nothing to do about it tonight, he decided as he put the SUV in gear and backed out of her driveway. Hopefully, she wouldn't change her mind. He really wanted those cards.

Tia left the baseball cards under the bed when she went to see the attorney a couple of days later but took the jewelry and the coins.

"Here you go, all done," Mark Jones said as he handed Tia a file a couple of hours later. "I've included a copy of her tax return for last year, so that's all done too."

Tia took the folder and shook Mark's hand. He was older, maybe in his late fifties, Tia thought, with light brown hair that was neatly combed. He was dressed in a dark blue suit with a striped two-tone tie, brown oxfords. Very classy, Tia thought. He was everything she expected a lawyer to be. He was also friendly and personable, she was glad her mom had hired him. He made the whole process easier.

"Oh, wait, here's the name of the jeweler I use when I need items appraised. I can call him if you want to meet with him right away."

Tia thought about the jewelry and coins pulling down her backpack and took the piece of paper from him. "That would be wonderful. I could just go there after I'm done here."

"He's in Minneapolis, so you would have to go there." Mark warned. "Are you okay with that?"

"I'm absolutely okay with that," Tia answered. She had only been to Minneapolis once since she had been home and that had been for the bike ride. She frowned thinking about it.

"Are you sure? You don't look convinced."

"It's fine, I mean, it's not like it's a two-hour drive." She smiled.

She waited while he called and left his office a few minutes later, directions in hand. She stopped at the coffee shop next door and picked up a coffee, then headed to Minneapolis. The jeweler was downtown, but not hard to find. She found a parking place and walked the short distance with her backpack slung on her back. It would be nice if a couple of the coins were worth something, she thought, so she could buy some new furniture, and maybe do some repairs on the cottage.

She looked up as she reached the door and noticed a couple walking down the street towards her. Nance? It was Nance, with a beautiful woman walking next to him, arm hooked in his. She was tall with blonde hair and spectacularly dressed in a slim dress and matching jacket.

Tia immediately felt a little inferior. She looked down at her tan slacks and white shirt covered with a short coral-colored blazer, then back at the woman with her head close to Nance, as though they were talking about something very private. She ducked into the jewelry store before they could see her, and took a deep breath as they walked by to wherever they were going.

"Can I help you?" the man at the counter asked.

Three hours later, Tia walked into the See-Food Inn and let Kahlia lead her to a table by the windows overlooking the river. The noon rush was over and there weren't many customers, but Tia had realized on her way back to Stillwater that she was hungry. She shrugged off her backpack and sat it on the chair next to her.

She was staring at a boat working its way out of the marina when she felt a touch on her shoulder. She stood and hugged Danny like she didn't want to let go. After a moment he leaned back and looked at her face. It was pale, even for Tia.

"What's wrong? Kahlia said you barely spoke to her."

Tia grinned and her face lit up. She sat back down, and Danny sat across from her. She put her hands on his.

"I might be in shock, but a happy shock, or maybe disbelief," she amended when he leaned towards her with a look of concern on his face. He relaxed and sat back.

"You're pregnant." It was a statement.

Tia laughed and a couple sitting nearby looked up from their meals to stare at them.

"No, I'm not, and you know it." She slapped at his hand. "I'm not even seeing anyone and you know that too."

Danny raised his eyebrows. "What about that weather guy? I see the way you look at him."

The shock in Tia's expression made him laugh. "See?"

"I don't look at him in any such way," Tia protested, "and he's not interested in me anyway." She could feel her face flush as she said the words and remembered the kiss from the other night. That's just the way he was, she justified. "Anyway, that's not why I'm in a state of shock."

"Your knee is okay?"

"It still hurts, but not like it did. It's fine."

"Did you win the lottery?" He laughed when she did a little happy dance right there, sitting at the table.

"Closer. I feel like it."

Over a meal of a chef's salad, Tia told Danny about the things she found in the attic, showed him pictures of some of the more interesting finds, like the pelicans. She dug in her backpack and pulled out the spreadsheet the jeweler and his assistant had made and printed for her, listing the jewelry and the coins and what they were worth.

"That's what he said he would pay for them," Tia added when Danny didn't say anything. She was quiet again while he read through the spreadsheet, but when he looked up and didn't say anything, Tia couldn't stand it.

"Well?"

"It's impressive." He gestured to the spreadsheet. "You really found all this in the attic?"

"Plus all the other stuff. It was like finding a hidden treasure."

Danny whistled. "That's a lot. You're rich."

"Oh, and that's not all." Tia leaned across the table a spoke in a low voice. "I found two cigar boxes full of old baseball cards." She paused, debating whether to say more. "I tried to give them to Nance, but he didn't take them."

"How old?"

Tia considered the question. "I think everything is from the 1930s and older, so old."

"And you tried to give them to the weather guy?"

"Nance, yes. He said he loved them, then got up and walked out."

"Okay, back up. He was at your house."

"Sunday," Tia explained. "He felt bad about my knee and brought me some lunch, so I showed him what I found. He helped me carry it all down from the attic a few weeks ago." She waved her hands in the air. "I thought he might enjoy the cards. They're really not my thing."

"Did you have those valued too?" Danny flipped through the pages of the spreadsheet.

"No." Tia furrowed her brow. "Should I have?"

Danny nodded. "Probably. And you tried to give them all to him?"

"Yes, and he looked at a few of them, and then, like I

said, just got up and left. I haven't heard anything since then. Do you think I offended him?"

"I doubt it." Danny shrugged. "He probably had something else on his mind. No man who's thinking clearly would turn down baseball cards. I know I wouldn't." He laughed. "But about the rest. All that stuff is probably worth a lot of money as well. What are you going to do with it?"

Tia answered with a grin. "The things I like I'm going to keep, and I'll probably sell the rest, maybe place a couple of ads online, I'm not sure." She leaned forward. "I sold a couple of coins and some of the jewelry to the jeweler, enough to do some improvements on the cottage. I'll have to get a safety deposit box for the rest of it, but I'll keep a couple of pieces of the jewelry for myself,"

"Good for you." Danny handed back the spreadsheet. She had enough in the coins and jewelry to do more than repair her house. She could build a new one.

"So, what about the weather guy?"

"What about him?" Tia was confused.

"Are you going to see him again?"

Tia shrugged. "I don't know. He just left without any explanation, and now I haven't heard anything from him, so I don't know." She didn't mention that she had seen him walking with the woman in Minneapolis, she didn't even want to think about that, let alone talk about it. She was already assuming the worst, that he was seeing someone else and that's why he didn't want her coming to his house.

She sighed and sloshed the water around in her glass.

"What about his family history? Are you done with that?"

Tia looked up. "Oh, well, I thought it was going okay, but Nance didn't seem very interested in the information I found the last time we talked, before the baseball cards. So, again I don't know."

"Hmm, maybe there's something else going on his life." Danny rose and pushed his chair in. "It'll sort itself out, I'm sure, but now I've got to get back to work."

Tia rose too and kissed him on the cheek. "Thanks for listening,"

"Always happy to listen to you. And congratulations on the unexpected windfall. Don't spend it all in one place."

Tia laughed as he headed to the kitchen, and she walked to the entrance. "You sound like my dad."

Tia thought about what Danny said as she booted up

her computer a little while later. She had lost most of the day and needed to get back to work. People were depending on her to identify remains of those who had died years ago.

Maybe Nance did have something else going on in his life, like the blonde. How well did she know him anyway? He didn't talk much about his past beyond the college stories and a little bit about his family. He was friendly and confident, but for all she knew, he could be in another relationship. She didn't know anything about his feelings, didn't know if he'd ever been in love, wanted a family or kids.

Tia cocked her head. Did she even know that about herself? She looked at the blank computer screen as it went through the motions of waking up and thought, yes, she did. She wanted a family of her own, kids and maybe a dog or a cat.

The computer beeped and Tia hit the button to bring up her email. She scanned through the new messages until one showed it was the sheriff's office in Bend, Oregon. They had just announced the identity of a woman who had been murdered fifty years ago. They had never been able to positively identify her. Until now. With her help.

"Oh my God." Tia cradled her face in her hands. "We did it," she murmured. "We found her." Tia's eyes filled with tears, they ran down her face as she looked at the photo on the computer screen. She was a young woman who looked so happy, so full of life.

She jumped when someone banged on the sunroom door, looked up to see Nance standing there, a look of fear on his face.

Tia wiped her face with her hands and stood up to open the door. Nance stepped through and started to take her in his arms.

"What is it? What's wrong?"

Tia wanted nothing more than to fall into his arms and stay there forever. Instead, she took a step back and hugged herself with her arms. She saw his look of confusion, and possibly disappointment, but she didn't move her arms.

"Look." She gestured towards the computer with her head.

Nance looked at the woman, smiling happily. He glanced back at Tia who was still hugging herself.

"I saw this on the news today. She's finally been identified. Did you know her?"

Tia shook her head as the tears started to fall again.

"You found her, didn't you?"

Tia nodded, wiped the tears away.

Nance sat down in Tia's chair and looked at the screen, then back at her. "This is what you do, isn't it? Find people."

"Technically, they've already been found, but no one knows who they are. I just find the names to put with the bodies."

"I suspect there's a little more to it than that. But, this isn't your first, is it?"

Tia sniffled, then took a deep breath before she spoke. "No, not even my second or my third, but it hits me the same every time the police verify my work. I send them my information and I'm pretty sure I'm right, but until it's confirmed, I'm never one hundred percent sure."

"I can understand that, but what you do, I guess I didn't really think about this aspect of it. I figured you looked at data and DNA files, but I didn't think about them being real people."

"They're real." Tia paused to grab a tissue off the desk and wiped at her nose before she continued. "They're always real people. Even those in your family tree, the ones we've been looking for, are real. They may be dead, and weren't murdered, but they're real. Even Helen. She's a real person and she had children and grandchildren who are out there, probably looking for relatives they know must exist."

Nance stood up. "I get it now, You've always so serious about your work and you're good at it too. And what you do is important, what you're doing for me is important."

Tia watched him walk over to the windows to look out at the river. Tia followed his gaze, sensing he had more to say. He turned back to her.

"I don't think I've been appreciative of the work you've been doing." He gestured towards the computer. "For these people and for me, especially for me."

Tia shrugged and looked away. "I've enjoyed helping you, probably more than you've enjoyed doing the research. But I guess we're done now."

Nance whipped his head around. "What? We're done?"

Tia looked him in the eyes. "I figured you were bored. When we talked the other day about the new information I found, you didn't seem that interested in it anymore."

"I'm interested, I really am."

Tia could almost hear the panic in his voice and wondered why he would feel that way.

"And I've enjoyed it, all of it."

Tia raised her eyebrows but remained silent.

"Okay, I admit, reading old records for hours and hours is hard for me, really hard, but I've enjoyed the company, and we've had some adventures."

Tia finally smiled, remembered being locked in the basement of the library. "You didn't think that then."

"Maybe I overreacted." Nance shrugged. "But I don't want to stop looking for Helen."

"Because your mom will be unhappy if you don't find her?"

Nance winced. "Partly that, but now we have a mystery. How do we find her?"

Tia finally stood up and walked over to stand next to him.

"You know, when I look at these people, it's like I get to travel in time, back to when they lived, when they worked and loved as they made their way through life. It's so fascinating to see how they managed to get through something like the Spanish flu, World War I, like your great-grandfather did."

Nance watched her face light up as she spoke.

"You really do love it all, don't you?"

"I do, and I like to help people find answers."

"So, what about Helen?"

Tia took a deep breath and released it in a heavy sigh. "I'll be honest, I'm not sure where we find her. Sometimes, even I hit a brick wall. So, maybe she can't be found."

Nance looked at her with surprise. "Really?"

"Yeah."

"I don't believe you," he replied. "Maybe we just need a new plan. Let's think about it, but I came over here for a reason."

It felt so natural to have him there that Tia had forgotten he hadn't told her why he was there.

"Okay?"

"Two things. I left kind of abruptly the other day and without the baseball cards."

"You want them?"

"Are you kidding? Of course, I want them if you're giving them to me." He searched her face. "You know some of them could be valuable. You could use the money they would bring if you just sold them."

Tia laughed and dug the spreadsheet out of her backpack that was on the floor by her desk, right where she dropped it when she came in. She handed it to Nance.

"What's this?"

"Go ahead, take a look. I took the coins and jewelry to

have them appraised today.”

While he glanced over the papers, Tia went to retrieve the baseball cards. He was still sitting there when she came back.

“Is this for real?”

“Yep. I’ve already sold a couple of the coins and some of the jewelry, so I can buy furniture, maybe give the outside of the house a facelift, maybe do some renovating in here like we talked about.”

This time when Nance picked her up and twirled her around, Tia was ready. She laughed, and when he stood her back up, she didn’t move out of his arms. He didn’t kiss her like Tia thought he would, but squeezed her in a hug. Those familiar shivers raced along her spine, but she didn’t move away, didn’t want to.

Nance finally let her go and led her to one of the wicker chairs, then sat down in the other one.

“When can we start?”

Tia laughed again. “I don’t know, I haven’t thought that far ahead.” She decided to change the subject. “You still didn’t say why you drove all the way out here to see me.”

“I didn’t, did I?”

“So?”

This time he took the deep breath. Tia decided he was nervous, but she had no idea why. It only took a few seconds to understand why.

“Would you like to go to my sister’s wedding with me?”

Tia was taken aback and knew the surprise showed on her face. “Excuse me, what?”

“I asked if you would like to go to my sister’s wedding.”

“With you?” She clasped her hands in her lap.

Nance grinned. “Yes, with me.”

Tia’s fingers moved to her hair. “Uh, I don’t think so.” She saw his brow furrow. He clearly wasn’t expecting her answer.

“Why not?”

“Oh, well...” She thought about the blonde woman she had seen him with earlier that day.

“You don’t want to be seen with me?”

“No.”

His eyebrows rose.

“I mean, I don’t mind being seen with you, we’ve gone places together, but...”

“You don’t like weddings?”

“No, I like weddings, in theory anyway,” she corrected.

“In theory?”

Tia blew her breath out. "Well, weddings themselves are nice, but..."

"But?"

Tia didn't reply.

"But?" he repeated.

"Well, you know..." She didn't want to admit it. "People." The word was barely audible.

Nance leaned in closer. "Did you say people?"

Tia lowered her head, nodding.

He put his fingers under her chin, raising it and forcing her to look at him.

"What about the people?"

Seconds ticked away.

"Lots of people go to weddings." She shuddered involuntarily. "There, I said it. I don't want to go because there'll be too many people there."

"You're afraid of being in a crowd?" Nance's tone was incredulous.

"Exactly, so no weddings." Tia's chin went up.

Nance considered that before he spoke. "No sporting events, no concerts?"

Tia shook her head.

"What about church? I know you go to church, we've talked about it."

She looked up at him. "I go to a very small church."

"You went to the fundraiser," Nance reminded her. "There were a lot of people there."

"Don't remind me," Tia said, shuddering again. "There were a lot of people there, especially at the beginning. Once we got started, it wasn't so bad." She shrugged. "But the whole thing made me pretty anxious."

That's what happened when she crashed her bike, Nance realized. She had been so anxious about the situation that she ended up hurting herself.

Tia thought he looked like he felt bad for a minute, but then smiled at her. Tia didn't like the looks of it, if a smile could be challenging, his was. This conversation was about to be over. Tia pushed her hair back and stood up, started to walk over to her desk.

Nance automatically stood as well, stepped back as she moved around him.

"You really are a hermit, aren't you?" he asked.

Tia stopped mid-step and bristled. "I'm not a hermit. I go places, I have friends."

"But you'd prefer not to go out, be honest."

"I like where I live, and I like working here too." She

pushed up her chin again, and he changed tactics, apparently realizing this line of pursuit wasn't going to work.

"This wedding's just a little affair. My sister Jan is hosting it in her backyard, so really, not that many people can attend."

Tia picked up some papers off the desk, started putting papers in a file. "Really?" She looked him straight in the eyes. "Just a little affair?"

Nance nodded and smiled. Tia felt her heart start to pound.

"Well, maybe I could think about it." She knew he could feel her indecision and knew as well that she was going to cave in and go to a wedding. After all, how bad could it be?

"It'll be fine, really. What have you got to lose?"

"I'll be there the whole time," he added when Tia raised her eyebrows, but believed him.

They moved on to other conversations, and when he left, Nance made sure the baseball cards were tucked under his arm. He wasn't leaving them behind.

CHAPTER FOURTEEN

The next couple of weeks went by quickly, too quickly for Tia, since the wedding date was looming closer with every day. She helped Erica with the book signing, and it was a good experience. There had been more people there than she would have liked, but she stayed in the background, pouring coffee, or offering cookies.

She also had to go shopping for a dress, and thankfully, Erica went with her, or Tia would have had to wear jeans and a t-shirt.

Reid and Nance came over and built the low shelves she wanted in the sunroom. They were fast and efficient, and as promised, it was only a few hours before they were done.

"We stained them, but I'll have to come back to add a clear coating on them," Reid told her, "and I can do that in the next day or two."

True to his word, Reid finished them the next day. They had a nice visit and didn't discuss Nance or Tia's feelings for him, instead keeping the conversation light.

Tia wouldn't discuss the wedding either, she was so nervous that she had a panic attack every time she thought about going. Even with Nance by her side, especially with Nance by her side, she worried it would be too much.

When he called the day before the wedding to tell her they would have to meet at his sister Jan's house, Tia nearly backed out.

"I'll be there to greet you before you get in the door, so don't worry about it," he told her before he hung up.

Nance wasn't there to meet Tia when she drove up to his sister's house. Tia saw his SUV parked on the street by the house, but there was no one out front. She wasn't sure what she was supposed to do, so she walked up the sidewalk to the front door of the sprawling mid-century home. She knocked and was just considering making a run back to her car when the door opened.

"Hi there, you must be Tia." The woman who answered the door spoke kindly. She was tall, with glorious red hair and was dressed in a very chic, navy-blue dress.

Tia suddenly felt inferior. She hadn't known what to wear, only had a couple of dresses and they were black, last worn for her mother's funeral. Erica had convinced her to go shopping and she had found a pretty, white linen dress with tiny pale blue flowers on it, but now she thought it was too plain.

Tia finally realized she hadn't replied and extended her hand.

"I am Tia. Nance said he would meet me here."

"I'm Jan, Nance's sister." She nodded and stepped back.

"Of course," Tia replied, suddenly remembering. "He showed me a picture of you and Jill."

"Well, come on through. Everyone's gathered in the back yard. I think they're getting ready to take pictures, but let me get you something to drink before I have to go."

Tia followed Jan inside and through the living and dining areas, then stepped out into the backyard where she waited for Jan and the drink. It seemed like there were a lot of people here, way more than she thought would attend, more than Nance had estimated. Maybe it wasn't too late to leave.

She was planning her escape when a flute of champagne appeared in front of her. She turned to thank Jan, then stopped.

"Oh," was all she could say. This wasn't Jan, or Jan had just changed clothes very quickly. She looked like Jan, but she was wearing an off-white wedding dress of satin. It had a dropped waist and was simple, not fancy at all. Tia felt a little better about her own dress.

"I'm Jill, Nance's sister ..." She twirled around, sending the dress fluttering. "... and the bride."

"Congratulations on your marriage," Tia said politely. "I hope you don't mind that Nance invited me." She glanced around for him.

"Of course not, I'm glad you're here. And of course, he's left you already. I'm going to have to have a talk with him about manners."

Tia looked around again, took a sip of champagne. "Oh, I came by myself. Nance said he had to be here early, but would meet me out front."

"Of course he did." Jill laughed again and Tia immediately liked her. Jill's green eyes sparkled with happiness, and her smile was genuine. Her red hair acted like it wanted to burst from its loose bun, Tia guessed that it was glorious down.

"I've got to go, but we'll talk later." Jill squeezed Tia's hand. "I'm glad you're here. Nance doesn't usually bring any of his girlfriends to family functions."

Tia could feel the blush rising on her face and gulped the rest of the champagne in her glass. "Not a girlfriend. We're just friends."

"Hmm, if you say so." Jill looked across the grass as a man shouted her name. "Have you told Nance?"

"Have I told Nance what?"

She didn't answer. Instead, she squeezed Tia's hand again and walked away. Tia wondered what she meant, but only for a moment.

"Hello, you must be Tia."

Tia turned to face an older lady with gray hair and bright eyes walking towards her. An equally older man walked by her side, with eyes just as alert as the lady's.

"I'm Ruth Hadley, mother of the groom." She held her hand out to Tia. "And this is my friend, Bill Weaver."

"I'm Tia Carnes, a friend of Nance, but he's busy with the wedding." She shook both their hands.

"Oh, that Nance," Ruth said, laughing, eyes sparkling. She was wearing a navy-blue dress like the other women in the wedding party, but hers was a sleeveless A-line dress that stopped just below her knees. The only adornment was four rows of square, white beads that followed the neckline of the dress. Tia thought they gave the effect of a pearl necklace without having to wear jewelry. She was wearing the same white square beads as earrings.

"He's a good boy, even if he's a little naughty." Next to her, Bill nodded and chuckled.

Tia raised her eyebrows in question and Ruth waved her hand in the air as if dismissing the topic. "That's a story for another day," she said. "You looked like you could use a friend."

"Thanks, I appreciate the company. Now, about Nance?"

"Oh, you never mind about that." Ruth changed the subject. "Jill makes such a beautiful bride, doesn't she?"

"She is stunning," Tia agreed. She looked at all the beautiful people in the bridal party getting their pictures taken at the edge of the yard and felt a stab of insecurity. Her eyes linked with Nance's, and he winked. Tia quickly looked back at Ruth and Bill.

"I've heard a story or two about you both as well, from Nance. Something about nightcrawlers?" He had mentioned it when he was talking about who was going to be at the wedding, but he hadn't elaborated.

Ruth and Bill looked at each other and burst out laughing.

"That was funny," Ruth said when she caught her breath. "That didn't have anything to do with Nance, but it was definitely funny. Poor Dillon. Bill and I were out one evening searching for nightcrawlers for fishing."

"We were in Ruth's yard, so it wasn't like we were trespassing or anything," Bill interjected.

"Dillon was at Jill's house... next door to me, you know... so, Dillon comes out of Jill's house and is walking towards my house..."

"We were trying to be quiet so he wouldn't notice us there," Bill added.

"Dillon wasn't paying attention and walked right into me," Ruth continued as if Bill hadn't spoken. "He thought I was a burglar, can you believe that?"

Bill chuckled. "The funny part is, he apparently had just told Jill that he wouldn't be surprised if his mother was lurking out in the bushes spying on him."

Tia couldn't help herself. "Why would he think that?"

"Oh, he always thought I was trying to get him matched up with Jill," Ruth replied. Bill nodded.

"Were you?" Tia whispered.

Ruth laughed. "Of course I was, and look, it worked." They all turned to look at Jill and Dillon, who were sharing a kiss for the camera.

"And now, they're getting married," Tia said.

"Oh, look, we're being summoned." Ruth waved back at Jill as she beckoned Ruth and Bill over. "It was nice to meet you, Tia. Enjoy the party and oh, try the chocolate chip cookies."

Bill nodded as Ruth pulled on his arm. "She made them

herself."

Maybe she would, Tia thought, but right now she was too anxious to eat anything. After they left, Tia stood there, wondering what she should do next.

"What was I thinking?"

"Excuse me?" A voice from behind her interrupted Tia's thoughts and she turned.

"Oh, hello, Paula. I was just thinking out loud."

Nance's mother was dressed elegantly in a mid-calf, navy-blue dress with elbow-length sleeves and a wraparound bodice. White appliqued flowers spilled from the waist down to the hem. Her dark hair was up in a elegant French twist, but her smile was friendly as she touched Tia's arm. "It's all a bit much, isn't it?"

Tia looked around at the people gathered in Jan's backyard. Tia thought that when Nance said it was going to be a small wedding, she should have asked more questions. This gathering didn't fit into her category of small. People milled around, waiting for the music to start, signaling the beginning of the wedding. A few had already taken their seats.

"I didn't realize there would be so many people here."

"You don't like crowds, do you?"

Tia looked at the older woman. "Not particularly. I feel like I shouldn't have come. Nance is busy."

"You never mind that." Paula patted Tia's arm. "You can hang out with Allen and I."

"But you have things to do." Tia felt like an intruder. Paula was so nice, but all Tia wanted to do was fade into the nearby bushes.

"I do, but not right this minute, and I'm not the star of this show. I'm sure Nance will be happy to see you. He wasn't sure you would come."

Tia smiled wryly. "He wasn't wrong. I changed my mind a hundred times."

"But you're here now, and I'm glad you came. I know Nance can be a bit..." she paused, "much, but he means well. He has a big heart and he's had it stomped on." Paula tilted her head at Tia's puzzled look. "But, of course, he hasn't told you about Missy yet."

"Who's Missy?"

Paula's expression mirrored a deer caught in the headlights of a car. "Oh, he can tell you about that, but don't tell him I said anything. Actually, I wanted to talk to you about something else."

Missy? Tia wondered as Paula took her arm and led her

toward the chairs that were set up on the lawn for guests. Who was Missy? An old girlfriend, who according to Paula, broke Nance's heart. The blonde from a few weeks ago? He didn't look like she had broken his heart, in fact, Tia couldn't see anyone breaking his heart. She smiled. She imagined Nance was the one who broke hearts and left them bleeding all over the place.

Once seated, Paula turned to Tia. "I was going through some boxes in the attic, and I found one that has a bunch of my grandfather's things in it."

Tia's eyebrows rose with curiosity, and Paula nodded.

"That's what I thought too. I found some more letters and pictures that were apparently from his time in the war. None of it means much to me, but I thought they might be useful to you."

"Absolutely." Tia lightly clapped her hands. "I would love to have a look at them, there may be more clues that would be helpful."

"And another thing..." Paula paused. "You probably could have solved this whole mystery pretty quickly, right?"

Tia bent her head forward, then looked up again. "Truthfully?"

Paula nodded.

"About eight hours of work, I figure."

"I'm guessing Nance is hindering your progress."

"Maybe. But I'm working for a flat fee."

"I'm not worried about that, I'm only worried about him taking up your time."

"He's pretty busy so we're working around his schedule, and I'm doing my regular work as well, so it's not a problem."

Paula nodded and smiled. "I'm just glad you're indulging him. He seems to be pretty interested in the whole mystery now."

"We're probably digging deeper than we needed to, but he does seem interested, and he's found he enjoys the war part of the story."

"Good," Paula replied. "I know he likes history, but he hasn't looked at it from a personal view."

"Exactly." Tia stopped and caught her bottom lip with her teeth.

"What?"

"Well, since we're talking...."

"You can tell me anything."

If that were only true, Tia thought, she might be walking down the aisle next week.

"It's more of a question."

"Ask away."

"I was thinking it might be a good idea for him... or you... or both of you, to have your DNA tested, you know, the mystery really is what happened to the little girl. I think John is her father, but I don't have any concrete evidence. We still don't know what happened to her, adoption for sure, but who adopted her? We don't have a last name, and we don't know if she got married and had a family. She's definitely still a mystery. Maybe you don't want to dig that far?"

"I do, if you've got the time and patience. Consider it done." Paula nodded as the pre-wedding music began.

Tia panicked. "I can't sit here," she whispered. "I need to move to the back."

Paula's hand kept her from moving.

"Nonsense, I won't have anyone to sit with until Allen comes along with Jill, so you'll be doing me a favor."

And so Tia sat in the front row, hugely aware that everyone could see her. She picked at the skirt of her dress.

Paula patted her arm and surprisingly, the action calmed Tia's nerves. Just a bit.

"Aren't you wearing the cutest dress?" Paula whispered.

Tia looked down at her dress. It was still the simple dress she had arrived in. She had agonized over the selection of a dress to wear to an outdoor wedding but luckily had taken Erica shopping with her. The older woman had made the decision in the end, assuring Tia the dress flattered her curves. She had added a pair of flat, white sandals and wore only a string of white pearls that had been her mother's and a pair of pearl bracelets on her wrists for jewelry.

Her hair fell in soft waves down past her shoulders, and she was sure she looked presentable, but Tia still felt out of place.

She stood with Paula and the rest of the guests when the bridesmaids started down the aisle.

They were beautiful women, Tia thought. Jan, with her glorious red hair pulled back from her face in a mass of curls, and the other bridesmaid, a tall, regal-looking woman with short blonde hair tossed back from her forehead and curls perfectly in place, framing her face, were wearing blue dresses as well. They were high-waisted, tea-length dresses in navy-blue like Paula's, but the white-lace bodices and cap sleeves were covered with white appliqued flowers that spilled down onto the skirts.

Tia smiled as she met the gaze of the blonde woman for just a moment, and for another moment thought she recognized her. It was gone in an instant as the two delightful and bouncing flower girls came down the aisle.

Penny and Peggy, Tia remembered Nance saying. Both with that same glorious red hair pulled back in half ponytails, red curls spilling out everywhere. They were wearing white dresses with light-blue, appliqued flowers spilling from one shoulder down to the full skirt and beyond. Adorable, Tia thought, although she had no idea which was Penny, and which was Peggy. They took their places next to the bridesmaids as the bride came into view, holding the arm of her father.

Jill's dress shimmered and shined as they walked down the aisle. Allen L'Breck handed her off to her groom where he and the groomsmen and minister were waiting.

Dillon's brother, Jason, Tia remembered, was his best man and Nance stood on the other side of Jason. All of them wore lightweight brown suits, with navy blue shirts and ties.

It was a unique color choice for a wedding, Tia thought, but the color combination was magnificent.

In what seemed like a blink of an eye to Tia, the couple was married and smiling as they preceded the group back down the aisle as the crowd, Tia included, cheered and applauded.

She followed Allen and Paula and stood quietly as they greeted guests.

"There you are."

Tia turned to face Nance and realized he was much too close. His eyebrows furrowed as she stepped back, but it was gone in an instant. He was holding two glasses in his hands.

"I thought you might like something to drink." He handed her a glass of champagne and kept one for himself.

"Thanks, but aren't you supposed to be doing something?"

"Not for a minute." He looked over the crowd. "They'll make some toasts in a minute, but I'm not a part of any of that."

Tia sipped as she followed his gaze. "There are a lot of people here, Nance. I thought you said it was going to be a small wedding."

He smiled as he looked at her and Tia had to put a hand to her heart to keep it from beating out of control. "I was misled, Jill said it would be small, but apparently our definitions of that word are different.”

His smile faltered when Tia didn't respond. She was staring off into space.

“Do you want to leave?” Nance touched her arm, and she jumped.

“Oh, what?” No, it's fine.” Tia smiled, just a brief movement of her lips. She turned back to the wedding guests and gestured with her glass. “I was wondering who the bridesmaid is.”

Nance followed Tia's gaze. “That's Suzanne Hall. She's Jill's best friend and her accountant. Why?”

Tia shrugged. “I don't know. She just looks familiar.”

Nance watched Suzanne as she talked to an older man who he didn't recognize. “Have you met her before?”

Tia shook her head and sipped from her glass. “I don't think so, it's just a feeling of recognition. It's nothing.”

“Hmm, maybe you know her from college,” Nance offered. “After all, she was at the University of Minnesota when we were.”

“True, but I don't recall ever seeing you there, so likely I wouldn't have seen her either.”   Nance   started   to speak, and Tia shook her head. “I know, we didn't travel in the same circles.”

“I just can't believe you never went to a football game. You missed some good times.”

Tia shrugged. “I didn't do much outside of going to class, studying and working. And in case you haven't noticed, I'm not exactly the sporty type.”

“You ride a bicycle,” he pointed out.

“That's relatively new. In Sacramento, I could go just about everywhere without a car. And I still can mostly, but I found that I just like riding.” Tia raised her glass. “And it's good exercise.”

“So is dancing, do you want to give it a try?”

The horror on her face couldn't be more evident, but Tia thought she handled the shudder that slithered through her body.

“I don't think so.”

Nance smiled and dropped it, but Tia was certain the subject would come back up later.

She turned around and looked at the food set out on several tables on the Humphreys' patio. Her stomach growled and Nance smiled.

“Hungry?”

“Not really,” she lied like they hadn't both heard the growl. “And shouldn't we wait for the bride and groom?”

"Not at all," Nance replied. "We were told to eat whenever we wanted, and look, there are others filling plates. Come on."

"I'm really not hungry, but you go ahead."

Nance shrugged and led her to a small round table, helping Tia with her chair before going for food.

He came back a few moments later with two plates piled with sandwiches, salads and fruit. He set one in front of Tia and took the chair next to her. Tia looked at the plate, then questioningly at Nance.

"I was afraid you would change your mind and steal off of my plate, so I brought you your own."

Now that the food was in front of her, Tia was suddenly hungry. Her stomach growled again and Nance grinned.

"Way to think ahead, and maybe I could eat." She looked at the fancy little sandwich and melon on her plate. "No cookies? I was told I should try them."

"I brought some." He took a folded napkin out of his suit pocket. "I love Ruth's cookies, wasn't about to come to an event where we have them and not have some." He opened the napkin and Tia took one, added it to her plate.

"You should have at least two." He continued to hold the napkin out.

"Fine, you convinced me." Tia took another and put it on her plate

Nance had opted for the same fancy sub sandwich Tia had. It was wrapped with parchment paper and tied with a string, which he untied and unwrapped. He took a bite.

"Mmm, that's good. And the pasta salad, mmm, good too."

Tia smiled and speared a chunk of melon. "You act like you haven't eaten all day."

Nance paused with his fork halfway to his mouth. "You know, I'm not sure I have." He gave it some thought. "I had breakfast before I left Minneapolis, and we had one of those cheese and cracker board things earlier, but I think that's it."

"Charcouterie."

"What?"

"It was a charcouterie board, fancier than cheese and crackers."

"Sure, if you say so." Nance plucked another sandwich off his plate. "This is better though."

They finished their meal and sat watching the dancers. Just as Tia predicted, Nance didn't let the dance go.

"So, ready to dance with me now?"

CHAPTER FIFTEEN

T ia's hand, holding a refilled glass of champagne, shook just a little. She had drunk just enough champagne to consider it for a minute, but she looked at the crowded dance area and then at Nance. With the alcohol in her, Tia thought she might be able to brave the crowd, but the thought of getting that close to Nance sent shivers through her. She was pretty sure that being that close would melt her into a puddle of want at his feet, and that wouldn't do. She shook her head.

Nance watched the shudder, like the one earlier, run through her, saw the slight shake of her hand and finally the shake of her head, and knew the answer before she spoke.

"Still a no, I'm afraid." She hoped he didn't hear the disappointment in her voice. "Anyway," she added brightly, and held up her glass. "Let's toast the bride and groom."

Nance obligingly clinked his glass to hers and let the subject of dancing go.

"Hey Nance, we need you." Dillon bumped him on the shoulder. "Apparently, we haven't taken enough pictures."

Nance raised his eyebrows. "I feel like we have."

"Me too, but the lady of the day says we need a couple more."

Nance looked at Tia.

She smiled. "Go on, I'll be fine."

He nodded and went with Dillon, but he wasn't sure

about leaving Tia, no matter what she said. He looked back. She was watching him, and still smiling, but her smile looked forced.

Tia wasn't fine. When Nance didn't come back, Tia stood up. There were too many people here, and she could feel the anxiety setting in. She walked into the house and went to the bathroom to wash her hands. As she stood there with her hand on the doorknob to go back to the party, Tia realized she couldn't do it. She needed to go. Home, preferably, but she would have to settle for the motel.

"Have you seen Tia?" Nance asked his mother a little while later. The pictures were done, but when he went back to the table, Tia was gone.

"I think she left," Paula said. "I saw her walk out the front door a few minutes ago."

"You didn't ask what she was doing?"

Paula shook her head. "She looked a little anxious, so I thought maybe she was just looking for some quiet."

Nance went to the front door, opened it and walked out, peering into the night. Tia wasn't there. Why would she have left? he wondered. And why hadn't she just said she was ready to go? He would have taken her back to the motel.

"Find her?" Paula asked when he came back inside.

"No." Nance's tone was short. "I guess she got tired of sitting alone and left."

"That's too bad." Paula patted his arm. "But I think there was more to it than that. Why don't you call her?"

Nance nodded but left his phone in his pocket.

By the time Tia got back to her motel room, she regretted her decision to leave the wedding without talking to Nance first. It was rude and wrong, and she knew it, but the panic that had been rising up inside her had been real. She needed to escape.

She sat on the edge of the bed and shook her head, then breathed deep. It was done and she couldn't change it. Nance probably wouldn't speak to her again, and she hated that, Tia thought as she took off her shoes and got ready for bed.

She wished she had stayed, wished she had accepted

the offer of a dance with Nance. Tia thought about that missed dance as she snuggled under the fluffy comforter in her motel room a few minutes later. What would have been the harm in one dance, really? Nance hadn't danced with anyone else, even the bridesmaid he was paired with, or his mother.

She supposed he didn't want to leave her alone for fear she might bolt. He probably wasn't wrong about that, she thought, and since that was exactly what she had done, he was probably reevaluating their relationship right now.

What relationship? Tia reached to turn off the bedside lamp. When they were together, he was kind, attentive and even flirted a little, affectionate with his friendly kisses, but it didn't seem to mean anything. She saw him interact with other women. He treated them all the same way, it was just the way he was.

Suddenly, Tia sat up in bed. The woman in Minneapolis. It was the bridesmaid, Suzanne something. Hall. Suzanne Hall. She was the tall blonde woman walking that day with Nance in Minneapolis, Tia thought as she pushed her hair away from her face, but why did Nance tonight act like he barely knew her?

Tia sighed and laid back down, trying to get it out of her mind. It didn't go away, and she tossed and turned as she thought about it. She finally decided she wanted to mean something to him, really be his girlfriend.

"That's not going to happen, now, is it?" She said the words aloud. "Because even if Suzanne means nothing to him, and that's not likely, you're still afraid you'll fall at his feet and beg him to take you to bed, and he will, and it'll mean so much to you, and be nothing but another fling for him."

Tia sighed and turned over. And that's fine for him, but not for me, she thought as she fell asleep.

"Why not?"

Erica posed the question to Tia the next day. They were sitting on the deck of the bookstore with mugs of coffee and watching the river go by. The sun was shining and there was little wind. It was a perfect Sunday afternoon. Tourists were out enjoying the weather, strolling along the river and stopping to take photos. All the leftover snow had melted, and boats floated up and down the river, stopping to wait for the old lift bridge to lift its movable section up so they could go to the other side.

"Why not have a little fling?" Erica repeated when Tia didn't answer.

"You're okay with it?"

Erica nodded over her coffee mug. Tia had stopped by to ask her out for supper that evening. They had already agreed to meet at the See-Food Inn later.

"Honey, when you get to my age, you tend to ask, 'what if?' What if I had done that, taken the risk?" She looked out at the river. "I've had a few times where, like you, I thought the risk was too great. Now, I wish I would have taken the chance." She wiggled her eyebrows. "I would totally take a fling now."

Tia laughed. She thought about Erica meeting Danny that evening. "I bet you would, but me, I'm feeling a little cautious."

"I'm just saying..."

"Yes, you are, and I'll take it under advisement." She held up her empty mug. "I'm going for a refill. Want one too?"

Erica handed over her mug and Tia went back inside for the refills.

Jamael looked up from the counter where he was checking out a young woman and a very young boy. He flashed Tia a brilliant smile.

The shop wasn't busy at the moment, but Tia knew that could change at any moment. Tia poured coffee into the mugs as two older ladies entered the shop. Tia smiled. They were discussing the luck of finding a little bookstore and what books they wanted to buy. They moved into the fiction aisle, now discussing whose favorite author was the best.

"Can I help you ladies?" She heard Jamael ask from the counter.

"Oh, no, thanks, we know what we're looking for," one of them answered. The other woman waved at him, then noticed Tia and smiled.

"Look, they have a place to read and a coffee bar," Tia heard her say as she carried the mugs back outside.

"What?" Erica asked as she took her mug.

Tia shook her head. "Oh, it's nothing. There are a couple of ladies inside shopping. I think they're sisters. They were talking and laughing. It was sweet, reminded me of my sisters."

"You miss them, don't you?" Erica blew on the hot liquid in her mug.

Tia sat down at the table across from her friend, "More than I like to admit." She waved her hand. "I mean, we've all been out of the house for years. They have families, lives and they have had for years. It was bad enough losing Dad, but we all had Mom. She was the glue that held our family together, and I guess I thought she would always be here. Now that she's gone, well…"

"You feel alone."

Tia nodded. "I feel like there's nothing to hold us together. Maybe if they lived closer, it would be better. But they were just here a few months ago for the funeral and I've talked to them both on the phone… a lot… more than we have for years."

"I understand completely." Erica gazed out at the river. "When we're young, our whole world revolves around our parents, our siblings, then we grow up, start our own families and that's where our focus goes. But when we lose our parents, that's tough, and it never goes away."

"To our families." Tia toasted Erica's mug.

"To our families, and enough about that. What are you going to do about that hunk of a weatherman?" Erica raised an eyebrow.

"Well…"

"You do want a fling." Erica clapped her hands.

"I will admit to considering it, but what if I get my heart broken?"

"You're worried about your heart? Are you in love with him?"

Tia shook her head vigorously. "Absolutely not. But I think I could be. I'm certainly lusting over him."

Erica laughed. "You and every other woman out there, so don't feel bad about that. If I was a few years younger, I might take a try at him."

Tia laughed. "I bet you would, but that doesn't change the fact that I'm so nervous around him that I can hardly think straight, let alone jump on him."

Erica laughed again. "Maybe you could try flirting a little."

Tia snorted. "I just said he makes me so nervous I can't think straight, and now you're suggesting I flirt with him? And just to make a point, I don't think I've ever flirted in my life."

"It could be fun." Erica stood up. "Maybe try to just think of him as a friend and see how that goes. Now, I've got to get back to work. Jamael probably thinks I've run out on him. I'll see you this evening for supper. We're going to the See-Food Inn, right?"

Tia nodded. "If that's okay with you."

"Absolutely, I haven't been there for years." She laughed. "I'm looking forward to it."

Tia was sure Jamael would never think such a thing, but she understood. She handed Erica her mug and went down the steps of the patio before turning to give Erica a wave. She pedaled away with a thoughtful look on her face and as she rode her bike across the lift bridge to the Wisconsin side of the river, she replayed the conversation with Erica.

She sighed. Flirt? She didn't think she could do it, but maybe Erica was right. She could be friendlier, and maybe she could try not to flinch every time Nance got in her personal space. She shrugged. But a fling? She felt like she was a long way away from that.

Tia met Erica in the parking lot later that evening and they entered the restaurant together. It was busy and Tia was immediately aware that she probably should have called ahead. A moment later, Danny stepped up to them.

"Hello, my lovely Tia." Danny hugged Tia and then offered his hand to Erica. "And who is this beautiful lady?" He looked straight into Erica's eyes and Tia could actually see the faint flush that quickly filled Erica's face.

"You don't know each other?" Tia looked from one to the other as they both shook their heads.

"Should we?" Erica asked, not taking her eyes off Danny.

"Erica, this is Danny Holcomb, the owner of this fine establishment. Danny, this is my friend Erica Helms. She owns Pages, the bookstore downtown."

Danny, still holding Erica's hand, raised it to his lips, never taking his eyes from hers. "The pleasure is mine."

Tia thought Erica was going to swoon, if women still did that. Erica broke eye contact with Danny just long enough to give Tia a startled look before she was drawn back to Danny. He slowly lowered her hand.

Tia had to hide her smile. Good for them, she thought, and she was going to have to point out to Erica later that she had nearly melted into that pool of lust they had talked about earlier.

"How could you not know each other?" Tia looked from one to the other. "I mean, don't you both belong to the local chamber of commerce?"

"I don't know," Danny replied. "I will admit that I don't go to many of the meetings, I send Micah when I can. But now…" He led them to a table, his hand on Erica's back, gently guiding her. He pulled out her chair and helped her sit.

Tia rolled her eyes as she pulled out her own chair and sat. They seemed to have forgotten she was there. She gently cleared her throat.

Danny apparently remembered where he was and looked around, nodded to the waitress who came and filled their water glasses.

"Thanks Kat," she told the waitress, then turned to Danny. "Do you have time to join us?"

He shook his head. "I would love to…" He looked at Erica. "But we're pretty busy tonight. I can bring you some wine though."

Erica spoke for the first time since they arrived. "We would love that." She looked at him and again, Tia had to hide her smile behind her hand. She wondered if they realized they were acting like lovestruck teenagers.

Luckily, Kat came back with menus and Danny was called to another table.

"Wow." Erica watched the tall man walk away. "Who is that man and where have you been hiding him?"

Tia laughed. "He's been here forever, since I was little. How could you not have known him?"

Erica looked down at the menu. "I have no idea. I've eaten here many times, but I'm sure I would have remembered him." She licked her lips. "So, what's his story?"

Tia didn't answer her until Kat had taken their order, fish and chips for her and a salad and grilled fish for Erica.

She filled Erica in on Danny's general background, but decided Erica could learn the rest on her own.

It was a pleasant meal and as they finished, Danny came back to sit for a minute. That turned into about fifteen minutes, Tia estimated, but who was counting?

Tia finally made a decision. "I'm going to head out now," she declared as she rose from her chair. Erica started to rise as well, and Tia put her hand on the older woman's shoulder. "No, you stay and have another glass of wine. Enjoy yourselves." She winked at Erica and headed for the door. She looked back and saw their heads close together, talking like old friends.

CHAPTER SIXTEEN

"I don't know Mom, I don't think it's a good idea. She doesn't really like me."

Paula L'Breck disagreed, but she wasn't going to tell Nance that. They had both just swabbed their cheeks for the DNA test Tia wanted, so Paula could send it to the company Tia had suggested. Now she was trying to convince Nance to take the box of John Beckwith's letters and other memorabilia that she had found in the attic to Tia.

"She probably doesn't even need this stuff," Nance continued. He stabbed around at the things in the box. "She likely solved the whole mystery the first day and has been waiting for me to catch up to her answers."

"That's not true and you know it," Paula scolded him. "I think she knows most of it, but she's shared everything she has with you. And she thinks she's figured out who this Helen is, but not what happened to her. It's likely my grandfather had another child that we didn't even know about. I want to know. We probably have more family out there that we don't know. I agree with Tia that the DNA samples are probably going to be what solves this."

"I haven't even talked to her for two weeks. She hasn't called or anything, and I couldn't even get her to dance with me at Jill's wedding. And then she just left." He ran his fingers through his hair. "It's like I have leprosy or something."

Paula sighed. "Didn't Tia tell you she doesn't like crowds? And yet, there she was, because you asked her to go with you."

"You know she shudders and moves away from me every time I get close to her."

"I expect she does." Paula cocked her head. "You know you can be a little intimidating, don't you?"

"I'm not intimidating. Am I?" There was disbelief in his voice. "Anyway, I feel like she should be used to me by now."

"You can be." Paula patted his arm. "Even when you don't mean to be."

"I didn't realize," he said softly. "I've only tried to be friendly. I mean, I like her. I like being with her, I want to know her better."

Paula's eyebrows arched. "Even if she's a hoarder?"

Nance smiled at that. "Turns out, she's not a hoarder. I forgot to tell you. Her mom moved into the cottage from a larger house and didn't have room to store everything. Apparently, after that, it got out of hand and now Tia's trying to get it all organized. I actually helped her deal with some of it a few weeks ago."

"Is that so?" Paula thought about it for a minute. "And she let you?" she finally asked.

Nance nodded. "I wasn't judgmental about it."

Paula raised her eyebrows.

"Okay, I wasn't judgmental after she told me the situation. There are a couple of rooms that are still a mess, but she's working on it."

"And the cats?"

Nance grinned. "She doesn't have any cats. She said she would like to have one, though."

Paula considered that. "And how do you feel about that?"

"I could totally see her with a cat."

"Really? If you had a relationship with her, you'd be okay with her owning a cat?"

Nance nodded again. "I think I would. You know I never hated them, but you've forgotten an important point here. She doesn't like me."

"Well, maybe you just need to get her to change her mind." Paula reached up and patted his cheek. "So, go and let her get used to you."

"I feel like she should be used to me by now." He noted his mother's exasperated expression. "Fine. I'll take the box to her, and I'll be friendly and not intimidating, and not judge her about the hoarding thing."

"You're a good boy." Paula gestured to the box. "It'll give you a good reason to see her again."

"Giving me dating advice, Mom?"

Paula nodded. "I am and I expect you to take it. Remember that time you didn't take my advice. She's not good for you I told you, don't get too close, I said."

Nance's smile faltered. She wasn't wrong. Missy had been a huge mistake. He hadn't done anything more than casual dating since then, hadn't had the stomach for it.

"I remember," he finally replied, shuddering.

"I don't think Tia is a Missy," Paula said, patting his cheek. "You can trust me."

"That's all fine and dandy, Mom, but it doesn't change the fact that she's not interested in me."

Paula helped him get out the door and watched him walk to his SUV with the box.

"Oh, she is, honey, trust me, she is," she said softly, and waved as Nance drove away.

It took all of Tia's nerve to pick up her phone and call Nance. A fling, Erica had suggested. She wasn't sure she could do it, but maybe she could start by calling him. She hadn't heard from him in a couple of weeks and decided he had given up on her after the wedding.

She was surprised when he answered on the first ring, and she couldn't help herself, she blurted out the reason for her call.

"I have to go into Minneapolis Thursday, do you want to have dinner?" The words all but ran together.

"Well, hello to you too."

"Sorry, hello. How are you?"

He laughed and Tia's nerves settled.

"Are you asking me on a date?"

Tia cocked her head. "Maybe? Or not? I was just thinking that you come here all the time, so maybe I could come there?"

The silence was deafening. Tia looked at her phone in surprise.

"Hello? No dinner out?" What was this? He didn't want to be seen with her? She imagined Suzanne walking down the street with him. "I could bring something and we could eat at your place if that would work better for you."

"No."

"No to dinner out, or no, don't bring something in? I thought it might be fun to experience the city at night, you know, take a walk, eat something fancy, see where you live and your world."

She heard him clear his throat. "Umm, let me give it some thought."

Tia furrowed her brow. He had to give it some thought? That didn't sound right. He was usually the one to suggest an outing, but she thought it might be nice if she did the inviting this time. Dinner seemed like a perfectly good outing to her.

"You act like you don't want to show me the city."

The silence was back.

"Nance? Are you there?"

"Yeah, yeah, I'm here. You know it's quite a drive for you, and you would have to drive home in the dark."

"I told you I'm coming into Minneapolis anyway. I'm a big girl, I think I can handle that. But it you don't want to, fine." She could feel tears of disappointment starting to form in her eyes. And that was stupid, because they weren't dating, they were working together. A thought stopped her. Suzanne.

"Maybe you have other plans?"

"Yes, that's it. Other plans. I have a meeting."

Tia knew Nance was lying as soon as he agreed. Embarrassed, she assured him she would see him around, talk to him later, all the things people said when they were trying to get out of an awkward situation, and hung up.

"So much for that fling thing." Tia looked at the phone. "I can't even get him to take me to dinner. Other plans, he says, another time, he says. Right."

He didn't have other plans. Nance looked at this phone after she said an abrupt goodbye and immediately felt bad. He should call her back, accept. She wasn't Missy, he reminded himself, was nothing like her. He knew that as a fact, and yet, once burned, twice shy, as the saying went.

Nance admitted there was something else. He liked being in her world. Liked the slower life she led. There were no honking cars in her world, no traffic, so he wasn't in a hurry to bring her into his world.

Nance was pretty sure he had hurt Tia's feelings, and that was the last thing he wanted to do. He liked her, really liked her. Maybe their lifestyles weren't exactly the same, maybe she was a little messy and was okay with clutter, but she had a good heart, cried for people she'd never met. Maybe he could compromise on the clutter. He went back to the conversation they had when he had stopped at her house to find her crying. His heart had nearly broken watching the grief on her face.

Nance walked out onto his patio and looked out over the city. He'd always lived here, not in this building, sure, but in Minneapolis, and he had always been happy. The draw to Stillwater was real, but he knew that was because of Tia.

Would he go there if Tia wasn't there? Nance could look right out at the Mississippi River from his patio, was doing it now. It was a perfect spring evening. The flowering crab trees were blooming, leaves were coming out on the other trees, birds were chirping as they flew from one perch to another. The setting sun glinted off the river below and reminded him of Tia's sunroom. Two different rivers not so far apart and not far away from each other, in fact, one flowed into the other.

The view was different at her house, a little wilder and uncontrolled, so much different than the person she was. He looked back inside. He liked his apartment, it was convenient and had everything he needed. He shrugged. Maybe it didn't have the personality of Tia's little cottage, but it was his.

He admitted that Missy had done a job on him, it was an experience he never wanted to repeat, and yet, as his mother had pointed out, Tia wasn't Missy.

He shrugged, then thought of Reid and the boys. He loved being with them, watching them grow from babies into the boys they were today, and thought maybe he would like children of his own. But that meant commitment and letting someone into his life. Like Tia.

He did like her, thought she knew it, but except for a few kisses he hadn't been able to get close to her. His eyes narrowed. He had told his mother she didn't like him, and he still stood by that opinion, but they had had some nice times together.

He missed her, he realized, and right now, he regretted his decision not to have dinner with her here.

"Crap." He just realized that her phone call was the first time she had reached out to him, the first time she had initiated something that wasn't related to his grandfather.

"And you told her no, practically ran the other way." He turned to discover his reflection in the patio door window, his scowl evident. "You know you're going to have to fix this, so figure it out."

It wasn't as easy as that, Nance discovered. He had given it some thought, but work invaded.

"Have you seen the latest computer models for later this week?" Adam asked from the door of Nance's office. Nance was sitting at this desk doing exactly that. The weather had been nice, but several days ago, he could see they were going to be in the bullseye for a potentially dangerous storm.

"I'm looking now," Nance replied. "It looks like it's going to be all hands on deck for the next few days."

"I know, isn't it great?"

Nance disagreed. He loved the changing weather, the rain when they needed it, the clearing and the beautiful days that came after a storm. He loved the lightning and thunder, and tornadoes fascinated him, but he recognized their fury and destruction. He had loved to chase the big storms when he was in college, even went to Oklahoma for a summer to study and learn to predict their paths.

Today, Nance recognized that he had been reckless and foolish in his youth, but he was glad he was able to have the opportunity to warn others now so they could stay safe.

Tornadic activity in the forecast meant long days and nights studying the track of the storms and keeping viewers up to date with watches and warnings. Most of those came from the National Weather Service, but he and his colleagues had a duty to get that information to the public.

He was going to call Tia back, had every intention of doing that earlier today and yet, here he sat. Maybe he could text her.

"We're going to get together in about ten minutes, just thought I'd let you know."

"Sure, thanks, I'll wrap this up and be there."

Tia sat in one of the wicker chairs in the sunroom and stared out at the water. She didn't feel like cooking dinner, didn't feel like cleaning or working. She was restless and she didn't know why.

She hadn't heard anything from Nance since the day she called him. She had gone to Minneapolis yesterday to do some research into a murder that had occurred in the 1970s. She met with a private investigator who was looking into a death of a Jane Doe. Tia agreed to help him, it would be her first case outside of the lab and she had been excited to get started. Today, she was just sad about it. Maybe that explained the restlessness.

She sighed and walked outside, padded down the steps to the edge of the water. The weather was probably on, with Nance talking all about it in that deep voice of his, but she was boycotting watching the weather. There wouldn't be much to watch, she decided. It was a little sticky and muggy out, Tia thought as she looked at the sky, but there wasn't a cloud in sight.

A heavy sigh left her as she stared at the water. Tia felt like her heart was breaking, which was ridiculous, wasn't it? She admitted to herself that she liked Nance, liked how he was full of life and fun, could poke fun at himself and laugh. She wasn't so sure about the Nance who was vague and didn't answer questions. He never talked about his past relationships. There were probably too many to mention. She couldn't see him without a woman in his life. For all she knew, he was living with one. Suzanne.

She bent down and picked up a little rock, sailed it into the river. Surely, she would have known that, if he was in a relationship, surely the woman would have been at the bike ride. Right? Right, she said to herself. So, what was Suzanne to him?

A flash of light and a clap of thunder brought her back to the present. She turned and looked up at the angry clouds gathering off to the west, gasped.

"Where did that come from?

The clouds had a greenish hue to them and they were moving towards her. If she wasn't mistaken, that was a tornado forming, or heavy wind and hail.

"Crap, crap, crap," Tia repeated as she ran into the house. She grabbed her phone and laptop and picked up her purse on the way to the bathroom. This house wasn't prepared for tornadoes. There was no basement, and it was too late to go to a neighbor's house.

She should have watched the weather, Tia decided as the wind picked up. She sat down in the bathtub and said a couple of prayers. She couldn't remember the last time there was a tornado warning in the area. She opened her phone and looked at the weather radar.

It was bad out there, according to the radar, and she regretted the decision not to watch Nance on the television. Just then the electricity went out and the room went dark. She lost her internet and could only hold her phone and hope the storm missed her. It was the most frightened she'd ever been, she decided, and she wished she had at least gone to the See-Food Inn so she wouldn't be alone.

She felt the house tremble and was sure this was going to be her last few minutes on this Earth. She poked out quick texts to her sisters and to Erica, then thought about it for a moment before texting Nance.

It was just two words.

"I'm sorry."

Nance read the text from Tia and was immediately alarmed. Sorry? About what? He didn't have time to deal with it, as Adam called his name.

He glanced up.

"Tornado indicated heading northwest to Stillwater."

"What?" Tia was in Stillwater. No. It couldn't be.

He started to run to the door and realized he couldn't leave. He had a job to do, but if she was hurt, or worse... He wouldn't think about that, he couldn't get to her. He couldn't even call her friend at the bookstore.

He pinched his nose with his fingers, took a deep breath, pushed the panic away and rushed over to Adam's desk.

"We've just gotten an update, the tornado pulled up and moved across the river, it's moving fast."

"It's missing Stillwater?"

Adam nodded. "Looks like it never touched down but there's some high winds and some pretty good-sized hail."

Nance breathed a sigh of relief. He would check on Tia as soon as he had a chance. She was likely with Erica anyway, and was fine.

CHAPTER SEVENTEEN

Tia was not fine. She was still sitting in the dark bathroom. The wind and hail had subsided. The bathroom was
still intact, but she was afraid to open the door and see
what the rest of the world looked like.

She took a deep breath and did it anyway. The house
was dark, but it looked like everything was intact. She went
to the front door and opened it a crack. It was just raining,
and it looked like a couple of tree branches had come down
in the neighbor's yard.

She went back through the kitchen and out to the sunroom. Again, everything was fine there. She sat down in one
of the wicker chairs and breathed out, had been unaware
she was holding her breath. The sky above her was lighter
than the dark angry mass across the river.

Nance was dead tired by the time the last of the storms
had moved out of the area. The stress could sometimes be
overwhelming. Trying to warn people about the possibility
of bad weather was hard enough, but when there was damage, it was even worse. Lives were affected, torn apart like
the trees.

One tornado had apparently taken a swath through a
rural neighborhood northeast of the city, and news crews
were on their way to investigate the damage. He had seen
the footage from some of the storm chasers and was glad he

wasn't with them.

As soon as the storms had moved out of the area, Nance tried calling Tia. It rang three times before it went to voice mail. He texted her to find out if she was okay, but there was no response.

He couldn't get out of the station fast enough. He jogged to his apartment in a light rain. He realized it was late, but he changed into jeans and a t-shirt and boots and got in his SUV. He would go make sure she was okay, had to.

Nance had driven through some areas that had branches down but finally made it to Tia's neighborhood. He discovered there was a branch blocking her street, so he parked on the side of the road, got his flashlight out and hiked in, knocked hard on Tia's door.

"What are you doing here?" Tia asked in surprise as she opened the door a moment later. "Aren't you supposed to be working?"

"I heard it was bad here, and I couldn't get hold of you, so I came to see if you're all right. You sent me a message."

"Oh, yeah, I forgot about that. That was my 'I'm going to die soon and don't want to leave people hanging' message."

"But, you're okay?"

She nodded. "Yeah, I really thought I was a goner, but someone somewhere was looking over me and I made it through."

He didn't wait for permission. Nance stepped inside and enveloped her in a big hug. Tia was surprised enough to take advantage of the warm male body next to hers and hugged him back.

He finally backed away but held her loosely. "I was so scared for you, and I couldn't get away."

"I knew that, and I was so scared too. I've never been in a tornado, never even seen one in person until today, didn't realize it was coming."

Nance scowled at her. "But you were watching the weather, right?"

Tia dipped her head, then shook it. "I was mad at you, so I decided I wasn't watching the weather this week."

"Two things. You were mad at me?"

"For not wanting to take me to dinner in the city."

"That's why you said you were sorry?"

Tia nodded. "I felt bad because I didn't try to call you again."

"I get it, I was going to call you and apologize, see if

you wanted to reschedule that, but then the weather...”

“I get that now, but I was still mad, I thought maybe we could be friends.”

“We are friends, aren’t we?”

“Are we?” The doubt crept into Tia’s voice. “What about Suzanne?”

“Suzanne?”

“Suzanne Hall, Jill’s accountant?”

Nance blinked. “What does she have to do with anything? I barely know her.”

Tia took a deep breath before she spoke. “I saw the two of you walking together one day in Minneapolis when I was there.”

Nance’s brow furrowed as he thought about it. “I did run into her one day. I was walking back to my apartment and she was coming from an appointment. We just happened to see each other, walked together for a block or so before we parted ways.”

He looked at Tia, puzzled. “You saw that?”

Tia nodded. “And I thought you and she, well, were a couple. The reason you didn’t want me to come to the city to see you.”

“I barely know her,” he repeated. “Why didn’t you say something?”

Tia looked away. “I’m saying something now.”

“You know you’ve been worrying for nothing, don’t you?”

“Maybe. Now. But you can see how it looked.” She put her chin up. “And you didn’t want me in the city.”

Nance took a step closer. “That’s another story, but it has nothing to do with a secret girlfriend.”

“So, we can be friends?”

Nance smiled. “I think so. We haven’t had much time to get to know each other, but we can be friends.” He leaned down to kiss her, his lips gentle, nudging hers, until Tia leaned into him and let nature take its course.

When they finally came apart, Tia was panting. “Does kissing go with being friends?”

Nance grinned, the smile reaching his eyes. “I hope so, as long as you’re okay with it. I like kissing.”

Tia leaned against his chest. “I guess I do too.” She breathed in the smell of him, closed her eyes and imagined running her hand up his hard chest, pulling his t-shirt out of his waistband and running her fingers along the hard lines of his muscles. She imagined putting her hands around his neck and pulling him down to kiss him deeply. She wanted to pull off his shirt and plant little love kisses on his chest, pull off his jeans. The erotic thought of it all made her heart race and her body tighten. Before she knew what was happening, her knees buckled, and Tia started sliding to the floor.

Nance barely caught her.

"Are you okay?" He looked at her face, it was red, and her breathing was labored. He backed up so his arms were outstretched but he didn't let her go. "You seem to fall a lot."

Tia turned and stumbled to the kitchen. She really needed to splash cold water on her face, but settled for getting a soda out of the refrigerator. "Do you want one?"

Tia handed one to him and wandered out on the patio. It was dark, pitch dark since it seemed the electricity was out all over the area. She sat down, put the cold can on her forehead for a moment before taking a drink.

"I'm really okay," she finally said. "I don't have any disease. I'm a little naturally clumsy, so..."

"Okay, as long as you're not sick."

She could hear in his voice that he wasn't convinced.

"So, number two?"

"Number two what?" Now his voice registered confusion.

"You said two things. First, I was mad at you. Second?"

"Oh." His voice was husky. "You said you weren't watching the weather."

"I did say that." Tia's chin jutted up.

"That's kind of irresponsible in this day and age, don't you think?"

"Yeah, but I was mad, remember?" The chin came down and Tia realized she couldn't put any heat into the words, mostly because he was right.

"That's no reason not to keep an eye on the weather. You could have watched another station, listened to the radio, something."

Tia turned away, looked out into the darkness. "You're right."

"What?"

She turned back. "I said, you're right. I wasn't thinking about it. I thought it seemed a little muggy out, but hey, it's spring, so you know. But I should have been aware of what was going on in the outside world. I came outside and looked at the sky. I didn't even see any clouds, and then it just came up so quickly."

"Okay. I don't mean to preach, but people die because they aren't watching and being aware of the weather. We're out there trying to save lives and that doesn't always happen."

"I get it." She smiled brightly in the dark, Nance could see the curve of her cheeks as she did so. "I promise to always watch you in the future."

"Good." He stood up. "I better get home. We've got more storms coming in a few days, so there's more work to do."

Tia stood up as well. Nance took her hand and led her back into the house. "Sleep well, and I'll call you tomorrow, I promise."

After a very chaste and quick kiss, he was gone. Tia sat down in one of the wicker chairs and rubbed her eyes. She didn't like being scolded and thought she should be angry. She wasn't though, because, as she had admitted, he was right. And it was sweet that he was worried enough about her to drive all the way out here to check on her.

Did he care about her? she wondered, and decided that was a stupid question. Of course he cared. Nance cared about people, it was in his nature. And there was that kiss. Tia's heart started beating hard and she tamped down the memory. She stood and went to her bathroom to wash her face.

Tia was still pondering the turn of events the next morning when Nance called, true to his word. They only spoke for a few minutes, mostly he checked to see if she was okay, but just hearing his voice made Tia's day.

"Oh, my God, Reid was right all those weeks ago," she told her blank computer screen. "You're in love with him. And does that mean a fling is out of the question?" She had to admit that a little part of her had wanted him to take her to dinner in the city, and after a romantic walk in the moonlight, they could have gone back to his apartment, and maybe she could have had her fling.

Just thinking about it had her mind wandering. She jumped when the computer beeped and the screen lit up to her background.

"What the heck?" Tia put her hand to her heart and peered at the computer. She moved the cursor and it followed. "That had to be a glitch, this computer did not just answer me."

She put it out of her mind and got to work, going over records and DNA reports until late afternoon. Satisfied she was at a good stopping point for the day, Tia shut down the computer. She glanced back once to make sure it really shut down, then got her bike out and rode down to Pages.

"Where have you been hiding?" Erica left the check-out counter and walked over to the coffee bar, her blue and pink paisley skirt swishing. She had matched it with a bright pink blouse and a shawl adorned with great big blue flowers. Just watching her raised Tia's spirits.

"Iced tea? Or soda?"

"Iced tea, please." Tia sat down at a little table. "Got any cookies?" She rubbed her eyes as Erica brought two glasses and a small plate of chocolate chip cookies.

"You've been working too hard." Erica sat down and picked up a cookie.

"Too long, anyway." Tia picked up her own cookie and ate it in three bites, grabbed another one.

"No lunch today?"

Tia bit into the cookie. "I was working and on a roll. I met with a private detective about a case the other day. It's the first time I haven't gone through the lab, but since it's a cold case, that's not an issue."

"At this rate, you're going to need glasses soon," Erica laughed.

"Probably." Tia shrugged. "But I didn't come here to talk about my eyesight."

Erica leaned forward and braced her chin on her palm.

"Really? What's on your mind? Are you having that fling?"

"Sort of?" Tia laughed at the surprised expression on Erica's face. "Okay, I'm not having my fling, as you call it, but I tried to."

"You tried to? Nance didn't cooperate?" Erica's expression was not only surprised, but it hinted of puzzlement as well.

"We haven't seen each other since the wedding, he hasn't called or anything, so I thought I would make the first move and invite him to dinner in the city, you know, go there."

"And?"

"And, he turned me down, made up a lame excuse as to why he couldn't go." Tia turned the cookie around in her fingers. "So, then my feelings were hurt. I guess there's no fling to be had."

"That's interesting, and yes, I suppose disappointing, especially when you reached out."

"Exactly." Tia pushed her bangs back. "Then I got angry, because, well, he kisses me all the time and..."

"So you thought he was interested." Erica nodded. "I get

that. Then what?”

“We had that storm last night and he came to check on me, and I guess we decided we’re friends, and then he kissed me, and I kissed him back.” Tia took a breath. “And I thought how I could touch him and...” She put her head in her hands. “And then, my knees literally buckled, and I would have hit the ground, but he caught me and now he thinks I have some sickness.” She peeked out through her fingers.

Erica couldn’t help it. Her laugh echoed through the store. Several customers looked their way.

She reached out and pulled Tia’s hands down. “You were embarrassed.”

Tia nodded. “It’s worse than that. I’m pretty sure I’m in love with him.”

“Pretty sure?” Erica’s eyebrows went up.

“Sure. I’m sure I’m in love with him.” She wrung her hands. “How can I have just a fling now? I’m pretty sure that would lead to a broken heart on my part.”

“There now, it’ll be all right.” Erica took Tia’s hands in hers. “It’s possible he feels the same way but is afraid of the same thing.”

“You think he’s afraid I’ll break his heart?” Tia asked incredulously. “I mean, he said we were friends. Friends, but with kissing. He’s always kissing me but not really like it means anything.”

Erica tried to hide her smile and her voice was gentle. “Love’s not easy, and maybe he’s had his heart broken before. Maybe he’s afraid to commit to another relationship.”

“Maybe.” Tia was doubtful. “Then there’s the problem of my house. He tries to ignore the mess, but I can tell it bothers him. I’m pretty sure there is not a hair out of place at his house.”

“Ah, well, you’re working on that, right?” Erica took a sip of her tea while she considered what to say next. “You don’t know for sure that he’s got OCD or anything, do you?”

“He actually said his mother told him he has OCD, but I don’t know for sure. He didn’t accept my dinner invitation, as you know.”

“He has to realize that not everyone is as neat as what he likely is, so there’s probably a compromise there some-where. Right now, I say you just go with it. He clearly likes you, so start as friends and the rest will work itself out. No hearts have to be broken.” She laughed. “And try to control your lust, at least until the time is right.”

Tia started to protest and ended up joining Erica’s

laughter.

"Okay, so now it's your turn." Tia leaned forward.

"My turn for what?"

"Spill it about Danny."

Erica didn't have to reply, her soft look said it all.

"That good, huh?" Tia smiled.

"I'm not going into details." Erica examined her fingernails. "But I will say he's pretty much perfect. We've spent some time together and we have a lot of shared interests." She looked off into space for a moment, then back at Tia. "I don't know how we went all this time without meeting each other, so thank you for that."

That was all she would say about the budding relationship, and that was okay, Tia decided. It was enough to see her best friend happy.

"Just go with it, she says," Tia muttered as she rode her bike back to the house. "Be friends, she says. Control the lust."

She could try, Tia decided as she put her bicycle in the garage. No, she would try. For now though, she was hungry and needed a real meal. She turned on the television to watch the weather, as she promised, and to her disappointment, Nance wasn't doing the weather. She chopped an onion and a pepper, took a chicken breast out of the refrigerator and put it all in aluminum foil to go on the grill. There was no bad weather forecast for the evening, so Tia was going to take advantage of it. She ate by herself and wished Nance was there to share.

The first thing to work on, she decided as the evening light waned, was controlling the lust. "No more backing up, no shuddering, no goosebumps," she told herself. "If you want the good stuff, you're going to have to let him get close enough to you to get it."

"I brought presents." Nance, wearing his usual jeans and black t-shirt, squeezed through Tia's front door, a large box in his arms.

Tia stepped back to let him in, looked at the box. "I don't need any more junk, as you well know."

Nance laughed, then stopped and stood there. He looked at Tia. She looked young and sweet in a pair of jean capris and a sleeveless blouse, her feet were bare. He pulled his gaze away from her to look at the living room, set the box on the floor.

"What happened here?"

"Isn't it great?" Tia strode over to the new, oversized couch and ran her hand along its back. "I got new furniture."

"I see that." He wandered around the room, touched the oversized chairs that matched the white couch, ran his hand along the small end table that looked like it was covered with wicker. There were two more of them, all the same, and big bowled white lamps sat on them. They all had some decorative piece on them, a bowl of shells on one, and three pelicans graced the mantle on the fireplace.

"I love it."

"I want to get new curtains, but I really would like to change the windows to make one big picture window to bring more light in."

"It already looks brighter with the furniture and the light blue area rug." He looked at the windows. "Maybe Reid and I can help get that done."

"That's not necessary." She walked towards the window. "Erica gave me the name of a contractor. I was going to call him to get an estimate."

"Seriously, I would really like to do this for you, and I'm pretty sure Reid would be happy to help. School's out for the summer, so he's got plenty of time, and he enjoys getting out and working with his hands."

"What about you? You work all week, and I can't ask you to give up your weekends."

"I would be happy to give up a couple of weekends to help you with this. After all, look at all the work you're doing for me."

"You're paying me for that."

"And you would have to pay for this too." Nance examined the two small windows, considered the work that would have to be done. "You would have to pay for labor and materials, just like any other contractor, at least for Reid. I would work for food." He smiled and shrugged. "The estimate just won't include any kind of markup on the materials, and I think it would only take a few days, so maybe Reid works during the week, and I help on the weekend."

"What about the repairs that will have to be done to the siding where the windows that are being taken out? Then the whole house will have to be sided with new siding."

"Good point, but we can take care of that too." He turned to Tia. "You said you wanted to change the siding anyway."

Tia bit her bottom lip. "But still..."

"Think about it, and I'll get Reid to come help with an estimate."

It was true. Tia wanted to do all of that and she had the money set aside for remodeling. She knew they would do a good job, their work in the sunroom was perfect.

"In the meantime, let's see what's in here." Nance hefted the box he brought.

He carried it to the sunroom and set it on the table, took out a woolen uniform.

Tia gingerly touched it. "His army uniform. It's in good shape except for a few little moth holes."

She smoothed out the fabric and laid it aside, reached back in for a pair of gaiters.

"Those are cool."

Tia agreed. "But they don't help us learn anything new."

"What's this?" Nance held up a small brass cylinder, then handed it to Tia.

"It's a trench lighter."

"A trench lighter?"

"Literally. The soldiers in World War I used them in the trenches. They could refill them with kerosene and gasoline."

"How do you even know that?"

As Tia started to speak, he held up his hands. "Never mind. I know that you know a lot about things I can't even imagine, but I thought John was a supply clerk. He wouldn't have been in the trenches, would he?"

"I don't think so, but maybe they were issued to everyone." Tia handed it back.

"I don't think he smoked."

"Even so, he probably would have had one." Tia peered into the box and pulled out a small metal box that contained a few buttons, a couple of military pins and several coins. She left them in the box and reached for a packet of letters.

"This looks promising." She untied the string holding them together.

"Let's sit." Nance gestured to the pair of wicker chairs they usually sat in.

They settled in and Tia sorted through the envelopes. There were several, two sent to his parents from Camp Cody and the rest postmarked Brest, France.

"Camp Cody first," she decided.

Camp Cody, New Mexico
June 2, 1918

Dear Folks,

I hope this letter finds you well. It's hot here and dusty, very dusty. What little rain we get barely wets the ground, then the wind dries it up and it's dusty again.

I don't mean to alarm you, but I was kicked by a mule and ended up in the infirmary with a couple of broken ribs. I was shoeing him and he managed to kick me pretty good before I could get out of the way. Imagine that. My first injury in the war effort was because of a mule. They're a little greener than the ones we see at home, so I guess I wasn't prepared. They say I will be better in a few days, but for now, I am laid up. It is cooler in here than in the blacksmith shop, and the nurses are sure prettier and nicer than those mules. There isn't much to do here except read and play checkers.

The food here is swell, and sometimes we go into town for a dance or a supper the townspeople host for us. I don't get to go now, but that's okay. I am not going to do much dancing until these ribs heal. I wish I was home. I miss everyone so much. The guys here are great, but they're not family.

I guess that is all for today, I will write again soon. Tell the rest of the family hello for me.

Your Son, John.

"That's interesting. Broken ribs." Nance took the letter from Tia and glanced over it. "I didn't know that."

"I would think your mom would have read these," Tia answered as she took the next letter out.

"Maybe, but if she did, she didn't say anything. It looks like they haven't been read for a long time."

"That's true." Tia gently flattened the creases in the next letter. "Ready?"

Nance nodded and Tia read.

Camp Cody, New Mexico
August 19, 1918

Dear Folks,

I hope you're all well. I thought I'd be shipped out by now, but my ribs were worse than they thought and one punctured my lung. I got pneumonia pretty bad and they thought I wasn't going to make it. I've now officially been in the infirmary for nine weeks, but they say I'm just about recovered. I tell you, coughing has been the fits with these sore ribs, but at least we don't have influenza here. I hear it's pretty bad in some places.

I've been reassigned to the supply depot as a quartermaster, so no more horseshoeing for me while I'm here. Guys are shipping out to France, I expect I'll be leaving in a month or so too. I don't know exactly when or where I'll be going, but I'll try to write once I'm settled.

I need a favor. I met a girl last summer at the Fourth of July celebration in LeSeur. Her name is Elizabeth Brownell and we spent some time together. I tried writing to her but my letters came back. Is there any way to get a message to her to let her know where I am? I think she lives in LeSeur, but I never met her parents and I don't know their names.

I have to go now, a nurse is bringing my supper. I say I'm well enough to go to the mess hall, but Nurse Stevens says I can't go. She's a pretty thing and knows what she's about, so I guess I'll eat my supper here. I hope to see you all soon.

Your Son,
John

CHAPTER EIGHTEEN

"Well, there's our nurse." Tia handed the letter to Nance.

"What do you mean?"

"Do you remember the letter he got from the lady in Chicago in 1929?"

"Vaguely?"

Tia stood and walked over to her desk, picked up the file, and shuffled through the papers inside.

"Here it is, Minnie Stevens Thomas. She was one of the nurses who took care of John in New Mexico."

"Oh, yeah," Nance said. "Do you think he found her attractive and that's why he asked about Lizzie? To see if she remembered him anymore?"

"Maybe." She put the folder back on the desk and came back and sat down.
"Next one." She unfolded the next letter.

Brest, France
November 15, 1918

Dear Folks,

I hope this finds you all well. I'm in Brest, France, working in the supply depot. It's not so bad, but the weather here is dreary, and there are a lot of men here who are sick.

I hear the influenza is bad back in New Mexico, they got hit just after I left. I hope you haven't had to worry about the sickness.

My ribs have healed finally and I've got a clean bill of health, but I'm in supply already, so they will leave me here. The job is easier than shoeing horses, I can tell you that, so I don't feel bad about it. I know you miss having me at home to help out, but I'll be back soon.

Thanks for checking on Elizabeth even if you weren't able to find anything. I was a little sweet on her and thought if she knew where I was, she might write to me. I guess it wasn't meant to be.

It's getting late, so I'll stop for now, give everyone a hug for me and hopefully, I'll be home soon.

Your Son,
John

  P.S. Don't publish this in the newspaper, I know some guys have, but this was personal, and the brass here don't want people knowing where we're at.

"So, he just gave up." Nance leaned back in his chair.

"It doesn't look like he had much choice." Tia folded the letter and put it back in the envelope. "And we don't know, maybe he wrote her, and she never answered. I know they used to be able to just put a name and town on an envelope and it would get there."

"I suppose if he had, the letter could have been intercepted." Nance shook his head. "Or, what if they did find her and her parents told them to go away? Either way, it doesn't help us much."

"That wouldn't surprise me. But, let's say Lizzie did get the letters. By the time John left for France, she had already had the baby and had given it up for adoption."

"It's sad really." Nance took the letter from Tia and put it with the others. "He was sick all that time, which we didn't know, by the way, and then to find they couldn't locate Lizzie."

"I guess we don't know for sure, but it seems like John didn't know about the baby."

"At least for another ten years or so."

"Right." They sat in silence for a few moments, then Tia picked up the last letter and started reading.

Brest, France

December 14, 1918

Dear Folks,

I hope everyone is well. The weather here is damp and I fear I may catch pneumonia again before we're done. I see long lines of soldiers every day and they all seem to have something wrong, from coughing to leg wounds and more. It is quite the thing to see all of them here, needing supplies, and I wish I could help them more.

I met a man from Duluth, he had only been here a few days, but he nearly cried when he found out I was from Minnesota. So many men here are young, younger than me, and this is the first time they've ever been out of the state, missing their families. I guess the same could be said for me, but maybe the advantage of a couple of years, and the time I spent in New Mexico helps me cope better than they can.

Don't get me wrong, I miss all of you, and I miss our small town and the friendly faces of the people I've known all of my life. I wish I could be there just to enjoy our freshwater lakes and clear, blue skies.

I don't know how long I'll be stationed here, but despite the weather and the food, I can think of worse places to be if I have to be involved in this horrid war. Don't get me started on the food. They try, but it's not the same as your fried chicken on a Sunday, Ma. I can smell it if I close my eyes.

I wonder if you can send me a new pair of boots? I know it's asking alot, but even being a supply officer can't get me new boots over here. They are reserved for the guys out there on the front line, and a high commodity around these parts.

I hear the dinner bell, so I must go now, but I'll try to write again next week.

I love you all, and say hello to all the folks in Henderson.

John

    "Not much in that one at all," Nance said when Tia finished reading.

    She folded it, then got up and took all the letters to her desk. "I'll keep these for now so I can copy them, if that's okay, but the rest of this can go back to your mom."

    She folded the uniform and put it back in the box.

    "Hungry?" Nance asked as he picked up the box.

    Tia looked at the clock on the wall. "How did it get so

late?" She turned to Nance. "And yes, I'm hungry, but unfortunately, I don't have much to eat. I was supposed to get groceries this afternoon."

"And instead, you sat and read old letters to me." Nance shifted the box in his arms. "How about I take you out for dinner?"

"We could walk down to the See-Food Inn," Tia suggested.

"Sounds good."

Nance put the box in his SUV while Tia put on sandals, then they walked down to the restaurant. Tia tried to walk as close to Nance as she could and not shiver, or worse, stumble.

Nance looked at the full parking lot. "Maybe we should have called ahead."

"It'll be okay, I know people."

The restaurant was crowded, but as soon as they stepped inside, Kahlia came over to them.

"Danny and Erica are out on the patio," she said, smiling. "Danny said to ask you if you want to join them."

Tia looked at Nance, and he smiled back at Kahlia.

"The patio it is."

He put his hand on Tia's back to guide her through the crowd and Tia immediately tensed. The bustle of the restaurant faded, and all Tia could think about was the pressure of his warm hand on her back.

You can do this, she told herself, just stay calm and breathe. Part of her wanted him to move away so she could get back on an even keel, but the rest of her wanted him to turn her around and kiss her, do more than kiss her, like lay her gently on a bed and slowly undress her, and...

She felt the flush on her face as Nance moved his hand away and pulled out her chair. Danny stood, and luckily, Erica was the only one who noticed anything off. She leaned in.

"Are you okay?"

Tia nodded and whispered back. "Just a fling thought," she confessed.

At Erica's laugh, Tia reached for a glass of water and took a large gulp, then coughed as she swallowed wrong. To make matters worse, Nance rubbed her back.

Erica finally contained her laughter and spoke to Nance.

"What brings you two out this evening?"

Nance stopped rubbing Tia's back as her coughs subsided and turned his attention to Erica.

"We were working on my great-grandfather's stuff, reading some old letters, and lost track of time." He glanced worriedly at Tia, who was dabbing at her eyes with a napkin.

"We decided we were hungry, but according to Tia, she forgot to buy groceries."

Erica smiled. "She tends to do that."

Tia finally spoke up. "I didn't forget, I was interrupted."

She didn't have a chance to say anymore as Kahlia stepped up to the table to take their orders.

"So, how goes the search?" Danny asked as Kahlia left.

"It's going okay," Nance answered. "My mom found some old letters my great-grandfather wrote during the war, so we were reading those."

"Anything useful?" Erica looked at Tia.

"Not really," she answered. "They were interesting, but they didn't shed any light on what happened to Helen after she was adopted."

"His daughter, right?" Danny asked.

"We're pretty sure, but we're having a hard time finding the family that adopted her."

"Really?" Erica sounded surprised. "I thought that's what you do every day."

"Sort of, but I usually have DNA as a starting point. Right now, I don't have any DNA, and I don't even have a last name for her."

She paused to let Kahlia serve their drinks.

"I think we need to go to Ohio."

Tia, Erica and Danny all looked at Nance.

"What?" they all asked at the same time.

"I've got the DNA in the works, but Tia says we might have better luck if we try to find the information in person, you know, adoption records and such."

"He's not wrong," Tia said. "The records we need aren't available online."

"She says the newspapers that might help us exist, but we have to go find them in person, in a real library. So, I say, we go have a look."

"Isn't that a little dangerous?" Erica looked from one to the other.

"Dangerous?" Nance asked.

"Yes." She grinned. "Aren't you worried you'll get locked inside the library again?"

Nance and Tia looked at each other and laughed.

"There is that," Nance finally admitted. "We'll be more

careful this time, I promise." He stopped talking as Kahlia and another waiter brought their food.

"Looks delicious," Tia stated as she cut into her steak.

"I hear the cook here is pretty good," Danny added as he picked up his fork.

They ate in silence for a few minutes before Tia circled back to the previous conversation.

"You really think we should go to Ohio?" she asked Nance.

"Sure, it'll be fun."

"You know, I could go by myself. You'll probably find it boring."

She winced as Erica's foot connected with her shin.

"I might, but I'll take plenty of snacks this time, maybe a pillow for a nap."

"Isn't it a twelve-hour drive?" Danny asked.

"Something like that," Nance replied as he speared a green bean. His phone dinged and he pulled it out of his pocket and looked at it. He typed in a response and put it back in his pocket.

"Something important?" Tia asked.

Nance shook his head. "Not at all."

Tia could see he wasn't going to say anything more, so she moved on.

"Flying might be a better option," she offered, "if you're really serious about going. It wouldn't take as much of your time."

"I kind of like road trips," he replied. "Limitless junk food, roadside stands and attractions." Nance shrugged and grinned. "It'll be fun."

"I guess you're going to Ohio then," Erica laughed.

Tia looked around the table at three smiling faces.

What just happened here? she wondered silently. If felt like she had just been railroaded. In a car with Nance for twelve hours, alone together for at least three days?

It was like Erica read her mind. She leaned over to Tia. "A great time for a fling," she whispered.

Tia pasted a smile on her face and tried to enjoy the rest of her dinner. A fling. It was a stupid idea. She couldn't even walk next to him, how was she going to seduce him? But maybe Erica was right. It would be a perfect time to get closer to him.

The sun was getting low in the sky as Tia and Nance walked back to Tia's cottage.

"That was fun."

Tia nodded. "It was, but Danny and Erica though, how about that?"

"What do you mean? They look like they're crazy about each

other."

"They are, but they've only known each other a few months."

"Really. I wouldn't have guessed it. They look like they're in love." He grinned. "Maybe we'll get an invitation to a wedding soon."

"You think?"

"I do." He smiled.

"Funny."

Tia stopped in the driveway. "Do you really want to go to Ohio, or were you just making conversation?"

Nance stopped too. "I meant it. First of all, you said yourself it was the only way to find the truth about Helen."

"That's true, and I'm happy to go, but you certainly aren't obligated to come along."

"I said I want to, and I do. I think it'll be fun."

Tia spread her hands. "Okay, we'll go. I'm flexible, so you just need to find out when works for you."

"I'll check with the station." Nance looked at his watch. "I'd better get back to the city. I'll talk to Reid, and we'll come back out tomorrow to work up an estimate for your window and siding."

"Tomorrow?" Tia walked with him to his SUV.

"Probably. Dad was talking about playing a round of golf, but we can do that in the morning."

"You should do that, and we can deal with the estimate another time."

"I'll see." He opened his driver's door to get in.

"It's not that late, are you sure you don't want to come in? We could have a glass of wine and watch the sun set on the river."

She knew what she was asking and was afraid of the answer. Fling be damned, she didn't want him to go.

Nance glanced at his watch again, smiled and kissed her on the forehead.

"Sounds good, but I need to get home. As it is, I didn't intend to stay this long."

Tia waved as Nance drove away and wondered why he had to leave. It likely wasn't because of Suzanne, but why? She wandered into the cottage and poured herself a glass of wine, carried it out to the patio and sat alone, watching the river.

She sipped her wine and wondered again why Nance didn't stay. She thought for sure he would, and although she hadn't said it, she thought she implied he could spend the night. Maybe he hadn't gotten the hint.

Tia sniffed and decided she was feeling a little lonely. Fling aside, she was getting used to having the man around, and now it was too quiet without him here.

CHAPTER NINETEEN

Nance barely had time to change into shorts and an old Vikings t-shirt before his doorbell rang.

He opened the door to Reid and his boys standing in front of him.

"Nance! We're here!" Benny shouted as he and Trey barged into Nance's legs.

"We came to have a sleepover," Trey added. "We brought our sleeping bags."

"You sure this is okay?" Reid asked Nance over their heads. "I mean, it is Saturday night, and still early enough to go out."

"No worries man, and I've already been out for dinner. I'm always here for you." He ushered the boys in and took the overnight bag from Reid.

They dropped the sleeping bags on the floor and kicked out of their Crocs.

Reid pointed to the bag. "Pajamas and clothes for morning. Are you sure?" Reid asked again. "I can still cancel my date, I mean, we're only going for a late drink. I depend so much on Mom that I didn't even think to ask if she had plans for the evening, and then I didn't want to tell her I had plans."

"Because she would have canceled them."'

"She would have," Reid agreed.

"This is only a set up, so I really could cancel."

"I thought you were seeing someone, another teacher,

Kayla Something.”

“You know that ended at the end of the school year when she moved to Duluth.”

Nance winced. “Sorry, man, I forgot.”

“Anyway, I can still cancel.” He ran his hand down his face. “I don’t know why I agreed to go in the first place.”

“You’re rambling, man.” Nance slapped him on the shoulder. “I got this. Tia and I went out for dinner, but we were done with plenty of time for me to get back here.”

“I knew it, it’s an inconvenience.” Reid pulled out his phone. “I’m going to call and cancel.”

Nance took the phone out of his friend’s hand.

“Go, I mean it. So, Tia did ask me to stay, but...”

“Oh man, really?” He took the phone back from Nance’s outstretched hand. “Now I feel worse.”

Nance laughed. “It’s all good, and I wouldn’t miss a sleepover with my best boys for anything.” He ushered Reid to the door. “So, get out of here and have fun, get lucky.”

Reid started to speak as the boys ran back over.

“Are you going to leave, or what, Dad?”

He laughed. “I’m leaving, I’m leaving.”

It took a flurry of kisses and hugs, but Reid finally left.

Nance closed the door and turned around. “Who wants a movie and some popcorn?”

Fifteen minutes later, the boys were wearing their pajamas and in their sleeping bags on the floor. They munched on their popcorn, clutching their favorite stuffies and watching a superhero movie.

Nance made himself a bed on the couch... he wasn’t up to sleeping on the floor. He kept one eye on the movie and the other on the boys.

He hadn’t lied to Reid, he loved spending time with Benny and Trey. They were awesome kids and watching them start to yawn and snuggle into their sleeping bags made him realize he was ready for his own family. With Tia.

Nance jerked up straight. Where had that come from? They were friends, finally, he thought, now that she didn’t act like she hated him, or shrink away whenever he got close. He liked her. A lot. But love? Enough to marry her?

He thought back to earlier, when she had asked him to stay for a drink. He was pretty certain that came with an invitation to spend the night and he was tempted, really tempted, but he had told Reid he would watch the boys and he wouldn’t back out of that, even for Tia. Nance suddenly realized he hadn’t told her why he was leaving, he hadn’t wanted to interrupt dinner, and then... he had been so surprised by her invitation, that he just ran away. He should text her, he thought. No. He wasn't going to have the conversation in a text message. He could call her tomorrow.

Nance rubbed his eyes, picked up his beer and drank deep. Missy was in his head again. Damn it. He had to get past her.

He could do it, Nance decided. He thought he was in love with Tia, and he shouldn't let Missy mess that up. There was only one issue. Tia. He ran his hand through his hair. Tia, the one woman who could resist him. They'd been working on this research project for months and she seemed to like him enough finally, but she never wanted to get close to him or touch him.

Nance went still as he realized that today she did let him touch her, let him guide her to their table at dinner, didn't stumble and fall. There was that coughing fit as they sat down, but that didn't have anything to do with him.

And she did ask him to stay for a drink. Maybe she was opening up a little. It was something, Nance thought as he stood up and took the popcorn bowls to the kitchen. He turned off the television, and made sure the boys were covered up, then turned off the lamps and settled on the couch.

"Umph." Nance came awake to find Benny trying to bounce on his chest.

"Benny, what's up?"

"I think he's ready for breakfast," Trey replied from the behind the couch.

Nance grabbed the little boy on his chest and tickled him, making him laugh. He held Benny up in the air and as he squealed, set him down on the floor.

Nance pulled Trey over the back of the couch and rolled him over to the floor with his brother. They were both laughing.

"Breakfast it is," Nance said as he stood up and stretched. "Who wants pancakes?"

Nance cooked pancakes for all of them, then took a shower once the boys were dressed and watching cartoons. He was just sitting down to join them when Reid showed up.

"Dad!"

Benny jumped up and ran to Reid, who hefted him up for a hug and let him down again. He immediately rejoined his brother.

"Hi Dad," Trey said without looking away from the television.

Reid grinned at Nance. "It's always good to be wanted."

Nance poured them each a cup of coffee and they settled at the kitchen island.

"How'd it go?" Nance met Reid's eyes.

"That's what I was going to ask you." He shrugged. "It was a bust. I met a woman, Lindsay, at a bar for a drink, blind date, so to speak, mutual friend."

"Pretty?" Nance sipped his coffee.

"Yeah, she was pretty, and smart. We had a nice conversation."

"So, what happened?"

"As soon as I said I was a single dad with two kids, she suddenly remembered she had to be somewhere."

"Ah, man, that's too bad."

Reid shrugged and sipped his own coffee. "It shouldn't be this hard."

"Trust me, there's a woman out there who will love your boys as much as she loves you."

"I don't know if that's true, but I would rather be alone than with someone who won't accept the boys as part of the relationship." He sat his cup down and looked over at the boys sitting close to each other. "They deserve that."

He sighed. "Anyway, we'd better get out of here, so you can get on with your day. Boys!" he called.

Nance stood up. "Sure, but before you go, Tia and I talked yesterday about some remodeling she wants done. I offered our services."

The boys came running.

"What, Dad?" Trey asked.

"Get your stuff together," he replied, and they ran off again. He turned back to Nance. "What does she want done?"

"She would like a bigger window in her living room. If we do that, we'll have to replace her siding too."

Reid considered it. "It would make her house a lot lighter and replacing the siding would be a good thing. The whole house looks a little run down."

Nance winced but didn't disagree. "I told her we would come over today to have a look, so we can put together an estimate."

"Hmm." The boys came running back.

"We're ready," they said in unison.

"Can we do it later this afternoon?"

"Sure, I'll let her know and I can pick up pizza on the

way, maybe have supper there.”

“Supper at Tia’s?” Trey asked, looking hopeful.

“Would that be okay?”

“Yay,” Benny shouted and threw his hands up in the air. “Maybe we can skip stones.”

Trey nodded. “I like Tia,” was all he said.

In the end, Tia said she would cook hamburgers and hot dogs, and they could eat on the patio.

It didn’t take long for the men to take notes and come up with a plan of attack.

“It’ll take me a few days to get all the materials together, and if you’re flexible on the size of the window, I should be able to get one without having to order it,” Reid said as they sat down to eat. “I could actually start work this week.”

“Good thing we kept our construction licenses up,” Nance said.

“Oh, agreed.” He turned to Tia. “I like to offer remodeling services in the summer, and I usually sucker Nance into helping.”

“You make the best mac and cheese,” Trey said as the adults paused in their conversation. He scooped up more off his plate and shoved it in his mouth.

“I’m not sure about that,” Tia answered with a smile, “since it came from a box, but I’m glad you like it.”

She turned back to Reid. “This week already?”

“If that’s okay?”

“Well, sure, I guess. Do you want the money now for materials?”

They went over the details as they ate, with Tia getting up a couple of times to get the boys more macaroni and cheese and refill their glasses with milk.

“You know you don’t have to wait on them,” Reid finally said.

Tia looked at him in surprise. “It’s no problem. I just want to make sure they get enough to eat.” She turned to the boys. “Who wants dessert?”

Reid and Nance raised their eyebrows at each other as Trey and Benny ran into the kitchen after Tia.

“She’s good with them,” Nance observed.

Reid nodded. “Maybe she’s the one for me,” he said, keeping his face straight.

“Don’t even...”

Reid laughed at Nance’s expression.

“Don’t even what?” Tia asked as she returned with the

boys and several bowls on a tray.

"Look Dad, Tia made us worm pudding." Benny set his bowl on the table and pulled out a Gummi worm as Tia handed out the rest of the bowls.

"Worm pudding, huh?" Nance asked as he picked up his spoon and dipped it into the chocolate pudding adorned with more Gummi worms.

"I thought it might be fun for the boys."

"And you were right, we love it." Nance and Reid tapped their spoons together.

She shook her head but smiled as all four of them slurped the candy like a straw.

After bowls were licked clean, Reid took Benny and Trey down to the beach to skip rocks. Nance helped carry plates and bowls to the kitchen and together he and Tia straightened up the kitchen.

They walked back out to the patio as Trey chased Benny up the stairs. Reid followed at a slower pace.

"I skipped my rock four times," Trey told Tia.

"Wow, that's pretty good."

"I skipped mine five times," Benny added.

"No, you didn't," Trey said and started after Benny, who ran. They made it halfway around the table before Reid stopped them.

After they were corralled and hugs were given, the three of them loaded into Reid's truck. Nance came back for a quick kiss, then got into the truck as well. With a wave, they were gone.

Tia straightened the chairs and went inside. Once again, it was too quiet.

Tia spent the next couple of days working long hours but still found time for a daily bike ride, usually down the trail and across the lift bridge. She would stop at the bookstore for a quick visit with Erica, and then ride home again.

Nance stopped by one evening to drop off the estimate for the remodel and Tia gave her approval. He only stayed a few minutes since he had to work early the next morning, but that short visit left Tia feeling lonely after he had gone again.

The next morning, Tia got up early and started work just as early. She was only on her first cup of coffee when the doorbell rang.

Tia looked up from her computer, annoyed that she was being interrupted, decided it was probably Nance. Who else could it be?

"I thought you had to work early..." Tia opened the door to find Reid standing there.

She stepped back. "Oh, you're here. That was fast."

Reid gestured toward the truck and trailer sitting in the driveway. "I'm just delivering materials, but I didn't want you to be alarmed that someone was lurking around your house."

"I'm not sure I've ever had anyone lurk around here, but thanks."

"I'll probably start tomorrow if that's okay with you."

Tia looked around her living room. "I'll probably need to move everything out of the living room today then, right?"

Reid smiled. "I just need the one wall, so I can put plastic over the furniture. Most of it can stay where it's at, and I can move anything that needs moving."

"Won't you have to put up drywall and all that stuff?"

Instead of answering, Reid turned to go outside. "Come on."

He gestured to the wall. "All we have to do is take out the wall between the two windows, then I'll replace the whole gap with the new window. The damage inside will be minimal."

Tia bit her lip as she considered. "It's going to be a big window, isn't it?"

Reid loped down the stairs and into the yard, then looked at the front of the house.

"It will look great with the proportions of the house." He looked up at Tia on the porch. "Having second thoughts?"

She shook her head. "No, of course not. It's just moving a little fast."

"Would you prefer we wait?"

Tia looked at the trailer, full of supplies and tools, then back at the house. She took a deep breath.

"No, let's get it done."

Reid saluted with a smile. "I'm on it then." He turned to walk to his truck, then turned back to Tia.

"Hey, Tia."

"Yes? You haven't changed your mind, have you?" Tia was sure the surprise could be heard in her voice.

He grinned. "Not at all. I just wanted to thank you for the other night, for being so nice to my boys."

"Oh, that was nothing." Tia smiled. "They're sweet boys."

"Not everyone thinks so, but thank you." His voice was serious. "They haven't stopped talking about your macaroni and cheese. Their grandmother is almost beside herself."

Tia frowned. "I'm so sorry."

Reid grinned. "No reason to be sorry. She's determined to win them back."

"She helps you with them, doesn't she?"

"She does, and I'm thankful for it. The boys adore her and I don't think I would be able to do it by myself."

"It's good you have her," Tia replied. "And they're always welcome here."

Reid dipped his head. "I appreciate that." He looked at the trailer and then at Tia.

"And now, I'd better let you get back to work and get this stuff unloaded. I'll have to use part of the driveway, so I don't tear up your yard." With a final wave, Reid walked towards the trailer and Tia went back inside, back to work.

Tia was a little surprised that Reid hadn't remarried. He was a good-looking guy with a great career and the sweetest little boys. She would definitely hook him up... if she knew anyone, she decided. With a sigh, she acknowledged she had her own problems.

The doorbell woke Tia up the next morning. She looked at the clock next to her bed and groaned. Seven a.m.

"What the heck?" she muttered. She pushed up from her pillow and brushed her hair out of her face. "It's only seven. I don't want visitors."

The doorbell rang again and Tia stumbled out of bed. She padded to the front door in her bare feet.

"This had better be good, L'Breck," she announced as she opened the door.

Reid stood there, wearing faded blue jeans and a button-down plaid shirt with the sleeves rolled up.

"You're not Nance."

"I'm not sure the world could handle two of him." Reid grinned at the sight of the disheveled woman wearing gym shorts and a well-worn white t-shirt that revealed more than she realized. She was certainly a sight, and he admitted to himself he was a little jealous of Nance.

"Were you expecting him?"

Tia rolled her eyes. "You know I wasn't," she grumbled, "and you know full well that you woke me up." She turned and walked away.

Reid, undeterred, followed her to the kitchen where he leaned on the door frame and watched as Tia fumbled to make coffee.

"Let me do that." He nudged Tia out of the way and took

over.

Tia shrugged and walked over to the table to sit.

"I thought you were usually up at this time of day," Reid said good-naturedly as he measured coffee grounds.

Tia yawned. "I usually am, but I had a late night." She propped her chin and watched his efficient movements. "I was on a roll putting together a DNA profile for a potential murderer, and about three, I found myself going in circles, had to call it a night."

Reid whistled. "No wonder you were still in bed." He rustled in the refrigerator and found a carton of eggs. He took them out and rummaged in a cupboard before coming up with a skillet.

"What are you doing?"

"Fixing you some breakfast," he replied. "You look like you could use something to eat."

"I can do that." Tia started to get up.

"I'm happy to do it," he said, and waved at her to sit down again. "Do you have some bread?"

Tia pointed at another cupboard, and before she knew what had happened, Reid had set a cup of coffee and a plate of eggs and toast in front of her. She wanted to protest again that she didn't need anything to eat, but the growl of her stomach stopped her.

"A murderer, huh?" Reid poured himself a cup of coffee and sat down across from Tia. "I didn't realize you did anything like that."

Tia smiled as she stabbed a bite of eggs. "It's not all dusty libraries and old papers." She paused to chew. "Actually, the DNA is the most important part of it. I can build a family tree, but I'm more interested in their relatives than when Grandma's aunt got married."

"That's interesting." He stood up and held up his coffee cup. "And I'm sorry I woke you. I like to get an early start so I can work while it's cool."

"I get it." Tia stayed seated, picked up a piece of toast. "I'll get started again in a few minutes, now that I'm up."

"Again, sorry. And I really just wanted you to know I was here."

"Acknowledged." Tia saluted him with her toast and smiled. "Feel free to get started."

"I'll try not to be too loud," Reid offered as he walked back to the living room.

"Don't worry about it," Tia called after him. "Once I get working, I won't know you're here."

Tia stood up and rinsed her empty plate, then headed to

the shower. Half an hour later, she was nursing her second cup of coffee and staring at her computer screen.

Three hours later, Tia looked up and around the room. The noise from the front of the house had stopped. She hadn't lied, the sounds of Reid working had receded into background noise. It was when it stopped that she noticed.

Tia stood up and stretched, wandered into the living room to check on his progress. She had a moment of panic when she saw the gaping holes where her windows used to be.

She jumped and put her hand over her heart when Reid popped up into the closest window.

"Well, hi, did you get your murderer yet?" he asked.

"Not yet," Tia replied. "You know you nearly scared me to death?"

"No, sorry though."

"I think I've recovered now, but for a minute it was touch and go." She stepped over to the window. "I needed a break and I heard the noise stop so I thought I'd come see how you're doing."

"It's good. Come out and have a look." He disappeared out the window.

Tia stepped out onto her front porch and looked at the house. Reid had torn off the old siding and black tarpaper was all that remained. A commercial dumpster was nearly full of debris. An array of tools sat on the porch, and saw-horses were set up in the driveway. Stacks of material sat at one end of the porch.

Reid's eyes followed Tia's.

"Organized chaos, I know." Reid said as he sat down on the step. "Have a seat."

Tia looked around for the chairs that were usually on the porch. They were gone.

"In the garage for safekeeping," Reid said. "Do you want me to get one back out for you?"

Tia sat on the top step. "This is fine. I didn't mean to interrupt, but the noise stopped, so I thought I'd better see if you were still alive."

Reid grinned. "Worried about me dying and leaving all this mess?"

"Oh, no, not at all. I didn't mean..."

"Just teasing," Reid said with a laugh. He pulled his battered Twins' ballcap off and ran his fingers through his hair before putting it back on. He sat silent for a minute.

"You know, I really meant it when I said I appreciate you being so kind to my boys. It meant a lot."

Tia looked at him in surprise. "I told you it was nothing, they're sweet boys."

Reid fidgeted with the pencil he had in his hand. "Not everyone is as kind as you, and not all women see it the same as you." He smiled. "If Nance hadn't already laid claim to you, I would seriously consider it myself."

Tia laughed, then turned serious. "And I'm flattered, but I think Nance just sees me as a friend. We're just friends."

"But you're in love with him, remember. I can see it every time you're together."

"No. Really?" Tia shook her head. "I mean, you're right, and I've accepted it, I'm in love with him, but I don't think he feels the same. He flirts, and he has fun, but that's just him."

"He does, trust me." Reid paused and looked up at her. "Maybe he just doesn't realize it yet."

"Hmm."

"Hmm, what?"

"You know I still trip over myself when he's around."

Reid feigned surprise, then laughed. "I've seen that for myself, but I thought you did a good job the other day when we were here."

"I've made a concerted effort, but you're right, sometimes it's easier than it was, especially when there are other people around to distract me." Tia laughed.

"What?"

"My friend Erica thinks I worry about it too much, and I should have fun, maybe have a fling."

"A fling? With Nance?'

"Yeah, just relax and have some fun, you know, a fling."

Reid considered it for a moment. "I don't think Nance is going to settle for a fling with you. He might have once but I think he's had his fill of flings. He's going to want more."

"More?" Tia bit her lip. "What more?"

Reid patted Tia's arm. "I think you just need to be you and the more will fall into place."

"That's not helpful." Tia did an uncharacteristic pout with her lips. "I'm always just me."

Reid laughed and stood up. "You'll be fine." He looked at the holes in the house. "Now, I've got to get busy. Nance is coming when he gets off work so we can put the new window in." He paused. "I do wish we had one more set of hands though."

Tia's eyes widened. "I hope you don't mean me."

"No I don't... unless..."

"Nope, nope, nope." She stood up as Reid offered his hand. It was warm and comforting, but felt nothing like the sensations Nance's touch gave her. "But I might know someone." She turned to go inside. "I'll get back to you."

CHAPTER TWENTY

Instead of going back to work, Tia got her bike out of the garage and rode to Pages.

"Hey lady," Erica greeted her. She looked at the clock on the wall. "What are you doing out this time of day?"

Jamael smiled and nodded his head but didn't say anything. The two were unpacking boxes of new books for the store's inventory.

Tia laughed. "You make me sound like a vampire or something."

"Not at all," Erica replied, unfazed. "You usually come earlier in the morning, before we're officially open."

"True, but today I started working early, and I needed a break. I thought I'd see if you could make me a sandwich while I'm out."

"We've got some chicken salad on croissants today, if you're interested," Jamael offered.

"I'm interested." Tia followed him to the counter. "I also have a proposition for you."

"For me?" Jamael stopped and his eyes opened wide.

Erica walked over to the counter. "What kind of proposition?" she asked. "You better not be trying to hire him out from under me."

"Oh, no, not at all." Tia looked from one to the other. "Well, maybe, but only temporarily. You know I'm doing some remodeling."

Jamael and Erica nodded.

"Well, the guys, Reid and Nance, are putting a new window in my living room."

They nodded again.

"They could use one more set of hands."

"But not yours," Erica said, laughing.

"Exactly. I was wondering if we could borrow Jamael later today."

Jamael finished putting the sandwich together. "Me?" he asked. "I don't know much about carpentry." He wrapped the sandwich and put it in a bag, added a small bag of chips and a chocolate chip cookie.

Tia laughed as he handed her the bag. She gave him several bills. "I think they're needing brawn more than skill for this."

Jamael looked at Erica, who put up her hands.

"Don't look at me," she said, backing up a step. "You're only scheduled to work until two, so after that you can do what you want."

Jamael turned to Tia and grinned. "Heck yeah, tell them I'm their guy."

Tia high-fived him, told him to come by after he was done with work, and thanked them both, then left with her lunch.

A few minutes later, Tia rode into her driveway and stopped.

"Hey there," she called to Reid as she got off the bike.

"Hey yourself."

"I found you a couple more hands, if you still want them."

Reid tossed a piece of old siding into the dumpster and strode over to her.

"That's great, who are we getting?"

"His name's Jamael, and he works at the bookstore part-time while he's going to college. He's free after two."

Reid looked doubtful. "Does he know anything about carpentry?"

Tia grinned. "Nothing at all. He's studying criminal justice but he's got muscles and he's willing to learn."

"And muscles are what we need, so okay, we'll take him." He looked at the mess that used to be Tia's lawn. "Maybe he could help out the rest of the week."

"You'll have to ask him about that," Tia answered. "I'm sure he can use all the money he can earn. I told him just to come over when he's done with work."

She gave him Jamael's phone number just in case he needed it and went inside. She ate her lunch with a soda while she peered at her computer screen, now fully concentrating on the job at hand.

Eventually, Tia had to stop for the day. She rubbed her eyes and decided this murderer wasn't going to be caught today. She thought she was getting close, but in her opinion, finding a murderer was harder than identifying a body.

She stood and stretched, noticed the house was silent except for the music she had on in the background. Tia walked into the living room and gasped.

The window was installed and she hadn't even noticed them working. Tia clapped her hands. It was exactly what she wanted. She walked over to it and looked outside. The three men were standing on the porch, each with a beer in their hand. When they saw her, all three toasted her with their bottles.

Tia laughed and went outside, her stomach fluttering as usual as she looked at Nance in jeans and a black t-shirt that fit his chest and arms like a second skin. The sight of him wearing a tool belt brought on a quick flash of want. She barely managed not to stumble when he spoke.

"What do you think?"

"I think I like it," she responded, missing the look Reid and Jamael exchanged.

"He means the window, Tia," Reid pointed out.

"Oh, yes, the window, of course," Tia stammered. "That's what I was talking about." She turned to look at the window. "It's exactly what I wanted."

"It didn't fit the opening exactly," Nance said, "since we didn't order it custom, so we will have to do a bit a drywall inside after all."

Tia waved her hand in dismissal. "No problem, since the whole room needs painted anyway."

"We'll do that for you once we're done with the exterior, if you want us to," Reid said.

"That would be great." Tia nodded.

Nance nodded. "Good. Reid and Jamael are going to start on the siding tomorrow and I'll come help after work again. I'll start finishing the window inside and install the drywall when I get here."

Reid clapped Jamael on the shoulder. "And thanks, Tia, for sending this guy to us." He looked at the younger man. "If you ever get tired of being a lawyer or whatever you're going to be when you're done with school, you'd make a great contractor."

Jamael grinned. "I appreciate it, man."

"Want a beer?" Nance asked Tia. He pulled a bottle out

of a nearby cooler.

"No thanks, I really just came out to put my bike away in case it rains." She started towards her bike.

"It's not going to rain," Nance called out behind her.

Tia just laughed and kept walking.

By the end of the week, Tia's cottage was unrecognizable. New, light-gray siding graced the exterior, and the men had added stonework to the lower half of the walls and around the concrete porch.

"I love it all," Tia exclaimed as she walked around the house. "I never thought it could look this good, this new, with just a couple of changes." She turned to the three men who were putting tools away. "I just don't understand how you were able to get it all done this quickly."

"It helped to have a customer that didn't have to have everything custom ordered," Reid replied. "I'll start painting your living room on Monday, and we should be out of here completely by Wednesday."

"Amazing." Tia couldn't stop admiring the new look. She walked around the house and when she came back, the guys were just finishing the cleanup.

"Do you want to stay for supper?" she asked. "I can put something together."

"Appreciate the offer," Reid replied, "but I've got to get home. I promised the boys we could go out for pizza."

"And I've got a date," Jamael added.

Nance squinted at Tia. "Like what something?"

"Umm, well, I have a plan."

The guys laughed, then Reid and Jamael finished packing up and strode to their vehicles. Nance stayed behind.

"So, if we had all agreed, what were you thinking to make?" Nance asked as he leaned up against the side of the house.

Tia lifted her chin. She didn't like his tone. "I wouldn't have offered to feed everyone if I didn't have a plan."

Nance straightened, then held up his hands.

"Okay, don't get mad. I didn't mean to offend you, in fact, I was hoping to invite myself for supper." He grinned and some of Tia's irritation faded. Some, but not all.

She turned to go into the house, then turned back. "I'll take that beer now," she called as she disappeared into the house.

Nance laughed, looked at the empty beer bottle in his hand, then looked around. Reid had taken the cooler with the beer in it when he left. He laughed again, and followed Tia into the house. She had her head in the refrigerator when he made it to the kitchen.

"Second thoughts about feeding me?"

Tia straightened quickly as she realized Nance was right behind her, and promptly hit her head on the shelf of the refrigerator. "Ouch."

"You okay?"

Only as okay as she always was when he was around, Tia thought.

"I'm okay." She turned around and handed him two yellow peppers, then reached back in and pulled out a package of steaks.

"I've got steaks, too many now, I suppose, and veggies for the grill." She looked around. "Did you bring me a beer?"

Nance laughed as he placed the peppers on the counter and held up the empty beer bottle.

"What?"

"Reid took the rest of the beer with him, so…"

Tia, still holding the package of steaks, stared at him, blinked a couple of times. Her brain felt a little foggy. She shook her head. Maybe she hit it harder than she thought.

"So?" she finally asked.

"I don't have any beer."

"Oh, well shoot, I was looking forward to having one." She was strangely disappointed.

"Let's do this." Nance stepped over to Tia and gently stroked her hair away from her face. She stood very still, the steaks forgotten, afraid to breathe.

"You start chopping vegetables and I'll run and get us some beer," he said softly.

Tia raised her eyes to his and he lowered his head. The kiss was long and hot, and all Tia could do was brace herself against his chest. Even when he raised his head, Tia stayed where she was.

"Your steaks are starting to leak," he said.

Tia was rudely jerked back to the present as Nance took the package, reached for a cupboard door, and retrieved a plate. He placed the meat on the plate, turned back to Tia and kissed her quick on the nose.

"I'll be back in a few with your beer." Nance waved and was gone.

Tia sank onto a kitchen chair. "What was that?" she asked out loud as she fanned herself with her hand. "First, he treats me like a sister, then he kisses my socks off, and then he just walks away. Just like that." She shook her head and pushed her hair back, then fanned herself again. "What is going on with him?"

Nance was asking himself the same question as he parked his SUV in Tia's driveway. He had nearly lost it in her kitchen. She felt good, she smelled good and it had taken all he had to step away, not take her right there on the floor. He wanted her, and it was getting harder and harder to keep their relationship from getting out of control. As Nance had told his mom, he liked Tia, really liked her, and he wanted her, really wanted her, which he had just discovered.

"But," he said aloud as he leaned his forehead on the steering wheel. There was always that one little word. Did he trust her? Yes, but did he trust her with his heart? Nance lifted his head. He wasn't sure about that. What he was sure of was that one of them could get their heart broken. Or both.

"You should text her and tell her something came up, and you couldn't stay for dinner," he told himself as he looked at his image in the rearview mirror. "But you're not going to, are you?"

He did not.

Tia and Nance worked together easily, the tension from earlier dispelled as they prepared the steaks and put them on the grill. Tia had cut up the peppers, and an onion, then added small red potatoes, and put it all on the grill as well.

They ate outside in the waning sunlight, then cleaned up the mess and went back out to sit and finish their beers.

"Happy?" Nance asked after they sat in silence for a few moments, watching the boaters on the river.

The question took Tia by surprise.

"Of course, why wouldn't I be?"

"No reason at all, actually." Nance shrugged. "You just act like there's something on your mind."

Tia shrugged. "Not really. My mind keeps winding back to the case I'm working on. It wiggles into my thoughts, makes me think I'm missing something." She shrugged again. "I don't know what though. I've spent almost two weeks working on it, and I still haven't solved it."

"Hmm." Nance looked out at the water. "Maybe you

need to step away from it for a minute.”

“I tried that today.” Tia pushed her hair back and took a deep breath. “You’re probably right though. I’d like to finish up your research if I could. What are your thoughts on going to Ohio?”

“Oh, yeah, I was going to talk to you about that.”

“Changed your mind about going?” Tia looked at him. “I can take a couple of days and go alone, get it done.”

Nance grinned. “Heck no, I’m all in. Actually, I can take two or three days off next week if you want to go then.”

“Do you want to fly to Columbus?”

Nance shook his head. “Drive, I think. I love road trips.”

“So, a day to drive there, and one back.” Tia mulled it over.

“And you’ll need a day or two to dig through records.”

They worked through the logistics and details, then Nance stood up.

“I’ve got to get home.” He picked up his beer bottle and walked back inside, leaving Tia sitting there.

That was abrupt, she thought. What was with the man, anyway? There seemed to be a pattern here. One minute they were talking and things were fine, then the next minute, he was gone.

After a moment, she followed, made a decision. “I was going to ask if you want to take a bike ride sometime this weekend.”

“That sounds like fun, and I’ve love to, but I promised Mom and Dad I would come help them with a couple of projects.” He tossed his bottle into the trash and turned around. “They think I’ve been neglecting them. Dad made a point to tell me how long it’s been since we played golf together.”

“Oh, sure.” Tia paused before she spoke again. “I could come help if you’d like. I mean, I don’t play golf, but I could help with your projects, depending on what they are.”

“No, that’s okay,” Nance replied. “It’s nothing I can’t do by myself.” He smiled at her. “How about a raincheck?”

“Okay, well, goodnight then.” Tia trailed after Nance as he walked to the front door.

He opened the door, then turned and kissed Tia, a quick kiss this time. “Thanks for dinner.”

After his SUV roared off, Tia wandered back to the patio and retrieved her own beer bottle, took it back to the kitchen, then wandered into the sunroom. He just did it again. They were talking and things were fine, then they weren’t. Tia narrowed her eyes. She didn’t like it, didn’t know why he did it, but it made her angry. She strode out to the sun-room, still mad, and stood with her fists clenched, looking out at the dark.

The anger finally drained from her, she rubbed her eyes. She wouldn't ask him again. Tia walked over to her desk and sat down at her computer, pushed the button to turn it on. It was late, but she hoped working would quiet her mind.

Tia didn't hear from Nance for several days, and she wasn't sure she cared. She might still be a little angry, if she was honest with herself, but when her phone dinged and she saw the message from him, Tia's heart did a little flutter. It was a false alarm, all he wanted was to tell her was when he would pick her up to go to Ohio.

Quite frankly, she was surprised he still wanted to go, but she was packed and ready early Sunday morning when Nance pulled into her driveway, met him at the front door.

"Ready to go?" His smile was friendly. Tia was instant-ly at ease. She smiled back and handed him her suitcase, then picked up her computer and a bag filled with snacks.

He laughed when he saw it. "I brought snacks too, and sodas for the road. I don't think we'll go hungry, will we?"

Tia followed him to his SUV and waited while he stowed her suitcase. He put the bag in the back seat, while she did the same with her purse and computer.

"What's all this?" Tia gestured to the totes on the back seat. They sat next to a cooler, one filled with sodas, she assumed.

"Snacks?"

Tia raised her eyebrows. "How many people are coming with us?"

"Just us, why?"

"There must be enough food here for twenty people."

"Or two people on a long road trip." Nance wiggled his eyebrows.

"I guess," Tia agreed as she settled into the front pas-senger seat.

"I booked us rooms at a little inn that makes a closer drive to Mt. Vernon," Nance said as he backed out of the driveway. "That's where you want to start, isn't it?"

Tia nodded. "The library at Mt. Vernon might be all we need. I called ahead to make sure they have their newspa-pers available."

"And?"

"They do. On microfilm, of course, but I can work with that."

Nance groaned. "Microfilm," he repeated. "I can't wait."

Tia's laugh filled the air. She patted his arm. "I'll do the heavy lifting, and you can watch the clock so we don't get locked in again."

Nance just smiled and pulled the big vehicle out onto the highway.

"Stop, stop, no more, I can't take it anymore."

Tia gasped for air, tears running down her cheeks. "Oh my God, you're killing me. Stop. I mean it, stop." She pulled her knees up and curled into a ball, banged her hand on her chest.

Of course, Nance had no idea of stopping. She had asked for this. From his position in the driver's seat, he continued speaking in a serious tone.

"So, there I was, sitting on the front steps, praying, and I mean PRAYING, that my dad would get there soon."

Tia tried to breathe normally. "Did he?"

Nance nodded. "As soon as the car stopped, I jumped the three steps from the porch to the sidewalk and ran. I was in the car before he could open his door."

Tia put her hand over her mouth but couldn't stop the laughter from welling up again. The tears started again.

"He must have wondered what happened," she choked out. "And what about getting paid?"

"By that time, I didn't care, all I wanted was to get out of there." He glanced over at Tia. "It's funny now, but back then, I was in another zone. Dad went back in and came out, got in the car and we drove away."

"And you didn't say anything?" She laughed uncontrollably, eventually calmed down enough to talk again.

"Nope, and neither did he. It was like it never happened."

Tia was laughing again. Nance was silent, but he was grinning.

When she could talk again, Tia gulped in some air to ask a question.

"Did you ever get paid?" She looked intently at him.

"My dad gave me the money when we got home, but I stuck it under my mattress." He glanced at Tia. "It might still be there. All three dollars of it."

Tia fell into laughter again. Miles later, when she had wiped her eyes and her nose and regained some sort of composure, it was quiet except for the music on the radio.

"My mom told me a few weeks ago that Dad went back over and brought the cat home, buried it in our backyard," Nance said.

Tia looked at Nance and then couldn't help herself, she burst into laughter again.

The rest of the trip, whenever Nance said something, even if it had nothing to do with cats, Tia laughed again.

As they were getting close to Mt. Vernon, Tia had a thought.

"I get it now."

Nance glanced over at her. "Get what?"

"Why you were worried about how many cats I owned." Then she doubled up with laughter again.

Nance just shook his head and smiled.

It was past seven when they finally drove into the parking lot of the inn Nance had chosen.

"This is nice," Tia said, looking around. It was an older building, made of natural stone, and surrounded by large oak trees. It looked like it could be hundreds of years old. "I like the looks of it."

"I really hate the cookie-cutter chain motels, so I looked for something that was close to Mt. Vernon but not far from a library in Columbus if we need to go there."

"This will do, then." Tia stretched, and shifted in her seat. "Ready to do some research then, as soon as we get checked in?"

Nance stopped in the process of unbuckling his seat belt. "Research? At this time of night?"

"Sure," Tia said. "I think I read that we have another hour or so before the local library closes. I looked it up."

He finished unbuckling. "Oh no, you don't. I'm not going into a library this late at night."

Tia giggled, actually giggled, as he got out and went to check them in. She smiled. The ride had been great, they had talked about their childhoods and teen years. The cat story had been the best, and thinking about it made Tia laugh again.

They ate breakfast at the inn, then headed to the local library. Tia breathed in the smell of books, old and new, and after they were shown to the research area, Tia sank into a chair and got busy.

"Need my help?" Nance asked.

Tia shook her head. "I've got it. It's going to take some time, but I think we can get there. You could check the cemetery records if you want, see if we can find death dates for Elizabeth's aunt and uncle."

The librarian, who introduced herself as Jess Myers, was a perky young woman with spiked brown hair that reminded Tia of Erica. She took them to the research room, showed them how to access the cemetery records.

"I'm on it," Nance said, and started looking.

The morning passed quickly for Tia, but finally she had to stretch. "Ready for lunch?" she asked.

When Nance didn't answer, Tia looked around. He was gone. She walked out of the research room to find him flirting with the perky librarian.

"Oh, there you are." Nance smiled at Tia and then at the librarian. "Jess here was just giving me some ideas for lunch. Are you hungry?"

Tia nodded. "I am, and I'm definitely ready for a break."

"Have you had any luck finding your person?" Jess asked politely.

"I've found a couple of articles, but nothing that tells us who our Helen is," Tia answered, "but I feel like we're getting close. Just a minute, I'll get my computer and purse and I'll be ready to go."

After lunch and a walk around the city's park to stretch their legs, Tia and Nance went back to work. Tia settled back into her seat at the microfilm machine and started scrolling.

This was Tia, Nance realized as he watched her work. She was happiest doing research, interacting with the dead, the forgotten, learning their stories, putting the pieces of an invisible puzzle together. Every time she put the last puzzle piece in, another hundred pieces were dropped on the table.

He was amazed at her tenacity, her dedication to her craft.

"What?"

Her voice startled him and Nance jumped. "What?"

She turned around to look at him. "You were staring at me."

Nance felt his face turn red, a rare occurrence since he was hardly ever embarrassed. "Sorry, I didn't realize I was staring. I was thinking about the way you work."

"The way I work?"

"You immerse yourself into it, and can block out everything around you, for hours."

"I suppose, but doesn't everyone? Don't you? When you're studying weather systems?"

Nance considered the question. "I suppose I do, to an extent, but I don't think I enjoy it the way you enjoy your work."

"I do enjoy it," Tia admitted. "It's like putting together a big puzzle, and there's always one piece missing."

Nance smiled. "That's exactly what I was thinking a few minutes ago. And I'm guessing that once you start a jigsaw puzzle, you don't stop until it's done."

Tia returned the smile, genuine with her passion showing in her eyes. "If you're talking about an actual jigsaw puzzle, you would be right, which is why I seldom do them. And if there is actually a piece missing, I will hunt on the floor and in the furniture until I find it. It's an obsession."

Nance nodded. "And I'm okay with a piece missing. I can see what it should contain and move on, admire the big picture that I've already put together."

"Aargh, nope, nope, nope. I couldn't do it. Wait, you're supposed to have OCD."

Nance laughed. "Apparently it doesn't include everything. How about that?"

Tia looked at the big clock on the wall and shook her head. "We're not getting very far and time is getting short, do you have any dates that could help me pinpoint where to look?"

Nance nodded. "As a matter of fact, I do. I found a Orvis A. Hanson, buried in a cemetery nearby. Born in 1891, and died, January 5, 1962. His wife Phoebe is buried there too. Died March 22, 1971. Aren't they Lizzie's aunt and uncle?"

Tia stared at him, speechless, for a few moments before she spoke.

"Why didn't you say so?"

"I was going to, but then I got distracted watching you work." Nance shrugged. "But now you know, right?"

"I do," Tia replied as she turned back to the microfilm reader. In a flurry of activity, she took the roll she had been reading off and put it in its box, then jumped up and went to the microfilm cupboard. After scouring in it for a few moments, she pulled out a box and held it up, triumphantly. "Got it."

A few minutes later, Tia was back at work, Nance forgotten.

He didn't have to wait long.

"Oh my God!" Tia shouted, then put her hand over her mouth, hoping no one heard her except Nance.

"What?" Nance looked up from the record he was reading.

"We've got it. A way to Helen."

"A way to her?"

Tia nodded. "Yes. Look at this. It's Lizzie's uncle's obituary. Why didn't I think of this sooner?"

Nance looked at the print on the microfilm Tia had up on her machine, but didn't see anything out of the ordinary,

"Here. Rev. O.A. Hanson of the Christian Church in Mount Vernon, Ohio, died Wednesday at his home. He was born in 1891... married Phoebe Hamilton... that's Lizzie's mother's sister." She ran her finger down the screen. "He leaves to mourn a sister, Mrs. Henry Dewey of Columbus, Ohio. What if they adopted Helen? Helen Dewey."

Tia pulled out her laptop and reread the obituary again while the computer was booting up.

"Wait." Nance read the obituary too. "You think another family member adopted her?"

Tia nodded vigorously. "It happened often back then. If his sister couldn't have children, this would have been a perfect solution."

"The obituary doesn't mention a Helen," Nance pointed out.

"They often didn't mention nieces and nephews in obituaries, or in this case, even his sister's first name."

Tia opened up a program on her computer and started typing.

"You have internet on that thing?"

Tia didn't look up. "Hotspot from my phone, but that's not the point."

"Here is it, the 1920 federal census, Columbus Ohio. Henry Dewey, age twenty-nine, wife Margaret, age twenty-eight, and daughter Helen, age two, born in Ohio. No other children. I think this is her."

"We found her, really?" Nance scooted closer to read the record.

"I think so, I mean, the age is right and the name is right. They're related to Lizzie's aunt and uncle." She went back to her search page and pulled up another record.

"Let's look at the 1930 census." Tia's fingers clicked on the keys. "Yep, she's here too, and it makes sense. That's how Lizzie was able to get a picture of her. She must have known all along who adopted the baby."

She jumped up, did a happy dance. "This is so exciting." She came back and pulled Nance out of his chair, then happy danced some more before she jumped and hugged him.

He enveloped her in his arms, and they stayed that way for a long moment. She stilled and Nance touched his lips to hers, tender and testing.

Tia leaned into the kiss before she knew what she was doing, then pulled away. She looked at him in shock, then took the initiative and raised her face to his.

Tia had known it would be like this from the first time she met him, melting into him and so limp she thought she would just slide to the floor. All the kisses before this were leading to something deeper.

Nance's arms supported her, held her close, and the kiss went on.

When he finally pulled away, Tia was afraid she was going down, but her legs held.

"Well," she breathed, and sat down.

"Yeah." Nance looked around and was glad they weren't in view of the front desk. "Are we done here?" His voice was low and husky.

Tia took a deep breath and tried to right her world. Her skin was still tingling and she really wanted nothing more than to push him to the floor and take advantage of him. Instead, she checked the time. "It's only about thirty minutes until closing time." She looked back at the obituary on the microfilm machine and took another deep breath. "I want to print it out."

"Do you think we'll need to come back tomorrow?"

Tia looked at the large man pacing the floor. He clearly had other things on his mind than research in a public library. She smiled. The kiss had caught him by surprise too, she decided.

"I don't think so, unless we want to see about getting a birth certificate, but I'm not sure that's necessary and I can always order one online if I need to." She paused. "If I can go through Helen's life and find her obituary, we might want to find her grave. Of course, she may have moved away from here and be buried somewhere else." Tia shrugged. "I think a trip to the cemetery might be in order, but when we get back to the inn, I can keep working and see what else I can find."

Tia retrieved the obituary from the printer, then helped Nance gather their things.

The drive to the cemetery was short, and finding the graves was easy with the use of a cemetery directory. The graves for the Hansons were right where they should be. Tia took some pictures, then wandered around, looking at nearby graves.

"What's wrong?"

Tia turned to him, her eyes sad. "I get this way every time I come to a cemetery. All these people, and few that are remembered, especially those that have been gone for a while."

Nance looked around at the cemetery. "I suppose you're right, but I don't remember the last time I went to a cemetery to visit my grandparents or anyone else. Do you visit your mother's grave?"

Tia nodded. "I do, as often as I can. I'm lucky, my grandparents are buried there as well, but I admit, I don't visit the graves of my great-grandparents or other family." She pushed her hair out of her eyes. "Anyway, I also thought I'd look to see if anyone else from the family was buried here."

"We can go back to the directory," Nance suggested.

They went back and looked but didn't find a Helen Dewey or any other Dewey family members.

"It looks like the Deweys didn't live around here."

"The obituary said Columbus, and so did the census record." She stopped to think. "I should have looked at the census record closer," she added, then shrugged. "I can do that later."

"Should we grab some dinner before you get started again?" Nance asked when they were back in his SUV.

"A celebration dinner?" Tia knew she sounded distracted, but she was still riding on a discovery high and trying not to think about the kisses.

"Sure."

"It might be premature." Tia started to add more but Nance cut her off with a kiss and she forgot what she was going to say.

"Just the fact that we've found her last name and her adopted parents is cause for celebration." He started the SUV and pulled out of the parking lot. "And we need to eat before you get involved in the research again."

"True," Tia agreed. "Count me in."

After they finished their dinner at the inn's restaurant, they walked back to their rooms, located just down the hall from each other.

"You really want to get back to work on this, don't you?"

Tia looked up at him and nodded.

"I really do." She paused. "Do you want to hang out with me, keep me company while I dig around a little more?"

"I'd love that, but won't I bother you? There won't be anything I can help you with, will there?"

Tia shrugged. "I don't think so, but you could probably find something to watch on television."

"The noise won't bother you?"

"Not at all, as long as you don't stare at me."

"Okay, then, let's do it."

Nance found a baseball game to watch but he preferred watching Tia as she worked. Of course, he had to be stealth about it, since he had been warned about watching.

She was just as intense using the computer as she was with the microfilm machine, but it was a different intensity. She occasionally consulted her notes, but was more focused on the computer screen in front of her. She was amazing, he thought, smart and funny and she loved her life. He didn't think many people saw this side of her, this intense scholar, solving crimes through puzzles. In this case, there was no crime, but she tackled it with the same intensity he imagined she did with her criminal cases.

Nance was just dozing off to sleep when Tia turned around in her chair. "I've got it," she said softly.

Nance opened his eyes. "What?"

"I've found Helen's family, the rest of your family's story."

"You don't look very excited about it." Nance sat up.

"I am excited, though." Tia looked back at the computer. "She married and had four children. Her husband's name was Charles Hall. Children were Charles, John, Margaret and Samuel. She lived in Columbus all her life and died May 14, 1983."

"Are there living relatives, can you tell?" Nance watched Tia's face.

"Yes, I would say you have some cousins." She finally grinned and stood up. "We did it, Nance, we solved your family's mystery of the coffee can."

She finally did her happy dance, jumped to hug him. The surprise of it forced Nance to fall back onto the bed.

Tia rained little kisses all over his face, and his arms automatically went around her. She lowered her lips to his and he let her. She didn't think, just felt. He tasted so good. He ran his hands up her sides and around to her breasts.

She tore her lips away and pulled back, despite Nance's efforts to keep her close. She pulled off her t-shirt and arched back to unfasten her bra.

She watched Nance's face, saw surprise and then want, a lot of want. He put his hands on the warm flesh, rubbed the newly freed nipples to stiffness.

Tia moaned and collapsed on his chest to kiss him. She was thrilled when he put one hand behind her head and pulled her into the kiss. He groaned when she pulled his shirt out of his jeans and ran her hands under it.

Tia felt almost triumphant at the reaction she got and decided to take it another step. She could do a fling after all. She put one hand on his belt and pulled it loose. Another tug and his jeans' button came loose. She was just about to tackle the zipper when his hand intercepted hers, brought it back up to his shoulders. She felt him shudder and he broke off the kiss, looked into her eyes.

"I don't sleep with women."

Tia's hands stilled. She sat up, her knees straddled across his lower body. His own hands fell flat against the sheets.

"You don't?" There was a pause. "I mean, you don't?" Her voice squeaked on the last word.

Nance's eyes that had been squeezed shut, opened to a slit. "I don't." He closed his eyes again. He couldn't look at her. He should never have let it get this far. He braced himself for what would come next.

Tia put her hand over her breasts, lifted one leg and moved off the big man. She grabbed her shirt and pulled it over her head.

"You can leave now." Her voice was cold as she walked to the bathroom.

"Wait. Let me explain." The bed creaked as he jumped off of it and strode towards her.

"No explanation is necessary." She stepped into the bathroom and shut the door. He could tell she was willing the tears not to fall.

"It's not what you think." Nance's voice was gentle. He was totaling screwing this up, heading down a hole he was afraid he wouldn't be able to get out of.

"You don't know what I think," Tia said from the bathroom. Her shoulders were starting to shake. "Please go."

CHAPTER TWENTY ONE

Tia heard the door close, heard his footsteps fade away, but she didn't move for several minutes. She finally walked out of the bathroom and sank down on the bed that now smelled like Nance and let the tears flow, humiliated. She had practically thrown herself at him, thought he was enjoying himself as much as she was, right up until the moment he wasn't.

He left her with one statement. He didn't have sex with women. What did that even mean? He was celibate? Tia found that hard to believe. Or he just didn't want to have sex with her.

She had been all in, and that wasn't something Tia took lightly. It had been a long time since she had a relationship with a man. That had been Brock, a officer with the Sacramento police force, just after she moved to Sacramento. They were together for three years and Tia thought he was going to ask her to marry her. Instead, his wife had called her one day and calmly asked Tia to stop seeing him. She had been mortified and hadn't made that mistake again. Until now. She knew Nance wasn't married, everyone knew that, and sure, maybe she was a little rusty, but she was pretty sure she had been doing things right. Until she wasn't.

It didn't make sense. Tia was sure he was interested, his actions over the past months had made that clear. Or, at least, she thought they had. Maybe it was clearer to her than to him.

Well, it wouldn't happen again. Tia sat for a long time, staring blindly at the wall, then finally wiped her tears away with the hem of her shirt and straightened her shoulders.

She would wrap this case up as soon as she got back home and email the jerk with her official findings. That would be the end of it. It would have to be, she was too humiliated to ever face him again.

Tia was gone when Nance woke up the next morning. He saw the text on his phone when he got out of the shower, saying she had purchased a plane ticket and was flying home.

"Damn, L'Breck, you've done it now," he said to the empty room.

What had he been thinking? Tia wasn't like any other woman he had met, he had spent enough time with her to know that she didn't take intimacy lightly.

He had a moment of panic when Tia actually decided to get physical. Missy had done that whenever she wanted something, and he fell for it every time. He had decided back then that it wouldn't happen again, and just that one moment, and with five little words, he had ruined everything with Tia, and she had sent him away.

Nance shook his head. "Now what?"

There was no answer. All he could do was get dressed and make the long drive home... by himself.

Tia got out of the ride-share car and hauled her suitcase and computer to the house. Her head was pounding and her eyes still burned. She thought she probably looked like she had gone on a drinking binge but didn't care.

The trip to the airport had been agonizing, she had cried most of the way but she was lucky she had been able to get an early flight out of Columbus. She also felt lucky that Nance hadn't actually come after her.

She snorted. Lucky. She certainly didn't feel lucky. Her heart was broken.

Tia opened the door and set the suitcase and computer inside the door, along with her purse. She went straight to her bedroom, so tired now that she was home. She had tried to sleep last night, but could only replay the scene from earlier in her mind, over and over.

She had tried to sleep on the plane, but it was a short

flight, and noisy. A baby in the back wasn't happy about flying and cried for most of the trip. She didn't blame the baby, she wanted to cry the whole flight too.

Tia used the bathroom, then went to her bedroom, fell on the bed. She hadn't heard from Nance, didn't expect to. Their relationship, or whatever it was, was over. She finally fell into an exhausted sleep, determined that when she got up, she was going to forget all of it and move on with her life, without Nance L'Breck.

"You said what?" Reid nearly shouted it.

Nance sat with his head in his hands. He looked up for just a moment.

"I know, I know, I'm an idiot."

"What were you thinking?" Reid sat down in the chair opposite Nance.

Nance looked up at his friend. "I wasn't thinking. I was enjoying every minute. And then, I couldn't do it. You know my rules. I don't sleep around because I don't want crazy women stalking me later when it's over." He stood up and paced the room. "Remember Missy? After we broke up, I came back from a business trip and found her living in my apartment. I had to move back with my parents, eventually find a new apartment. It's why I don't get serious... or take women to my apartment."

"But you took Tia."

Nance shook his head. "No, I never did."

Reid raised his eyebrows. "Really? But you introduced her to your family, took her to a wedding."

Nance nodded.

"You went to Ohio with her."

Another nod. "That was just business. Part of the work she's doing for me." He stopped pacing. "That trip was so much fun. She a great person, smart and funny, and kind."

"And you've been working with her for months on this family history stuff."

"Yes."

"But not dating."

Nance shook his head. "Not dating. We were just enjoying each other's company."

"Let me get this straight." Reid looked directly at Nance. "You've taken her to dinner, went for walks on the river, to a fundraiser where she met your family and friends, to a family wedding, and who knows what else. You know what?"

Nance looked away. "I'm sure you're going to tell me."

"Man, you were seriously dating," Red pointed out, "whether you want to admit it or not. You've made her believe you like her and want to be with her. You've probably kissed her through all of this."

Nance felt the red run up his neck.

"You did." Reid shook his head. "So, you did everything a man does when he's pursuing a woman, and at that crucial moment when she decides to take a chance on you, you push her away."

"I know, I know." Nance sat back down. "I had a moment of panic, a flashback so to speak. I don't think she's going to want to see me again." Nance pinched his nose with his fingers. "We're almost done with the family history stuff, so she wouldn't have to see me if she didn't want to."

"So, how are you going to fix this?" Reid crossed his arms and leaned back again the cushions.

Nance sat back down. "I don't know," he sighed, shaking his head. "I just don't know."

"Hey, what's up Nance?" Kendall met him in the hallway to the studio. Her question stopped him in his tracks.

He pasted a smile on his face. "What do you mean?" He hadn't seen or heard from Tia since he got back, not that he really thought she would contact him. The two days felt like two months.

"Oh, I don't know, it's just a vibe I'm getting from you, and you know how I am about vibes." Kendall cocked her head. "It's not really any of my business, but you look like a man with something on his mind." She paused. "You're not upset about that story we're doing on Tia, are you?"

Nance flashed a bigger smile, shook his head. "Not at all, and I'm glad the station's letting you produce it."

Kendall's smile lit up her face. "Thanks. It's taken a while to put it all together, but I think we're getting close. You know, she's a pretty private person, so I'm glad she finally said yes."

As they walked together down the hall, Nance made a decision.

"Actually, I could use your perspective with a problem I'm having."

Kendall stopped and put her hands on her hips. "I knew it. Vibes. So, what is it, a woman problem?" Kendall eyes squinted. "Like, well, a Tia problem? You're not going to kill my story, are you?"

Nance wiped his hand across his face. "Yeah, it's a Tia

problem," he admitted, "but your story's safe. I may have inadvertently insulted her."

Kendall's eyes widened. "Why would you do that? I thought you liked her, in fact, I thought maybe the two of you were in, you know, love. And maybe you were close to proposing to her."

Nance put his hands on his hips. "Where would you get an idea like that?"

Kendall opened her mouth to answer, but Nance cut her off.

"Never mind that, but I did insult her and I know it now, but I don't know how to make it right."

"Did you ask your mom?"

"Why would I do that?"

"You always talk to your mom, you've said so, and don't get me wrong, she seems to always give you good advice."

"Well, I didn't." He lowered his voice. "She loves Tia, and she wouldn't be happy to hear I've screwed it up. So, can you help?"

"How exactly did you insult her?"

Nance frowned. "I don't really want to discuss the details."

"Was it a hated her shoes moment, or did you tell her she was fat?"

"I would never say either of those, and you know she's not fat. It's actually worse."

Kendall considered for a moment before she spoke. "Is she speaking to you?"

Nance shook his head.

"So, flowers aren't going to cut it, and I don't think she's a jewelry kind of person." She looked him in the eye. "Have you thought about just apologizing?"

"Of course I have, but I think it's going to take more than an apology."

Kendall whistled. "Are you thinking a bribe?"

"A bribe? What? No, and she's not the bribe kind of person either."

"I suppose not, but is there something she wants more than anything in the world?"

"Like her house being remodeled? I thought of that."

"And?"

"Nah, it would take too long." He straightened. "Wait, I've got it." Nance lifted her up, kissed her on the forehead, set her back down. "Thanks Kendall, you're great."

"What did I do?" Kendall called after him.

Nance waved his hand behind his head and kept going.

Kendall smiled and shrugged. "Good luck!"

Nance put his new plan in motion as soon as he got to his office but decided to wait until the weekend to implement it. It would take a few days to put all the pieces in place.

He grinned as he finished his phone call, frowning when it immediately rang. He almost let it go to voice mail, but after a glance at the caller I.D., he hit the talk button.

"Tia?" He resisted the urge to jump up and do a victory dance, hoped the surprise wasn't evident in his voice.

"Hi Nance, do you have a minute?"

He had the rest of his life for her, Nance thought, but didn't say it out loud. He was just happy she called him.

"I do, and I'd like to apologize for the other night. I'm really sorry."

"I've already forgotten it. I mean, hey, if you don't want to sleep with me, I get it."

"I do want to sleep with you," Nance protested a little bit louder than he meant to, gaining him an odd look from an intern passing his open door. He stood up and shut it.

"Whatever."

Nance was sure she shrugged but continued on.

"Maybe I could swing by this evening, take you out to dinner."

"Oh no, that's not necessary. This is just a professional call. I just wanted to let you know I got you and your Mom's DNA results back and I've put everything together."

"Hello?" Tia asked when Nance didn't answer.

"I'm here." Nance cleared his throat. The news made him strangely emotional. He didn't want the journey to end. "You know who Helen is and what happened to her daughter?"

"I do, and I found a couple of her descendants."

Nance stood up. "Then I should definitely come by, take you to dinner. This calls for a celebration."

"Umm, actually, I'm busy tonight, but maybe I could meet you and your mom in the city sometime."

Nance couldn't be sure because it had been awhile, but that edge that Tia had in her voice when he had first met her, seemed to be back.

"We could, I guess, but Mom and Dad are at the lake for the week. We could face-time them, I suppose."

And thank God for that, Nance thought, or it would ruin his surprise on Saturday.

"I could come by on Saturday."

"That's not necessary." There was a pause. "I can just email the information to you both."

"You could, but I'd really like to see you, explain what happened in Ohio."

"Again, not necessary."

Nance sighed. "Could you just let me do this?"

Tia wandered out to the patio and sank into a chair, sighed. Making that call to Nance was one of the hardest things she'd ever done. She hated to admit it, but she missed him. So, she gave in and said he could come get the results of the investigation on Saturday. That would be a surprise he wouldn't see coming.

She hadn't forgotten the night in Ohio, but once the humiliation of his rejection faded, she started to question his motives. It didn't make any sense, so why had he said it?

"I don't sleep with women."

Tia was sure he did, and maybe he meant he didn't sleep with women like her, or women he didn't know well.

She had to discard both of those theories, or at least the second one. They knew each other well enough, she was positive about that.

"We've spent the last few months together, and you've had whole relationships that didn't last that long, so it has to be the first," she said to the absent Nance.

Maybe he meant women with her body type, Tia thought, and decided not to go there. She was who she was and wouldn't change that for anyone.

'So, I guess you'll let him explain on Saturday."

Tia held up a frilly blouse, surveyed it and hung it back in the closet.

"Good grief, make up your mind." She wasn't sure why she was fretting over what to wear, it was Nance, and he was just coming over to get the research results and, oh yeah, to apologize.

She grabbed the next shirt and took it off the hanger, pulled it on. It happened to be a t-shirt in olive green. She smoothed it down over her favorite pair of old jean shorts.

"Good enough."

Tia slid into a pair of flat canvas shoes and called it good.

She surveyed the house. It would never be a showplace, but it was so much better than it was when she moved in with her mom. She had ordered new curtains for the living room, and couldn't wait until they were up.

Tia ran her hand over the antique dining table she had added in the corner of the living room. It matched her mother's buffet, and she had spent hours polishing both, and the matching chairs.

The doorbell rang as she straightened one of the chairs and Tia forced herself to walk and not run.

When she opened the door, Nance stood there with a huge bouquet of flowers. They were shaking. Tia was touched. Nance L'Breck was nervous, probably not more than she was, but nervous.

"I brought you flowers."

The flowers shook again.

"I see that, and thank you, but why are they shaking?"

Nance handed Tia the bouquet and pulled out of his flannel shirt a tiny bundle of white fur wrapped in a small blanket. It looked up at her with big blue eyes and meowed.

"Is that a kitten?" Tia stepped inside and set the flowers on the little table next to the door.

Nance passed the kitten to her and Tia held it up to eye level. She glanced at Nance.

"You brought me a kitten? I thought you didn't like cats."

"I don't like dead cats or so many cats that you can't walk through a room, but I can handle one or two." His voice was husky. "You said you'd like to have one."

Tears filled Tia's eyes as she smoothed the kitten's fur. It was pure white except for orange fur on its ears and tail.

"She's so pretty. She, or he?"

"She." Nance stepped closer and the kitten squeaked out a meow. His shirt meowed in return.

"Nance?"

He stepped back and retrieved another bundle from his shirt. "I guess this one woke up from her nap."

"You brought me two kittens?"

Nance smiled and shrugged. "What can I say? I was afraid one would be lonely."

"Do they have names?"

"Not yet. I thought you would like to name them."

"Hmm, I'll have to think about it." Tia juggled the kittens, then reached up and kissed Nance on the cheek. "Is this your apology?" she teased.

"Is it working?" Nance grinned as he picked up the flowers. "How about I put these in some water since you have your hands full?"

Tia and the kittens led the way to the kitchen.

"This doesn't let you off the hook," she said, shifting the kittens that had curled up together. "Ohio still happened. And there's a vase in that cupboard."

Nance reached in and pulled out a vase, arranged the flowers and set it on the table.

"Come sit down and I shall tell you a tale." He guided her into the sunroom.

"You shall tell me a tale? What?"

"Nothing. I was trying to be funny."

They sat and the kittens shifted but settled back into their naps on Tia's lap.

"So, your explanation?"

"Remember when were talking about our most traumatic experiences?"

Tia nodded. "The dead cat."

"That was disturbing, but it was a childhood thing, nothing like my experience with Missy Langston."

"Missy. I know that name. Someone told me about her."

Nance's eyebrows rose. "They did? Who?"

Tia thought about it. "I don't remember, I just recognize the name. An old girlfriend?"

"We were dating, casually, I thought, and then one day, I discovered she was living with me."

Tia didn't move. "You didn't know? I mean, she was spending time with you, probably brought her toothbrush over..."

"Not even. We were having fun, but I never thought it was serious." He shrugged. "She was fun and bubbly, and we went out for dinner, to the theater and I'll admit, I took her shopping. It was fun."

"And then?"

"I came home from work one day and she had literally moved in, with boxes and more boxes."

"And?" she asked when he paused.

"I let her stay." Nance grimaced. "She told me this big story about not getting along with her roommates, and so on, so I let her stay." He shook his head and looked out at the river. "Worst mistake of my life. The apartment was a mess all the time and all I did was pick up after her. Then she quit her job and started charging all sorts of stuff on my credit card."

"You gave her your credit card?" Tia asked in surprise.

"I did not." Nance pushed his hair back. "She took it out

of my wallet when I was in the shower, and I didn't notice it was gone right away."

"Ahh."

"Don't judge. I bet you've done something equally stupid in a relationship."

"Point taken. I dated a married man for about three years and never knew he was married until one day when his wife called me."

"Really?" Nance leaned back in his chair, making the wicker creak.

"I broke it off immediately, but that's a story for another day." Tia idly patted the kittens. "Continue."

"Yeah, well, I broke it off and made her move out."

"That sounds about right."

"Yeah, if that was the end of the story, things would have been great, but two weeks later, she was back with some sob story about her roommates not letting her stay there anymore, and she didn't have anywhere to stay. And I fell for it, let her come back." He put his head in his hands. "It just got worse, so I finally had to tell her I was moving out. Missy finally left and I thought that was the end of it."

"But I take it, it wasn't."

"I went to a conference in Seattle and when I got back, she was living in my apartment. I finally had to get the police involved, had to get a restraining order."

Tia listened intently, holding her hand over her mouth.

"It's not funny."

"Of course it's not." Her voice was muffled by her hand, but she didn't laugh.

"I finally gave up my apartment and moved back in with Mom and Dad, stayed there for about eight months," he continued as he shook his head. "It was humiliating. Living with my parents."

Tia removed her hand, but had to bite her bottom lip. "I'm sure they enjoyed your company."

"You know, this is serious stuff. It killed my ego and I swore off women, all of which led to that unfortunate incident in Ohio."

Tia hadn't forgotten. She breathed deep. "So, go on."

"I finally got up the nerve to get a new apartment, one with better security, and I've never told any of my friends or co-workers where I live."

"Not even Reid or Kendall?" Tia was astonished.

"Of course Reid knew." Nance shook his head. "But not Kendall. She knows I live somewhere close to work, but even now I don't take a direct route to and from work."

"Couldn't a person just search for your address on the internet? I mean, not that I've tried, but…"

Nance looked at her in surprise. "Well, I suppose they could. Now I'm worried."

"Well, hopefully Missy isn't smart enough to do that," Tia said. "But the bottom line is, you don't bring women to your apartment."

"I don't even introduce them to my family, or sleep with them." He shrugged. "Now it's just kind of ingrained in me not to get too intimate."

"But I met your family."

Nance nodded. "I made an exception, but when you suggested dinner in the city, maybe at my place, I couldn't do it."

"And in Ohio?"

"I haven't slept with a woman since Missy."

"Wow." Tia considered that. "Then when I jumped all over you…"

"I panicked, pure and simple. I'm so attracted to you, and I know you're not Missy, not even close, and I knew I'd made a mistake, a big mistake, the minute I said it, but I couldn't take it back. You wouldn't let me take it back."

They sat in silence for a few moments and the only sound was the purring of the kittens on Tia's lap.

"So, what happens now?" Tia finally asked. She wasn't sure she wanted to hear the answer. She knew she couldn't do a fling, didn't want to, but she was in love with him, so yeah, now what?

Nance leaned forward and took her hands. "That's the thing. I want to sleep with you. I want to love you and hold you all night, and wake up in the morning with you in my arms. I want to spend the rest of my life with you."

Tia felt her heart swelling, her eyes welled up with tears.

"Do you mean that?" she whispered, then straightened up. "Is that a proposal?"

"I do, and yes, I guess it is." He ran his fingers through his hair. "That wasn't exactly how I was going to propose."

"You came here planning to propose?" Tia was confused. "I thought you were just going to explain, apologize."

"I wasn't going to propose today, so I don't have a ring or anything, I mean, you were barely talking to me. What if the kitten gift hadn't worked?" He stood up. "But I meant it, I want to spend the rest of my life with you, I love you and want to marry you, and if you come here, I'll prove it."

"I love you too." Tia stood and Nance pulled her into his arms, his lips met hers and they tasted and teased, he pulled her to him to deepen the kiss, but squeaking from between them made them pull back.

They both looked down at the kittens, clearly upset that their naps had been interrupted.

"Well, it looks like we've got a problem with Fluff and Puff." Tia smoothed their fur.

Nance laughed. "Fluff and Puff?"

"Sure," Tia answered lightly. "I don't know how I'm supposed to tell them apart, so Fluff and Puff it is." She considered them before she spoke again. "I really love that you brought me kittens, but I'm not even close to prepared to take care of them. I don't have anything that they need, you know, food, litter, everything else."

"Oh, yeah, wait, I've got it covered." Nance went back out to his vehicle and reappeared a few minutes later with a cat carrier, litter box and litter, and food and water dishes. He set them down in the kitchen and went back, returning with food and cat toys, while precariously carrying a cat-scratching stand.

"Oh my," Tia said, still holding the kittens. "You've thought of everything."

Nance grinned as he put litter in a state-of-the-art litter box. "Made specifically to reduce odor and stay clean."

Tia sat Fluff and Puff down on the floor and showed them where to go to get into the litter box. They did their business while Nance went back for another load.

"Got to have a bed for them," Nance explained as he put a cute little bed in the sunroom near Tia's desk.

"You've definitely thought of everything." Tia watched as the kittens wandered around, exploring, then found their bed and curled in together.

"There, good kittens." Nance pulled Tia back into his arms. "Now, where were we?"

Tia put her arms around Nance's neck. "About here, as I remember."

The kiss was more potent this time, as love and passion bubbled up in both of them. When their mouths broke apart, Nance lifted Tia into his arms and walked out of the sunroom towards Tia's bedroom.

Nance resumed the kiss, then slid her down his body and caught the hem of her shirt as he did so, slid his hands up her ribs and around to her back.

Tia arched against him and moaned as he unfastened her bra and moved his hands around to her breasts. She lost track of time and place, could only feel Nance's lips, his hands, warm on her skin. Her knees buckled and Nance's hands went back to her ribs to support her.

He drew back. "You okay?"

Tia laughed nervously. "You seem to have this effect on me. You get near me and my knees buckle, I collapse."

Nance's brow furrowed as he considered her.

"You mean...."

Tia nodded. "All those times I almost fell, even when I fell off my bike."

"All this time." The light came on. "You were in love with me, and you didn't want me to know."

Tia stepped away. "Well, to be honest, lust first, I suppose, but as I got to know you, yeah, I fell in love with you somewhere along the way."

He moved them both to the bed and sat down with Tia still in his arms.

"And I thought I could have a fling, but Reid told me it was a bad idea."

Nance raised his eyebrows. "You confided in Reid?"

"Yeah, but only because he figured it out. Obviously that didn't work, since you didn't cooperate, but I've decided I'm not really the fling type."

"That's good." Nance shifted them so she was lying under him. His lips met her again for a deep kiss.

"You know I don't want a fling either." He drew back to say it.

"You already proposed, so no take backs," Tia reminded him before he lowered his head again.

Tia couldn't think as he nuzzled her neck, planted little kisses there, gently brushed his hand against her breast. She shivered and set her hands to exploring his hard, muscled shoulders. Passion rose up in Tia, and she couldn't think of anything but the man above her.

A buzzing in her ears brought her back from the edge.

"What the...?" Nance raised his head. The buzzing got louder.

"I think it's your phone."

"Just ignore it."

Tia pushed at him. "What if it's your mom, and there's an emergency?"

Nance sighed and fished his phone out of his pocket. "There had better be," he muttered as he sat up.

"Hello, Mom," he answered.

Tia raised her eyebrows and rolled off the bed, adjusted her clothing and walked back to the sunroom. The kittens yawned and looked up at her. She took the water and food dishes to the kitchen and filled them. The kittens followed her to see what she was doing, then helped themselves to a snack.

She was watching them when Nance came into the kitchen.

"Emergency?"

"No, just as I suspected. They're home now and Mom wants to know when I'm going to get together with you to go over DNA and the other stuff." He moved to her and pulled her close, kissed her lightly. "So, can we go back to the other room now?"

Tia tapped his nose and stepped away. "Let's do the DNA," she said excitedly.

He groaned.

"You're going to find it interesting," Tia teased.

Tia picked up the folder that held her research.

"I found the bedroom interesting."

She took his arm and guided him to the wicker table. The kittens followed and started a game of tag under the table as Nance and Tia sat down.

"So, about Helen."

"Yeah, we know about Helen."

"Helen Dewey, to be exact. Lizzie's daughter. But did we know that she married a man named Charles Hall and had four children?"

"I think you said something about that?"

"They were Charles Jr., John, Margaret and Samuel. Samuel died as a young boy, but the other three married and had their own families. I'll get to John and Margaret in a minute, but the interesting one is Charles. He married a woman named Phoebe Martin."

Nance started to open his mouth to ask a question.

"Hang on a minute, I'm on a roll. Charles and Phoebe had one daughter, Suzanne."

"Okay." He considered the statement. "Suzanne."

"Suzanne Hall," Tia said.

"Suzanne Hall. Jill's accountant? The same Suzanne you thought I was having an affair with?"

Tia nodded. "The very same." She held up Helen's picture. "Remember when I told you at Jill's wedding that Suzanne looked familiar? Look at this picture."

Nance examined the photo. "I see it now. She looks just like Helen."

"So, she's your cousin. The DNA proves it." Tia passed him the match that showed the DNA connection. "There aren't many other matches that are current, and although I've traced Margaret and John's families down, apparently none of their descendants have provided DNA to any databases."

"So, Suzanne Hall is my second cousin?" Nance asked tentatively.

"Actually, yes. You and Suzanne share a great-grandfather, John Beckwith. Your grandfather, Lloyd Beckwith, and Helen were half- brother and sister because they had different mothers, but the line from John is true. Helen's son Charles is your mom's first cousin."

"That's interesting." He picked up the charts showing the pedigrees of Susanne and himself. "Helen is my great-aunt?"

Tia nodded. "Exactly."

He looked at the charts and sighed, then looked up at Tia. "You know what we're going to have to do now, don't you?"

"Call your mom and tell her?" Tia guessed.

"I don't think calling is going to cut it," he said, sighing again. "I think we're going to have to take a trip to see her."

"You mean go to Minneapolis now?"

"I'd rather go back to the bedroom, but if she finds out I knew this and didn't tell her right away, I'll be in trouble."

"Oh. Well, we don't want you to be in trouble." Tia looked at her shirt and shorts. "I guess I'd better change then." She started towards the bedroom.

"I can help." There was hope in his voice.

Tia laughed. "That will take too long." She circled back to kiss his nose, then moved quickly back as he reached for her. "We've waited this long, another couple of hours isn't going to matter."

"I'm pretty sure it will."

Tia just laughed. "Can you make sure Puff and Fluff will be okay while we're gone?"

She heard grumbling and laughed again as she changed into jeans and sandals. She kept the t-shirt, and just ran a brush through her hair. Tia held up her hand, looked at the empty ring finger. Engaged? That wasn't what she was expecting when she got up this morning, but it seemed right, and a ring didn't matter.

She smiled. It didn't. They had pledged their love to each other and were going to spend their life together. She was so happy.

"Ready?" Tia stepped out of the bedroom and picked up her purse. Nance was leaning up against the kitchen door frame, watching the kittens.

She peeked around him and saw them playing on the

cat scratching stand.

"Do we need to put them in a carrier?" She looked around the living room. "I'm not sure I want them roaming the house while we're gone."

"Done." Nance picked up a baby gate and put it up in the doorway to the sunroom.

"Where did that come from?"

Nance smiled as he came back to her and took her hand. "I had it in the truck."

"What if I had said no to the kittens?"

He shrugged as he opened the front door. "I guess I would have had two kittens living at my house."

"Really?" Tia stopped and looked at him.

"Really. I mean, when we're married they'll be living with us, right?"

"Married."

Nance pulled her into his arms. "Married. I have a ring, you know, it was my grandmother's. I just don't carry it around with me."

"Is that right?" she teased.

"We can stop and pick it up on the way to my parents."

"We probably should." She reached up to cup his face, met his lips with hers, pulled back. "Or do you want to keep a secret from your mom and dad?"

"We'll stop and pick it up on the way." He traced her lips with his finger. "I'll never hear the end of it if I keep this a secret."

"Exactly."

He kissed her again, then took Tia's hand to lead her out the door. "I am the luckiest man ever."

THE END

About the Author

Neesa Lee is a pseudonym for Denise Andersen, a former journalist and professed reading junkie. She has been writing most of her life, and holds a BA in journalism from the University of Nebraska-Lincoln. She spent years in the newspaper and print businesses, and has written everything from hard news to sports and a farm column, using those experiences to hone her writing style.

She enjoys traveling and treats every trip she takes as a new adventure with new experiences, incorporates those experiences into her writing, telling stories with unique characters that she would want to read about.

She and her husband live in eastern Nebraska with their three dogs. They also have three adult daughters, and six grandchildren.